CLOUD COTTAGE

Barbara E. Bull

Sweet
cloud
Dreams...

Barbara E Bull

Cherry Point Publishing
9600 West Buchanan Road
Shelby, MI 49455

cherrypointmarket.net
barbaraebull.com

Cloud Cottage is a work of fiction. Some of the characters are inspired by historical figures; others are entirely imaginary creations of the author. Apart from the historical figures, any resemblance between these fictional characters and actual persons, living or dead, is purely coincidental.

ISBN: 978-0-9857278-6-4

Printed in the United States of America
Signature Book Printing, www.sbpbooks.com

From the Author

During the very snowy winter of 2014, I picked up my pen and attempted to write a novel. *Cloud Cottage* and the MacLeod family came to life in my heart and mind.

Eight years later, on the eve of ordering a second printing, I faced a dilemma – do I edit and re-write *Cloud Cottage*, or let it stand as my first effort? My decision is to leave it as is. My hope is that all the love I wrote into the pages overpowers the awkward sentences, split infinitives, misplaced commas, and other grammar infractions.

So, with apologies to all of my English teachers, I humbly submit for your enjoyment the second printing of *Cloud Cottage*. May it transport you to the special place where you find peace and joy, and where good times with family and friends become treasured memories. It matters not whether the location is a cabin on a pristine inland lake, a home on an ocean shore, a campsite in the mountains, or Little Point Sable. *Cloud Cottage* celebrates time spent together.

Barbara E. Bull

To my readers –
Because you loved Cloud Cottage,
the MacLeod family story continues.

1

1863

Young Aonghus MacLeod was on deck, seasick from the short chop of rough Lake Michigan swells. He felt the schooner shudder, heard the creaking of timbers, and realized they had grounded. Men began to emerge from below deck and were yelling. The schooner was swept broadside, listed, and a wave crashing over the deck swept Aonghus into the water.

The impact with the cold water took his breath away, but he was a boy from the northwest islands of Scotland; he was not a stranger to cold water. Aonghus was also quick-witted. He had to make a decision whether to try and regain the ship or swim for the beach. As he had been bent over the rails retching a short time earlier, he had seen a light along the shore. He looked back toward the ship; lights were no longer visible and the crack of timbers echoed over the waves. He started to swim toward the sound of the breakers, praying as he stroked that there would be no rocks. His feet hit bottom. Surprised and thankful, he crawled onto a wide sandy beach. It was no wonder they had grounded; they were so close to shore.

He didn't dare lay still long. Aonghus knew he would die from the cold, so he got up and started walking. He counted 200 paces in each direction. All night he counted and walked back and forth along the beach. Sometimes he would hear a different pattern in the waves as they broke upon the sand. He would run to see what or who had made it to shore. It was a long night for the 14-year-old boy as he pulled debris and bodies higher onto the sand. Of the six men on board the schooner, all washed ashore that night. Five had drowned when he found them. One was alive – barely. He frightened Aonghus with haunting words as he gasped his last breath; words that Aonghus never spoke, or forgot.

When dawn broke the next morning, he was thankful to be alive but still terrified of dying. He was cold, wet, hungry, exhausted, and overwhelmed with responsibility. There were six dead men stretched out on the beach. From the schooner, Aonghus had seen the light the night before, but he didn't know how far down the shore it might be, or who was there. He felt alone, utterly alone.

He found a piece of wreckage he could use as a shovel and dug six shallow graves just below the tree line. On top of each one he piled wooden planks from the schooner. He also managed to collect a few items for himself – an extra coat he dried in the wind, a tin plate and pot, and some canvas from the sail for shelter. One of his greatest finds, however, were some apples that floated in. For the rest of his life he said nothing would ever taste as good to him as those bruised apples.

As the sun set at the end of that long day, Aonghus had done all that he could. He had done it alone, no one or no ship had passed by. He climbed up the dune to make a shelter for the night among the trees. He covered himself with leaves and allowed himself to sleep, a prayer of survival on his lips.

Aonghus did survive that night, and as morning dawned he gathered his few salvaged items into a bundle of sailcloth and started to walk south. The wind was from the north, and the beach was wide and easy to walk. Fate was kind to him once again. After three or four hours he encountered human activity where a small stream emptied into Lake Michigan. Aonghus was never sure who was more surprised, he or the men working on the short pier. He only knew, once again, he was very thankful. The men worked at a nearby lumber camp and took him to their bunkhouse. They were experienced in weather exposure so they stripped him of his clothes, wrapped him in a blanket, placed his feet in a bucket of cool water and his hands around a mug of hot stew. While his clothes dried, he relished the hot food as the men plied him with questions. At the conclusion of his tale one man shook his head and commented that only a lad from the north islands of Scotland would have survived. He told Aonghus to get some rest and to come find him tomorrow.

In the morning, Aonghus rose at 4:30 with the men in the bunkhouse. After a breakfast of flapjacks and venison gravy he approached the man who had spoken to him the day before. The man was the foreman in the camp at Stony Creek and asked the young lad what he planned to do. Aonghus responded that he first needed to work to pay for the meals and lodging he had shared. The foreman nodded in approval and offered Aonghus a job for the winter, which he in turn accepted. His life in Michigan had begun.

2

Present Day

March days are often blustery and raw on the shores of Lake Michigan. Sometimes, when a gentle breeze flows from the southwest, they can be temperate. Today was temperate. The sun, almost at its point of equinox, was bright and cast a spring warmth through the car window. Katherine MacLeod was driving north and the afternoon sun felt wonderful on her left arm. As she crossed the Oceana County line she opened the car window part way. She inhaled the rush of fresh air and thought, ah, yes, that's it. Ever since she was a child and made this trip with her family, when they reached this stretch of road, where the land began to roll, in forest and orchard-covered hills, they would crank down the car windows and take deep breaths. They had been convinced that the air was better here than a few miles back, south of the county line. Everything was better when they came to this part of the world, when they came to Cloud Cottage.

Katherine rolled the window back up, the air was wonderful, but it was still very cool. She smiled as she thought about all the other times she had made this trip. She shifted her position in the seat, she was almost there. She exited the expressway, drove ten miles west, then turned off the paved road onto a two-track driveway. Shifting the car into park she got out. She stretched to limber up her muscles after the long drive, then walked to the gate. This was it, the day she had been waiting for. The day she returned to Cloud Cottage to live year-round. With a sharp twist, she turned the key in the padlock. It sprang open. See, she thought, you're as happy as I am. I'll find someplace else for you. Your service out here is done. The gate is now open to Cloud Cottage.

Katherine threw back her head and gleefully hollered, "Woo-hoo!" She glanced around. The likelihood that someone would have heard her was remote, but oh well…who cares. She climbed back in her car and started up the long grade.

Tall white pines and hemlocks interspersed with oaks, sugar maples, black cherry, and beech trees created the top canopy of the woods on both sides of the driveway. Even with no leaves their branches formed a tunnel. In the understory, Katherine noticed a slight touch of green on the twigs of the Serviceberry. There were still piles of snow on the shaded slopes but Mother Nature was awakening. It wouldn't be long before the Serviceberry would bloom white and another cycle of growth would begin.

One curve at the top of the hill and there it was, just as it had been for over a hundred and forty years, Cloud Cottage – she was home. The two-story stone structure seemed to rise from the crest of the hill as if it had roots and had grown there. Tall windows recessed in the thick walls balanced the massive stone with light, and two chimneys were an indication of warm hearths within. At one end of a porch a huge multi-trunked lilac spoke of fragrant shade for the swing that creaked quietly in the breeze. The porch extended across the southern face of the house, where it embraced sweeping vistas of Lake Michigan, which stretched to the horizon on the south side of Little Point Sable. To the north, one could see the long curve of sand dunes that defined the shores of Silver Lake.

The old house had witnessed many changes through the decades. It had weathered storms, held celebrations, and sheltered sadness. It was solid and strong, warm and welcoming. It was what its builder, Aonghus MacLeod, had hoped it would be when he named it Cloud Cottage; an ancestral home on the shores of Lake Michigan for his clan, MacLeod.

Katherine debated whether to stop at the front or pull around to the garage in back. This is a front door day, she decided as she turned off the motor. She sat still to absorb the moment. When one anticipates something for so long the actual event too often passes in a rushed blur.

Katherine resolved to savor every day, to set aside time to 'be,' and to not just 'do.' After all there was so much to do, the water had to be turned on, a fire built, the car unloaded, but that could wait. This was a 'be' moment. Katherine stepped out of her car, then reached back in for her coat. The breeze coming right out of the north was beyond fresh or brisk, it was bracing. As she buttoned her coat with one hand she reached for the large ring that held the keys to Cloud Cottage. It had ridden all the way in the passenger seat on top of her favorite pillow. She had placed them there in a casual act, but during the drive had smiled at the appropriate place of honor.

Katherine drew in a deep breath and walked up the path to the cottage. Every few steps she paused, took in another deep breath, and surveyed the scene around her. Dried leaves rustled as they were blown into windrows angled across the lawn. The young apple trees she had planted last year and protected with a tall deer fence seemed to have survived the winter. The deer had worn a distinct path across one lower corner of the clearing. She must remember to watch for them at dusk. As she approached the porch she reached down and brushed her hands across the dormant leaves of the lavender plants she had placed along the path. Katherine raised her fingertips to her nose to inhale the fragrance. After one more deep breath, she placed her foot on the bottom step. She stopped and looked up at the strong stone walls.

"I'm here," she whispered. "Dad, Uncle Gus, Great-Grandfather Aonghus, I'm here. Today I will rekindle the fires on the hearth of Cloud Cottage. I commit to welcome here all the family, not just in summer, but year round. I will do my best to 'hold fast,' to instill values of traditions, commitment, and loyalty, just as you did by demonstration and example. I am grateful to be here. I am proud to be a MacLeod."

She climbed the remaining steps, placed the key in the lock and opened the door to her ancestral home. Cool air escaped the front hallway as the door swung wide. Yes, thought Katherine, I will need to light the fires. These massive stone walls will take a while to warm up. She sought the thermostats and turned them all up one notch, then went back outside into the sun. The porch swing was creaking with a slow motion.

"Do you need to be sat upon?" Katherine asked.

She didn't wait for an answer, but turned towards the swing. A giggle escaped her lips, and on impulse she grabbed a post supporting the porch roof, wrapped one knee around it, and swung around. Her free hand and leg extended in open air.

"Wheeee, I haven't done that in years, but I can still do it." And just to prove it, she did it again!

Ok, Katie Ann MacLeod, she heard in her head. You are all grown up now – go sit in the swing! She heard her own voice answer out loud.

"Uncle Gus, I'll go sit in the swing but not because I'm too grown up to swing around the post."

Katherine smiled as she settled her lithe frame on the sunny end of the swing. She leaned back into the corner, stretched one long leg out the length of the seat and left one foot on the porch to effect a gentle movement. She was very agile for her sixty years. Thanks to yoga, a regimen of swimming, and a monthly bottle of hair color, she looked, moved, thought and acted younger. Katherine started to reach down to brush some sand off her jeans. Why bother, she thought, here sand is a way of life. Instead she tipped her head up to the sun, released her shoulder-length blond hair from its clip, and closed her eyes.

The porch's southern exposure sheltered it from the main force of the north breeze, the sun was warm and soon a warmth penetrated her being. Katherine slipped into a half-conscious reverie of thought. Images of her childhood played through her mind: adventures on the beach and in the woods with her siblings and cousins, building steps down the bluff with her dad, making wild blackberry jam with grandma, and Uncle Gus, dear Uncle Gus. Tears welled up in Katherine's eyes. No image of Cloud Cottage could ever be complete without Uncle Gus.

7

Angus MacLeod II had been her father's older brother and she had been a very favorite niece. It was because of Uncle Gus that she was sitting in this swing at this moment. It was to Katherine that Uncle Gus had deeded Cloud Cottage.

Uncle Gus had been the eldest son of Aonghus MacLeod's only son, Daniel. He had never married and had lived his entire life at Cloud Cottage. He had four siblings, three sisters who married and contributed cousins to the clan and Katherine's father, Daniel II. Katherine was the eldest of three children. She had a brother, Daniel MacLeod III, and a sister, Gillian.

As a child it had been Katherine who followed Uncle Gus like a shadow. It had been Katherine who had listened to his stories, and in later years had recorded them. It was from Uncle Gus that Katherine learned about a rebellious young Scottish lad who ran away from home and ended up shipwrecked during a November storm on Little Point Sable. She also heard the stories of how he had built Cloud Cottage. How he had built a home that would withstand the fires that frequently raced through the timber slashings. How he had built it as he had seen his father and grandfather build homes in Scotland. How he collected the stones from his property and his neighbors', hauling stone boat after stone boat loaded with stones out of newly plowed fields. How he built it double-walled and then from the beach hauled clean sand to fill between the walls as insulation. There were no other houses like it, and it was as solid now as the day it was built.

It had been a stout and warm home for Aonghus, his wife, Moira, and their five children. It became the home of his son Daniel and his wife Emma. Aonghus lived in Cloud Cottage with his son's family until he died in 1935. His eldest grandson, Angus II had been born in 1910 and for 25 years young Angus, Uncle Gus, listened to his grandfather's stories and learned the clan heritage that he later passed on to Katherine.

With Cloud Cottage came an unspoken role of 'head of the clan.' Female leadership was not unknown in the MacLeod clan, and after all

8

it was the 21st century. Yet, even without a title of Chieftain at stake, some male feathers had been ruffled. Cloud Cottage was a valuable piece of real estate in today's market. It sat on one hundred and sixty acres of land that extended down to the shores of Lake Michigan. For Katherine, the value of the property was the heritage and tradition it represented. She would not and could not ever sell it or pass it to someone outside of the family. Uncle Gus knew Katherine's heart, she understood and accepted what he had given her. His gift had legal recognition by a land deed, but in reality he had passed to her the custodianship of hearth and clan.

A vibration interrupted Katherine's reverie on the swing. Startled, it took the third or fourth pulse before she realized her cell phone was on vibrate. Wow, I have reception here, was her first thought. When she found the pocket that held the phone, she had missed the call. She glanced at the phone number; it was one she could return later. She was more interested in how many bars her phone had. Three, no two, well, it probably wouldn't be reliable but it was interesting to know she might have service sometimes. As much as Katherine loved Cloud Cottage, she knew there would be many adjustments as she made it her year-round home. She wasn't in 'metropolis' any more. She felt a pulse pass through her again.

"That was not my phone," she said. "That was a chill. Swing, I love you, but until another day …"

Katherine got up, stretched, and went to get another load from the car. Upon reentering the house, she thought, well, it is warmer. She rechecked the thermostats and pushed them up another five degrees.

The sun was low in the sky when she finished unloading the car and parked it in the small garage attached to the rear of the house. She carried in an armload of wood and built a fire in the kitchen fireplace. She started to strike a match then decided to watch the sunset before she lit the fire. With phone in hand she went back to the front porch to enjoy the last show of daylight.

It didn't matter how many sunsets she watched, it was always a beautiful moment to close a day. This one promised to be spectacular. Low wispy clouds hung in striated layers above the horizon. They were the kind that would reflect any color thrown upwards by the setting sun. As the sun began to sink below the horizon, the flaming yellows became orange and then almost a burnt sienna while the tops of the clouds above were a multitude of purples edged in shades of 'gone pink.' What a fitting sunset for this special day, Katherine thought. She raised her phone to snap a quick photo to email friends later. She didn't want to miss a single shade of the unfolding kaleidoscope. When all had melded into a deep midnight blue and the grays of night descended, she exhaled one long breath.

Later, over a cup of soup by the fire, Katherine looked around the kitchen. It was a room she knew very well, but she wanted to look at it as if she were seeing it for the first time. The fireplace dominated one end. It was a raised hearth fireplace with heatilater vents that warmed the whole kitchen. To either side of the fireplace was a door. One went to the back porch and one went to the mudroom that connected to the garage. On an adjacent wall a door opened into the dining room and on a third wall a door entered the front hall. A drop-leaf table was positioned in front of the fireplace with two cozy wing-backed chairs at each end. Additional slat-backed chairs stood against the wall for extra seating when the table became round. This end of the kitchen was almost unchanged except for the wing-backed chairs. Katherine had purchased them the year before, anticipating her retirement and cozy hours by the fire.

The other end of the kitchen had been remodeled by Uncle Gus about 15 years before. Looking back now Katherine realized that even then he was preparing the transfer of Cloud Cottage to her. He had asked her opinion about cabinet styles, countertops, and appliances. She had never caught on that she was designing her own dream kitchen. Uncle Gus had spared no expense. It had been state of the art then, and with only summer use for many years it was like new. The galley end easily accommodated three cooks and the dining end allowed for family activity at the same time. Katherine loved this room. One end was lit by two side-by-side sets of double hung windows that filled the room with the morning sunrise from the east. The other end was lit by the warm glow of the fireplace.

The fire was beginning to die down. Katherine checked her watch. She probably could and should clean a cupboard or two while the fire burned out. The guilt of needing to accomplish something would always prevail. Katherine sighed, got up, and started to clean cupboards. The ash in the fireplace was cold by the time Katherine quit for the night. Once on a mission she just kept going.

"There, ancestors," she announced. "I have now atoned for daydreaming this afternoon in the porch swing. I'm going to bed and I might just sleep until noon." Katherine laughed and wondered if talking to herself and to her ancestors was going to become a habit. "I'd better be careful, people may talk."

She chuckled all the way upstairs to her bedroom. 'Her room.' That still sounded funny to her. It was the second floor bedroom always occupied by the most senior family member in residence. It was the largest and had an attached bath. Twenty years ago the fourth bedroom upstairs had been converted into two bathrooms, one for the master en suite and an enlarged one for the family. Up to that time, like many old farmhouses, there had been only one small, functional bathroom.

Katherine entered the bedroom and looked around. It had not been redecorated in years. She had purchased a new comforter and sheet set that updated its look, but she actually liked the bluish gray walls and 18th century sheer tieback curtains. It fit the house. Her suitcases were piled together in the middle of the room. There would be time enough tomorrow to unpack. She found what she needed and went to bed.

3

Every house has its sounds, creaks, refrigerator compressors, well pumps, pipes that clang. The sounds are the same regardless of how many people occupy the house, but when one is alone they seem ten times louder. Katherine, at least this first night, was oblivious. She slept the sleep of relaxed contentment. She knew she was where she was supposed to be.

The next morning she was startled awake by a knocking. It was rapid, insistent, and persistent.

"What in …? Who would be here at my door? Who even knows I'm here?"

She stumbled as she tried to dress. The knocking stopped.

"Oh well, I guess I missed whoever it is."

She peered at an angle out of one of the bedroom windows. There was no sign of anyone. Then the tapping began again.

"Is it at the back door?" she said. "But it sounds like it's coming from the front."

Just then movement caught her eye. Katherine burst into laughter.

"You city slicker. Don't you know the sound of a woodpecker when you hear it?" she asked.

She couldn't believe she had been so silly, but there on a tree, just 20 feet outside her window, was a huge pileated woodpecker having breakfast, his red head working like a jackhammer as it searched for insects. Katherine was mesmerized by its beauty and thrilled to observe one so close. She would feel sorry for the tree later. At that moment she was enjoying a spectacle of nature. Wow, she thought, when it flew away. She had never been a bird watcher, although she did remember sitting together with Uncle Gus after sunset and listening to the whippoorwills.

"Perhaps I should pick up a bird book and put out a birdfeeder," she said out loud. "How many hobbies can I juggle in my retirement? Easy girl. Right now you have a house to clean and put in order, you want to plant a garden and ..."

Over her morning coffee Katherine worked out a plan. She would attack one room at a time until it was finished. Allow some time every afternoon for a walk and personal respite. There were eight weeks until Memorial Day weekend and the house had eight rooms plus three and a half baths and hallways. It would be a busy eight weeks. She had started the kitchen so she would finish it first.

The following weeks were a balance of cleaning, long afternoon walks, and gardening. Evening brought a cup of tea either by the fireplace, or on the porch swing at sunset. Katherine loved finding new descriptive words for the colors of the sunset, striped fuchsia, or lemon orange.

She reveled in watching the world of nature awaken around her. She had always been observant, but now every day she noticed changes in growth and colors. She had never thought about the various shades of greens as they emerged. She watched the birch first send forth its leaves, and then the beech extend its long brown buds that unfolded to yellow-green leaves. Each tree took its turn greeting the spring season until finally the red oak would uncurl its first leaves, as red as any fall foliage.

Katherine was invigorated by the demonstration of each species as it began its annual growth cycle. She too wanted to burst forth with fresh new expression. She wanted to paint a watercolor, to write a novel, to design something, anything, she didn't yet know what. She wanted to volunteer, she wanted to learn Spanish, she wanted to express herself anew as nature did every spring.

Granted, the trees sent forth leaves every year, but they grew branches and roots too. They stretched and extended in new directions with a purpose of enriching themselves and in so doing enriched the world. Katherine also noticed qualities in trees she wished she possessed. As she walked the deer runs in the woods she found favorite trees she visited along the way. One was a hemlock, the bottom fifteen feet was a shell she could step inside, yet at the top of the hollow trunk one branch grew vigorously upward seeking light. Another was actually three trees, two beech and an oak that had sprouted too close together. In their growth they had intertwined. They each survived by finding an uncommon way to co-exist.

Her favorite was a tall white pine very near Cloud Cottage. One night during a thunderstorm a loud clap indicated a lightning strike close by. The next day Katherine noticed the bark of this pine had been split in a spiral all the way down its trunk. The gaping wound was a three-inch-wide path of destruction. She was sad to think this beautiful tree would die until she noticed about two feet distant from the new wound was an old wound. The scar was healed and difficult to see, but it was there. The spiral of the new wound paralleled the scar of the old wound all the way down the trunk. The tree had survived before. It would survive again. Katherine developed an appreciation in general. She admired the way trees seemed to accept things the way they are and find a way to grow, overcoming any obstacles.

Katherine followed with equal enthusiasm the growth of the forest floor. She remembered one Easter accompanying her grandmother to look for a little flower called Trailing Arbutus. Katherine scouted the hillsides and one day a group of broad flat green leaves that she recognized caught her eye. She brushed away the oak leaves and gently lifted the vine-like plant, Trailing Arbutus. The tiny pink and white buds were just ready to open. Katherine lay down alongside them and as she watched, the blossoms responded to the warmth of the sun and opened. Her first inhalation of their fragrance was pure heaven and, for a moment, she felt like a midwife.

The Arbutus was followed by a carpet of Spring Beauties, Violets, Adder Tongues, and then Trilliums. She had seen the Trilliums before on spring visits but this year they seemed more beautiful than ever. They flowed like a carpet of white, down the hill, along the path to the beach. She also found a patch early on of Bloodroot, and later, a patch of big thick-leafed May Apples.

Katherine spent many hours that first spring walking the beach. She watched the last of the icebergs disappear. She thrilled at the wind patterns created by the blowing dry sand across the wet sand. For a week, the thawing beach was a blank canvas and the wind a true airbrush. She collected driftwood of all sizes and always carried a bag to pick up trash. The best part of these walks was that her footprints were the only ones on the beach. This sand was her corner of the world. She thought about her great-grandfather and the night he crawled ashore. She wondered how he felt, what he thought, and if he came to love this stretch of sand as she did now. Katherine's head was full of new observations and insights. She felt she was experiencing spring for the first time; it was a season of new awakening.

Then the day came that as Katherine emerged from the woods, and crossed the sand, she stopped in her tracks. There were footprints on the beach. She felt like her space had been violated, just as if a thief had entered her home. She didn't know to whom they belonged; she didn't want to know. She had reveled in the solitude, in the pristine qualities of unadulterated nature. Now the footprints were an indication of change. She knew it was coming and she would welcome the joy of sharing the beauty of this space with family and friends. She just hadn't wanted it to come yet. Perhaps, Katherine reflected, I have become too good at living alone, maybe it's time I encourage the family to come.

The first family to visit arrived Memorial Day weekend. It was Katherine's nephew, Daniel, and his ten-year old twins, Connor and Caitlin. She was ready for their company.

4

Katherine heard the car in the driveway long before she could see it. The sound of the car engine, the tires crunching on the gravel, seemed amplified to her ears, but no doubt Daniel was driving too fast! In the two months since she had come to live at Cloud Cottage there had only been one visitor. Her brother, Daniel's father, had come one weekend to help her with a project.

Car doors slammed. Katherine said a wistful mental goodbye to her spring solitude and went outside to welcome the raucous, yet joyous chaos that would soon envelop her world. The visiting season at Cloud Cottage had started.

"Aunt Katie, Aunt Katie," greeted her as she stepped onto the porch. Her grandniece and grandnephew came bouncing up the steps. Caitlin wrapped her arms around her Aunt Katie. Connor held back a little until Katherine put her arm around his shoulder in a 'sideways squidge.' It immediately became a group hug when their father, Katherine's nephew, stretched his arms and pulled all four of them together.

"I'm squished," a muffled voice pleaded.

"Sorry, Caitlin," he relaxed his embrace and the little girl wiggled free. "I'm just so happy to be here I got carried away."

"Can we go to the beach?" Connor asked.

"Yeah, can we?" echoed Caitlin.

Their dad grinned and turned to his aunt. "Remember when I asked that question?"

"As soon as you got out of the car," Katherine answered.

"What do you think? Is there time for these two beach bums to hit the sand before dinner?"

"Of course," answered their aunt smiling. "After all it's tradition!"

"Ok, now listen – you stay out of the water, stay together, walk – dash – or run as far as the lighthouse, then come right back. Got it?" he asked, his voice intense and serious.

"Got it," the twins answered as they raced toward the beach path.

Their father, still grinning, turned and gave Katherine another hug.

"How are you, Aunt Katie?"

"Wonderful!"

"Come sit, tell me about retired life at Cloud Cottage."

Katherine sat down on the swing next to him and looked at her nephew. One should not have favorites, but somehow with Daniel, or 'Dano' as she had affectionately called him since he was a little boy, there had been a special bond. He had been quiet, sensitive, and like a little sponge, he had absorbed everything around him, the good and the bad. When his parents divorced it had been difficult for him. He had harbored a lot of anger for many years. In some ways Katherine's home had been his escape hatch. She had lived close enough for after school visits, frequent sleepovers and long weekends. His younger sister Jennifer sometimes came too, and also spent overnights by herself. But it had been Dano who was at Katherine's side in the garden, or antiquing, participating with gusto in whatever project was at hand.

"Aunt Katie, what are you thinking?"

"Oh, just how much I love you and how glad I am you are here."

"Me too, me too! Now, tell me, does life here agree with you?"

"Yes, Dano, it does. I feel invigorated, yet content at the same time, and I have been surprised how much I've enjoyed the solitude. Yet I think it was time human activity came back into my daily routine. Just now, sitting here, looking at you, I realized how much I miss you. I've become so self-absorbed that I don't know what's happening in the lives of people I care about. I never thought, nor do I want, love of solitude to lead to detachment."

"Aunt Katie, your love of people and family is too strong for that to happen. You've been surrounded by people for decades, engaged in relationships of all kinds that placed demands upon you, at a cost to your personal life. Now this is your time to be 'Katherine.' If you find there is a quality to solitude you enjoy – enjoy it – and tell us to back off."

"Is that my Dano, or Dr. MacLeod the psychiatrist speaking?"

"Both! You will always be my very special Aunt Katie, and from you I learned to be insightful. I just honed my skills in medical school."

Laughter, the sound of pounding feet and panting announced the return of Connor and Caitlin. They rounded the corner of the house and collapsed on the porch steps.

"I do believe there is a tickle pile on your porch, Aunt Katie." Dano jumped up adding his lanky limbs to the children's and started tickling anyone who wasn't moving.

"Let's get Aunt Katie," a little boy's voice called out. At once, wiggling fingers surrounded the swing, and to the children's delight Katherine joined in.

"Truce, truce," the children's father called out. Four bodies froze in place, then collapsed where they were. Katherine was still on the swing, but she hadn't stopped laughing.

"That was fun," Connor announced, "and Dad, you've got to see the beach, it's really wide this year." Without taking a breath he continued, "What's for dinner, Aunt Katie?"

"You're always hungry," his father teased. Then he asked, "Do you have something planned, Aunt Katie, or should I order a pizza?"

"Chili is simmering on the stove."

"Johnnycake too?"

"A double batch of johnnycake," Aunt Katie answered.

"Yay!"

"Yay," Dano agreed.

"We'll do pizza tomorrow night."

"We have to have a beach fire and roast hot dogs," Connor said.

"And S'mores!" echoed Caitlin.

"Weather permitting," their dad answered, smiling at Katherine.

They were just finishing the dinner cleanup when the phone rang. Katherine was up to her elbows in soapy water cleaning the chili kettle.

"Would you like me to answer it?" Dano asked.

"Go ahead."

"Cloud Cottage," Dano said as he picked up the phone and smiled at Katherine. "Oh, hi Dad, how are you?"

Katherine only heard one side of the conversation, but she could tell her brother Daniel, wanted to come up the next day.

"Just a moment, I'll ask." Dano covered the phone with his hand and said, "He wants to know if he can come?"

"How do you feel about it?"

"Oh, it's fine, Aunt Katie. It's good for Connor and Caitlin to see him."

Katherine nodded in understanding. "It's fine by me, if it's all right with you."

Dano spoke into the phone again, "Your favorite big sister said there's room at the inn. Great, we'll see you then." Dano hung up, aware that Katherine was looking at him.

19

"What? It is what it is." In a more serious tone he said, "Aunt Katie, before Dad gets here I would like to speak with you, perhaps after the kids have gone to bed?"

Katherine nodded in affirmation as the twins entered the kitchen.

"Can we play a game now?"

"Go choose one and set it up. We'll be right there," Daniel answered with a grin; and then asked, "Are you ready, Aunt Katie?"

"'Let the games begin,' is the cry of the clan," she answered.

The children picked out two games not one, and both were played with competitive gusto.

5

It was almost eleven when Dano came back downstairs after tucking Connor and Caitlin in bed. Katherine was waiting for him with a pot of tea at the kitchen table.

"Aunt Katie, it's late," he started.

"Daniel Angus MacLeod, I am retired, not ancient. I can tell something is bothering you. Now sit down, let's have it!"

"Yes Ma'am!" They both laughed as Dano filled his mug with tea. "Hey this is good, what is it?"

"Lavender mint," Katherine answered, then continued, "Dano?"

"Well, Aunt Katie," Dano began. "This is a little tough, because I never want you to be angry with me, and of all the people in the world you are the one I never want to disappoint." He paused and looked up.

"Ok, Dano," Katherine responded quietly. "That said, and now that you are at least looking me in the eye – whatever it is – we'll get through it. Talk to me."

Dano took a deep breath. "Caroline and I are having some problems. She wants a trial separation this summer."

"And you?" Katherine asked.

"I recognize the issues," Dano replied. "They are real. It's just that after everything I went through as a kid with my parents' divorce it's the one thing I said I would never ever do to my kids. I think I'm more willing to work toward a solution. Sometimes I think Caroline is too willing to walk away. Anyway, she has agreed to go through counseling this summer as long as I agree to a trial separation."

"Hmmmm," was Katherine's response.

"Yes, hmmmm."

"Has she moved out, Dano?"

"No, and at this point the kids know nothing. Or at least I don't think they suspect. We have been very careful about anything in front of them. It hasn't been hard to minimize our contact. Our schedules are busy; we have become good at juggling work, and conferences out of town, so one of us always seems to be away. We haven't sat down as a family of four for a meal in weeks."

"And you don't think Connor and Caitlin suspect anything? Give them credit, Dano."

"Well, maybe, but sometimes one or both of them are gone at dinner time too. Family life is just different today, even in the most cohesive families."

"That I understand," agreed Katherine. "Well, what are you going to do?"

"Aunt Katie, that's one of the reasons I wanted to talk with you." He took a deep breath. "Would you, could you, have Connor and Caitlin here with you at Cloud Cottage this summer? I do realize what I am asking and …"

"Yes," Katherine answered, saving him the agony of further justifications. "But how is this going to help you?"

"Our thought," he began…

"Our thought?"

"Yes, Caroline is on board with this. The children will come here as soon, and for as long as you agree to. Caroline and I will both stay at the house – in separate rooms. We'll participate together and separately in counseling. My hope is we'll have some space to work on the issues yet not so much that we feel we have moved on and started new lives. I'll come to Cloud Cottage every weekend I can, and when it's okay with you."

"Is this really what you want, Dano?" Katherine asked.

"Given the circumstances, yes. There is no better place for Connor and Caitlin this summer than here with you. There's no better place for Caroline and me than to be in our own home while we work through this."

Katherine was quiet for a moment, then spoke. "Ok, Dano, here's what I think. Connor and Caitlin should come as soon as they are out of school, and stay until school starts or you and Caroline are ready for them to come home. Whatever comes first. You are welcome here any time. Only understand when other families are here you may find yourself sleeping on an air mattress."

"Aunt Katie, that's perfect! More than I could have hoped you could agree to."

"Hold on, Dano, I'm not finished. I have one condition."

Dano watched his aunt's expression; it was very serious. He knew too well that stern look.

"Yes?" he asked.

"My condition is that for one week before this summer is over, before you make any final decision to divorce – if it comes to that – you will spend one week here at Cloud Cottage as a family."

"Caroline might not ..." Dano started.

"Don't close doors," Katherine interrupted. "Talk with her, not to her, but with her!"

"Got it! I'll call her in the morning."

Dano said goodnight and went up to bed. He had chosen to bunk with Connor in the traditional boys' room instead of using the sleeper sofa in the den that functioned as the fourth bedroom at Cloud Cottage. Caitlin

23

was tucked in bed in the girls' room. Katherine checked on her before she went to her own room. It was late but no way could she fall asleep. She was saddened by Dano's situation and knew he would indeed work hard to preserve the marriage. Katherine remembered too well the little boy who arrived at her house after having witnessed arguments between his parents. It wasn't what he wanted for his children.

Connor and Caitlin! What had she agreed to? Two energetic ten year olds for the entire summer? Well, some weeks there would be cousins for them to play with, but they would need some structure too. Perhaps a project to complete… Katherine was morphing into teacher mode as she fell asleep with ideas floating through her dreams.

The next morning Dano gave Katherine a 'thumbs up' to indicate he had spoken with Caroline and all systems were go.

The children were excited to see their grandfather and upon his arrival led him to the beach. Katherine was pleased to see her brother interacting with his grandchildren. Relating to people, young or old, had never been easy for him. It was one of the major differences between them, yet Katherine and Daniel had always had a strong connection.

The weekend passed quickly and there were no opportunities for serious conversations, which was fine. These days were about making memories and family bonding.

Monday morning Katherine took Dano aside and proposed that before they left she would sit down with Connor and Caitlin and invite them to spend the summer with her. Dano thought it was a great idea. Later two excited children piled in the car anxious to ask their mom if they could stay with Aunt Katie at Cloud Cottage all summer.

Dano winked and gave her a big hug as he whispered, "I'll see you in a couple weeks."

Katherine nodded, smiled, and winked back. By her side her brother, Dano's father, was watching her. After the car was out of sight he turned.

"Kate? Are you going to tell me what that was about?"

"What?"

"You and Dano are scheming. I know you."

"Don't be silly. Cloud Cottage is about family. Connor and Caitlin are your grandchildren, but they come close to being my grandchildren too. I think it would be fun to have them here. Besides, this way you can spend time with them."

"What about Jennifer's kids?" he asked referring to his other grandchildren.

"When they are old enough I would love to have them for a summer too."

Her brother grunted in response.

"Oh, don't be an old grump. Just enjoy the evening. I'm glad you didn't have to leave before morning."

6

Katherine had meant every word she said to her brother. She was also aware that the 'open door' policy she had created at Cloud Cottage did pose some issues. There were very few days from the middle of June until Labor Day that there would not be guests in the house. They were family, but Katherine realized she would need to establish a schedule of responsibilities for cleaning, laundry, cooking, buying groceries, and yard work. Cloud Cottage was an ancestral home, not an all-inclusive resort.

Another issue that now concerned her was sleeping accommodations. Traditionally there had been the master bedroom, the bunkroom for girls, the bunkroom for boys, and the den as a second master if two families were present at the same time – which was often. Now that Katherine had claimed the master bedroom as hers, there was only one other room for double occupancy. Katherine sighed; she wondered if this was how Uncle Gus had felt when the families had all descended upon Cloud Cottage. She knew what she needed to do – exactly what Uncle Gus had done – and Great-Grandfather Aonghus before him. She hadn't yet been to the third floor attic this spring. She had been too busy getting the first two floors ready.

Katherine opened the hall door that led from the second floor to the attic and peered up the stairs. She could probably count on her two hands the number of times she had been up there. As a child it had been strictly off limits. Sometimes children are tempted to enter forbidden territory, but not at Cloud Cottage. No one went up those stairs, not even adults, only Uncle Gus.

Katherine took a deep breath and climbed the steps. Halfway up, the stairway turned so that the top step was just under the roof peak. The morning sun was streaming in through two side-by-side double hung windows in the east gable. Wow, thought Katherine, it's really light and airy up here. In the west gable the beautiful stone of the chimney formed a wall and on each side there were double hung windows as well. It will be just as light up here in the afternoon, she thought. Who knew? The roof was steep enough to allow six-foot head clearance about five feet to either side of the peak.

The position of the stairs divided the space into two areas. It appeared Uncle Gus had used the smaller area west of the stairs, approximately eight by ten, as a sitting area. There was an armchair, a sofa, and a bookshelf. The larger area on the east end, approximately twenty by ten, had been his sleeping area. There was a bed, a bureau, an old washstand, several trunks, and another comfortable armchair. Katherine felt like *Alice* when she stepped through the looking glass. How could she not have known? Does anyone else know this space is so delightful? No one ever said anything, and Uncle Gus certainly didn't, but then we didn't ask. Any glimpse up the stairs through the open doorway had looked dark and creepy, perhaps because the stairway turned. Whenever she had come up a couple times to get Christmas decorations it had been dark and shrouded. It would have been much darker in winter, and Uncle Gus had draped sheets over all the furniture to keep it clean – old timers always did that.

"Well, Uncle Gus, it isn't creepy up here now. I'm moving up for the summer, just like you did. All it needs is a good cleaning and some fresh air."

Katherine stepped to the window and tried pushing on the sash. It responded to her touch and slid up. The windows were even screened. She went to each of the windows, and in a couple moments all four windows were open and a wonderful cross-breeze flowed from end-to-end. Katherine paused and looked out. It was the best view in the house. Suddenly an idea came to her and she went to the east gable to check. Sure enough she could see a sliver of Silver Lake. That's why, she marveled, Uncle Gus referred to this window as 'Silver View' and the other on the west was 'Golden View' – he always said sunsets were golden moments.

"Have I got it right, Uncle Gus?" She didn't need an answer.

The attic needed a top-to-bottom cleaning. After all it had been at least three years since it had been used. Katherine also rearranged and organized. She didn't have time to open boxes and sort. Items stored there would need to be examined at another time. For the moment she just pushed them back under the eaves.

She found folding dividers at a yard sale and painted them. She bought a new mattress for the old iron bedframe, and chintz slipcovers for the sofa and armchairs. Her biggest challenge was electrical outlets, but an electrician was able to run wire and installed several. Obviously Uncle Gus and Great-Grandfather Aonghus did not have the same need she did for electrical outlets. The one issue she could not solve was the bathroom. She did regret giving up her master bath, and if the need arose in the middle of the night, well, she would deal with it. Otherwise her attic had become an oasis under the eaves. She would be very comfortable and she felt good about the extra bedroom being available for guests.

Katherine had worked in the attic during the mornings and evenings of those early June days. In the afternoons she finished planting her garden. She had planted peas and potatoes much earlier, and during a warm spell in May, had set out a few tomatoes and peppers. She remembered too late Uncle Gus telling her to wait until after the last full moon of spring to plant tender seedlings. Sometimes that full moon was late May, sometimes it was early June. This year it had been late May and, sure enough, it frosted. There was even frost on her hilltop. It looked like the tomatoes were okay. The peppers, she had lost. They were more susceptible to cold temperatures. She was glad she hadn't planted anything more.

Katherine knew she was planting too big a garden, but the seed catalogs had been so interesting she got carried away. Now she had to get those seeds in the ground or it would be too late for the crop to mature. She wondered if she was going to be able to keep ahead of the weeds during the summer. Then she remembered the twins and grinned. They may not be enthused, but we'll make a game of weeding, she thought. Katherine was looking forward to Connor and Caitlin's arrival.

Katherine pulled her hoe along one last row, covering bean seed as she did so. There, she thought, that's it. I'll plant one more row of beans in ten days and a hill of zucchini and summer squash in a protected spot by the house. If I'm lucky, I'll still have some veggies in October. Then that's it. The garden will be planted. She looked over her rows of plants and furrows of covered seeds with great satisfaction. Now begins the battle with the critters. She grimaced. Her entire garden, as well as her fruit trees, were inside a deer fence, but that didn't mean raccoons, woodchucks, bunny rabbits, whatever might not go under, through, or over!

The twins were due to arrive in two days. They were coming earlier than expected, but Katherine had everything done to her satisfaction. She still had to move her things up to the attic oasis, but she wouldn't do that until other guests arrived and her room was needed. Therefore, Katherine thought, I officially declare tomorrow a holiday. I will do whatever I like – or nothing at all. She extended the holiday to the next morning as well, and slept in. How decadent, she felt, as she snuggled in her bed until nearly noon. But if Dano and the twins should arrive she would be embarrassed. She threw off the cozy covers and got up to dress.

Perhaps it would be a good idea to move a few clothes upstairs. After Connor and Caitlin are here, free time will be short. She stacked the contents of one dresser drawer into a tall pile and started up to her oasis. She had cleaned the bureau drawers and lined them with fresh paper, so they were ready. She filled the bottom drawer with sweaters then pushed to close it. It jammed about two-thirds shut. She wiggled it free and pushed to close it again. Once more it jammed.

"What's going on?"

A third time she wiggled and wrenched on the drawer. Finally she heard a thud under the dresser and the drawer closed. She opened and closed the drawer a couple times in succession and it worked fine.

"All right, this is good," she said. "But do I really want to look under the bureau?"

Something was causing that drawer to catch and whatever it was, was not there anymore. Not feeling very brave, and with visions of all kinds of critters populating her thoughts, Katherine backed across the room and bent down to look under the bureau from the safe perspective of distance. There was something there all right – but it was flat – it clearly did not have legs. Feeling braver, at least a little, she looked around for something to use to scoot out whatever it was from under the bureau. Along one wall she spied the dust mop, perfect. In a moment 'the thing' was at Katherine's feet. The threat of danger was benign. It was a book, an old book. This is interesting, Katherine thought, as she picked it up. She turned the book to read the spine but it was blank. Puzzled, Katherine thumbed the pages.

"Well," she said aloud. "It is a real book, not a hollow replica that hides secret treasures. Perhaps it's a diary."

She opened a page or two that appeared to be the front. There was no title page, no printer's information, just blank pages. She started to leaf through blank page after blank page. An unused journal, she wondered?

Why was it secured with some kind of adhesive to the bureau? The spots on the four corners of one cover were sticky. The bleach water she had used during cleaning the drawers must have penetrated through the wood and weakened the adhesive. It must have been glued in place, but shifted with all the cleaning and jiggling. There probably were four sticky spots on the bottom of the bureau drawer too.

30

While these thoughts were going through her mind Katherine kept turning pages – nothing! She was about to put the book down when she thumbed the remaining pages. She stopped. There was writing. She flipped back to where she had seen ink. Sure enough, she found writing, but it was very faint. She started to read.

7

Frantic voices echoed through the house.

"Aunt Katie, Aunt Katie."

The twins! She had been so engrossed she hadn't heard them. She balanced the book in her hand wondering what to do. She so wanted to read it but that was not an option.

"Lousy timing, book," she muttered under her breath. "Why didn't you drop out last week?" She laid the book inside another dresser drawer and headed for the stairs.

"I'm on my way down," she called.

Dano met her at the bottom of the stairs, a concerned look on his face.

"Aunt Katie?"

"What?" Katherine answered.

"We knocked and knocked. Then I found the kitchen door was unlocked and when we called inside you still didn't answer. I, well ..."

"Dano, I'm fine, " Katherine interrupted. "I'm sorry I alarmed you, and very sorry I wasn't downstairs to greet you. I guess I just lost track of time."

"Aunt Katie?" a hesitant little voice called upstairs.

"I'm up here, Caitlin," she answered, realizing the kids had been disturbed too.

"Come on up, Connor, Caitlin," their father called.

The twins bounced up the stairs. "Where were you, Aunt Katie?" they asked.

"Well," she began, then stopped. She sat on a step and motioned for them to sit on the step below her. Dano leaned against the door and listened as she explained about the attic. How Great-Grandfather Aonghus and Uncle Gus had always slept there in the summer when the house was full of family. How it had always been off-limits. No one else went up these stairs. She further explained that this summer she would be sleeping up those stairs but it still would be off limits to everyone else. If they needed her they could open the door to the stairs and call, but not come up. The children listened, the concern on their faces replaced with serious attention.

"Does that apply to me too?" Dano asked.

"Absolutely! The attic is off-limits." Katherine was stern. "Everyone understand?"

Three heads nodded in affirmation.

"Then let's go unload your car."

The kids raced back downstairs, but Dano still leaned against the door. Katherine raised her eyebrows, but waited for him to speak. He didn't, so she spoke.

"Dano, surely you remember Uncle Gus sleeping upstairs and the 'No Entry' policy?"

"Sure," he answered, "but Aunt Katie, I can't help feeling like we've pushed you out of your bedroom for the summer."

"No, Dano, it's a decision I would have come to eventually with all the family visiting in the coming weeks. My bedroom is needed for guests. Other than the sleeper sofa in the den it's the only double bed in the house. I am just going on vacation in the attic – and trust me it is fine."

"You aren't going to let me go up and see for myself, not even me?"

"No," Katherine replied, "not even you, Dano. Perhaps it would help you to think of the attic as my oasis under the eaves, I'm sure it was for Uncle Gus."

"Okay, Aunt Katie, I get that, but can you really be comfortable up there?"

Katherine smiled. "Dano, I'll be very comfortable. I have fixed it up a bit, I bought a new mattress, and an electrician added a few outlets. That's all the attic needed. I will be fine as long as everyone respects the boundaries. Agreed?"

"Agreed!"

Sounds of suitcases being dragged upstairs interrupted their conversation. Dano shrugged his shoulders then went to help the twins. Katherine was relieved. She did want to preserve the sanctity of space in the attic, but now she had another reason for not wanting other people up there. What was the story behind the book?

"Oh, Katie Ann MacLeod," she laughed. "That's a good one for even you – the story behind the book." She went to join Dano and the children.

A discussion was underway in the boys' room about sleeping arrangements. Katherine stopped in the doorway. The room was not huge, but good-sized. There were two sets of offset bunk beds in each corner. It was designed to sleep four, but with sleeping bags on the floor it often accommodated six or seven. The discussion seemed to revolve around whether Connor could choose a top bunk. Was it fair for him to monopolize it all summer?

"What do you think, Aunt Katie?" Connor asked when he realized she was listening.

"I think you and your Dad are both right. How about if you take a top bunk with the understanding that you let a cousin sleep there if he wants to?

"Okay," Connor nodded.

"Caitlin, how about you and I go choose your bed?"

The little girl nodded and skipped ahead of Aunt Katie. The girls' room was set up to accommodate six. It had one set of bunk beds and two trundle beds.

"I like all the beds in the girls' room, Aunt Katie."

"Then that's easy. Choose a bed to start in and each time we wash your sheets you can choose which one you will sleep in next."

A happy Caitlin placed her suitcase on a bed, then chose a drawer in the dresser for her clothes. Katherine smiled at the little girl. She was sure there would be times during the summer she would be challenged by the twins, but overall they were easy children to have around.

Dano stuck his head in the door. "All settled in here?" Caitlin nodded, smiling. Katherine acknowledged with a nod too. "Okay, then come give me a big hug. I have to be on my way."

"Now, Dano?" Katherine asked surprised. "You're not staying the night?"

"Sorry, Aunt Katie, something came up that I have to be back for in the morning, but I will come up early on Saturday. Alright kids? That's only four days away."

"Aunt Katie," Connor spoke up. "Daddy thought we should all come on Saturday, but Caitlin and I wanted to come today. After all, you said we could spend our whole summer vacation and this is our first day."

"Then we aren't going to lose a day, are we?" Katherine responded. "Let's walk your daddy to the car."

Dano wrapped his arm around Katherine, as they all headed for the stairs. Once again the twins raced ahead.

"Thanks, Aunt Katie." When the kids were out of earshot he added, "Caroline and I have our first counseling sessions tomorrow, together and separately. It may be a very long day. Given Connor and Caitlin's enthusiasm to get here, well, we thought perhaps they were better here. I hope it's okay."

"Of course it is, Dano. Have you outlined the ground rules we discussed so we are all on the same page?"

"Connor and Caitlin have been briefed – thoroughly!"

Together they walked the last few steps to the car where the twins were waiting. Each one had gathered an armful of possessions from the back seat. Katherine was pleased to note each one held several books. Connor, however, was very cautiously juggling a tablet. He was trying to secure it on top of his armload with his chin.

"Connor," Katherine suggested, "how about if I carry your tablet to the house?"

"Please, Aunt Katie," Caitlin asked, "he's going to drop it."

"Well guys, this is it, group hug," their father said. It was a good thing, Katherine thought, her nephew was tall and lanky with very long arms. There were many in the family who thought he looked more like her than his father.

8

In true Cloud Cottage tradition, Katherine and the twins stood waving goodbye until the car rounded the curve and disappeared down the hill.

"What may we do now, Aunt Katie?" Caitlin asked.

"Is there something we can do to help you?" Connor added. Katherine couldn't help smiling. They certainly had been briefed and prompted on the proper use of 'can' and 'may.'

"Thank you both for asking," Katherine answered, "this is your first day. What would you like to do?"

"Go to the beach!" was shouted in unison.

"Okay, to celebrate your arrival, I think that's a capital idea." The twins turned to run. "Whoa, what are the rules?"

They stopped, turned back, expressions of chagrin on their faces.

"Stay together. Stay out of the water. Never be gone more than one hour," they answered.

"Who's wearing a watch?" Katherine asked.

"We both are," as they proudly held up their arms to show off fancy new waterproof timepieces.

"Awesome," Katherine said. "Are those walkie-talkies too?"

"No, Aunt Katie," Caitlin answered, "just watches, but they do have a stop-watch function. Dad told us to always set it to remind us of the hour limit. Connor, did you set yours?"

"No, I forgot," he answered, as he looked up at Aunt Katie, dismayed.

"I was going to set mine when I got to the beach," Caitlin continued.

"Well," Aunt Katie responded. "If you set it on the beach you'd be gone from Cloud Cottage more than an hour. Set it when you leave here. How long does it take you to get to the beach?" Connor and Caitlin looked at each other. "Why don't you time yourselves going down, then be sure to allow that much time to come back up, within the hour limit. Got it?"

"Got it, Aunt Katie, we'll do it."

"Good, now go. I'll have dinner ready when you get back in an hour."

Katherine watched them disappear as they started down the path. They were wonderful children, but they were children. She was more than a little concerned about the beach rules their father had established. This was a different age than it had been for previous generations at Cloud Cottage. She would have to trust that all would be well and enjoy the summer.

There were going to be adjustments and one would be meals. If she were alone she would have had some fruit and yogurt for dinner, but tonight she was cooking. Perhaps she could do grilled cheese with apple slices. That would be easy and fast. Katherine was desperate to go back upstairs and check out the book; instead she headed for the kitchen. She sliced and buttered the bread, cut the cheese, and set the table. All that was left to do was grill the sandwiches and cut up the apples. She had at least a half-hour.

Katherine washed and dried her hands and headed for the attic. She wondered if she should be wearing gloves when she handled the book. Maybe tomorrow, she decided. One, she had already handled it with her bare hands, and two, she couldn't think of where she had a pair of clean gloves. No doubt it would be a good idea if she at least held it in a pillowcase. Katherine retrieved one from the linen closet then climbed the stairs. She opened the bureau drawer and carefully wrapped the book in the pillowcase. She wanted to sit down right there and start reading, but after the experience of the morning she didn't dare. She needed to be downstairs where she could hear Connor and Caitlin. In the living room she chose a chair by a window that looked out toward the beach path.

"Now," Katherine said out loud, "tell me your story, little book! Why were you hidden in the bureau?"

She found the pages where the writing started and began to read. It was a hard go. The handwriting was difficult to read, the ink was faint, and often she had to skip over words she could not decipher. By the time the twins returned, she was frustrated but intrigued beyond her wildest imagination. She did not yet know the story behind the book, but she was confident that it was either by or about her great-grandfather Aonghus. With a sigh Katherine wrapped the book back up and had just placed it high on a living room bookshelf when Connor and Caitlin burst into the room.

"Aunt Katie, you got to see them, they are so cool," Connor said.

"Way cool," Caitlin picked up where her brother stopped to catch his breath. "Will you come to the beach with us tomorrow?"

"What's way cool?"

"Kite surfers," Connor chimed back in. "They were down by the lighthouse. They were jumping and racing and everything."

"They had on wetsuits," Caitlin said.

"I've seen kite surfers there too. They like the wind currents around the Point, and I agree with you, they are 'way cool.' Come on, let's go to the kitchen."

Kite surfing continued to dominate the conversation all during dinner. Katherine was pleased the twins remained at the table and talked as she sat, enjoying her tea.

After a while Connor nudged Caitlin, who asked, "May we be excused?"

Given her nod of approval, both children picked up their dishes and carried them to the sink. While Caitlin loaded them in the dishwasher Connor came back to the table to get Katherine's.

"Thank you both."

"Sure," Connor answered. "Dad told us to help you. He said Uncle Gus had a saying about being useful."

" 'You're no ornament. You might as well make yourself useful,' " Caitlin said.

Katherine laughed, "That's right. He did."

"Aunt Katie," Caitlin asked. "Will you tell us a story tonight about Uncle Gus?"

"No," Connor interrupted, "I want to hear about old Aonghus."

"I think we have a lot of nights for stories," Katherine said. "Why don't we start with Great-Grandfather Aonghus? Let's go to the living room."

"I get the couch," Connor called as he raced ahead.

Caitlin walked beside Katherine. "Aunt Katie, may I sit in the storybook chair with you?"

"I'd like that."

Katherine positioned herself in the big oversized chair by the fireplace and the little girl climbed up next to her. Connor was sprawled on the couch.

"Once upon a time," Caitlin began with a giggle.

"Hey, who's telling this story?" Katherine asked.

9

"Once upon a time," Katherine began, "there was a Scottish lad from the Isle of Skye," and so the story went on. She shared the family legend of how young Aonghus, one day in the spring of 1863, angered his father while backing up a horse and cart. His father berated him. Aonghus, in an impetuous moment of youthful rebellion, ran away.

"Just because his dad yelled at him?" Connor asked.

"That's the story," Katherine answered. "It does seem pretty drastic, but we don't know how often he might have been punished by his father, or if there were other issues between them. The bottom line is Aonghus ran away, found his way to a seaport on the Isle of Skye. He secured passage as a cabin boy and worked his way across the Atlantic."

"How old was he?" Caitlin asked.

"Fourteen."

"And he never saw his family again?"

"No, he did not."

Katherine watched the intent faces of the twins as the reality of leaving home at that age sank in. Katherine continued the story. Sailing or following orders on a ship apparently didn't appeal to Aonghus either because as soon as he arrived in New York, he jumped ship. Just how he lived or what he did for his first months in this country she did not know. Somehow by early November of 1863, just a few months later, he found himself in Chicago. The story Katherine had heard was he wandered around the city and fell in with a group of young boys.

One day something happened that Aonghus never shared. The group took off running and when Aonghus realized the police were in pursuit, he split off, dodged into City Hall, and climbed his way to the observation tower. He had evaded the police but was apprehensive and he stayed in the tower the rest of the day. Katherine thought he must have been homesick and scared because he always said the view of the distant Michigan shore from that tower reminded him of home. He resolved then and there to get out of Chicago. He knew he had MacLeod cousins who lived in Montreal. From the tower he could see the docks, so when it felt safe to leave, that's where he went.

"Did he find work as a cabin boy again?" Connor asked.

"He secured work on the first ship he found headed to Canada. It was a schooner and sailed that same night."

Katherine paused for a moment, and reflected on the impulsive nature of this young boy, which was so different from the methodical stalwart Aonghus she thought she knew. He certainly had made rash decisions with hefty consequences. At fourteen he had been old enough to think he was a man but was not yet tempered to maturity.

"Aunt Katie?"

Katherine continued. She shared the story of the shipwreck, how young Aonghus found himself on the beach at Little Point Sable and of his walk to Stony Creek. When she got to the part about working in the lumber camp all winter, Caitlin interrupted her.

"Didn't he have to go to school?"

"No, instead he worked long hours all winter. Because of his size and age he did not have the strength to wield an axe all day in the woods, so he was given jobs around the camp."

She explained that in the cookhouse Aonghus built the fires in the cook stoves at three in the morning so breakfast would be ready for the men at 4:30. He ground coffee beans, peeled lots of potatoes, washed dishes, and did whatever the cook needed help with. He was known as a 'cookee.' Because the Stony Creek camp was small he also cleaned the barn and helped with the livestock.

Katherine shared with the twins that the foreman took an uncommon interest in this hard-working Scottish lad who had washed up on the beach. His own heritage was Irish, but as a child, like Aonghus, he had spoken Gaelic. At every opportunity he had Aonghus work with him, helped him improve his English, taught him elementary arithmetic, and how to write. He realized Aonghus was bright and very clever with numbers.

When spring came and the lumber camp closed for the season, the foreman offered Aonghus a job for the spring, summer, and fall, if he would also go to the local school. Aonghus would live with the foreman's family and work when school was not in session. Aonghus liked the foreman and considered himself very fortunate. Just a few months before, he had shipwrecked and was alone and starving in a strange country. Now he had survived the winter, had money in his pocket, an offer for a job, and an opportunity to go to school. When he asked how much school would cost, he was amazed that it was free. He only had to buy a slate and a book or two. He couldn't believe his good fortune. He accepted the foreman's offer!

During the first winter in the camp Aonghus listened when one of the men read the serial novelette on the front-page of the newspaper, news items, and sometimes a joke or two. He always wondered what information they were not reading. Perhaps next winter, when a newspaper came into the bunkhouse, he could read it himself. Katherine had heard that for the rest of his life Aonghus read every page of every newspaper.

One topic in the bunkhouse, whether from the newspaper or other sources, was always the war news. The men talked about the draft, bounties being paid, and where the last battles had been fought. Aonghus listened to each exchange about the war to preserve the union, kept his own counsel, but he wanted to know more. He would study very hard! At this point Katherine paused again.

"Don't stop Aunt Katie." Connor said, "Did he ever learn to read?"

"Yes," Katherine answered. "He did and throughout his life he emphasized education for his children and grandchildren. Look around this room, what do you see?"

They answered the usual: sofas, chairs, rugs, lamps…Caitlin figured out the answer Katherine was waiting for – books.

"That's right. See how on both sides of the fireplace the entire wall has built-in bookshelves?"

"Yeah, and they are full of books," Connor said.

"Old books," added Caitlin.

"Great-Grandfather Aonghus' books," Katherine continued. "He bought books from every peddler, on almost every trip to town, and through the mail. If you look you will see there are books about everything from how to grow fruit in Michigan to Shakespeare to history – lots of history, but particularly about the Scottish Highlands and the American Civil War."

"Did he read all of these?" Connor asked. He had gotten off the sofa and was reading titles as he walked along the bookshelf. "There must be a million books here."

"Not a million," Caitlin said, "but maybe a thousand."

Katherine smiled. Caitlin was the realistic, factual twin.

"Did any of these belong to Uncle Gus or Grandpa?" she asked.

"Yes," Katherine agreed, "but they're on the bookshelves on this wall." Katherine motioned to the wall opposite the fireplace. "The bookshelves here are mirror images of the bookshelves that flank the fireplace, right down to the spacing between shelves. On this wall, instead of a fireplace we have a nice wide arch to the front hall. You see, Great-Grandpa Aonghus was something of an architect too. He liked to design and build things."

"Like Cloud Cottage?" Connor asked.

"Like Cloud Cottage."

"I'm glad," Caitlin announced as she slipped her hand into Katherine's. "Now we can spend the summer here with you, Aunt Katie."

"What kind of wood is this?" Connor asked looking at the shelves.

"Walnut," Katherine replied. "He was very partial to rich dark wood. If you look around you will see it in other places in the house."

"Like the alcove at the top of the stairs by the bedrooms?" Caitlin asked.

"Exactly," Katherine answered.

"I like that little room," Caitlin continued, "especially the window."

"That is a very special window. It is called a 'leaded window.'"

"The one at the other end of the upstairs hall is leaded too. Are they supposed to be mirror images?"

"Very clever, Connor, you're right. They are the only two leaded windows in the house and they are opposite each other."

"Cool," Caitlin said.

"Cool," Katherine laughed. "Now I think it's about time for bed."

Connor protested. "But we have to hear more about Ancestor Aonghus."

"I like that," Katherine said. "Ancestor Aonghus, that is much easier to say than 'Great-Great-Grandfather Aonghus.'" Connor grinned, very pleased. Katherine went on, "but the adventures of Ancestor Aonghus will continue another night."

"Come on, Connor," Caitlin said as she extracted herself from Katherine. "Remember what Dad said."

"Good night, Aunt Katie," they said in unison. Katherine wondered how they did that. It must be a twin thing.

"You go on, I'll be up in a few minutes to say goodnight."

10

This has been an interesting evening, Katherine thought. She hadn't been sure how much history they would tolerate, but they absorbed it – every bit. She reached for the pillowcase-wrapped book on the top shelf of the bookcase.

"I'm glad they didn't spot this. I'm not ready to answer questions about this book yet."

Katherine walked through the downstairs, checking doors and turning off lights. Upstairs, she said goodnight to Connor and Caitlin and entered her own room. Anxious to open the book again, she rushed through her nighttime routine.

At last she was settled in her bed with the book in her hands. She continued to decipher some words, but there were so many she couldn't, it was impossible to put together a sequence of thoughts. The only content she could distill out of what she had read was a confession. The words "guilt," "sin," and the haunting phrase "God have mercy on my soul" had appeared several times. On some pages she couldn't pick out words at all. Frustrated, she leafed ahead.

"I can't make any sense of this," she said. After a few more pages the writing stopped in the middle of the page. She was about to close the book when a few more pages flipped open. There was more writing, and it was more legible. "Alright, this is more like it. Let's see what we have."

Katherine began to read. She read and reread. Often she turned back pages to reread them a third time. She was struggling to grasp all the threads of the story. She turned the last page and finished. Hopeful for more, she flipped through the remaining pages but they were blank. As she was about to close the book, she noticed a loose page. When she opened the book in order to straighten the page, it fell out. It wasn't a page at all—it was an envelope. My, thought Katherine, this is becoming even more bizarre. On the back of the envelope was written 'Clan MacLeod.'

"Well, I guess that includes me." She opened it, withdrew what appeared to be a letter, and read.

I am trusting to fate that a true member of the Clan MacLeod finds this letter. The facts I have to share are simple. On his deathbed my grandfather Aonghus MacLeod bared his soul to me, the specifics of which I have written in this book. The first pages of the book he wrote. What secrets they contain I have not discovered. I promised my grandfather I would find, value, and protect that which he describes in the book. I have failed. I have not found it. I hope at least I have protected it. I pray that you who are reading this will honor my oath to Aonghus MacLeod as if it were your own.

Angus MacLeod, II

Katherine sat motionless. Questions erupted in her thoughts, foremost, why? Why didn't Uncle Gus tell her? Why didn't he tell someone else – or did he? Does anyone else in the family know, she wondered? If they do, they have kept silent. Katherine had never heard this story about Great-Grandfather Aonghus and she was the acknowledged historian of the clan. Another question was – what should she do now that she knew? Share the information at the upcoming family reunion in August? That could start treasure-hunting hysteria. There were many in the family who would put money above clan. Greed could just breed discontent and chaos. Perhaps that is why Uncle Gus kept quiet. He had simple needs, a good home, and had been thrifty his whole life, as were most people who had lived through the Great Depression. He would have

47

had little use for wealth if, in fact, there was a valuable treasure. No, Katherine thought, Uncle Gus would rather not find it than have trouble in the family. I wonder how hard he looked for it? In the note he sounds contrite about having failed in his promise to find it.

"Well," said Katherine, "this has indeed been an interesting evening. I'm not going to make any decisions tonight. This will require some thought. I think it is safe to assume that whatever 'it' is isn't going anywhere. After all these years, another day, week, or month isn't going to matter."

Katherine turned out the light and snuggled down to sleep, if she could. The one issue that really troubled her was why Uncle Gus had left finding the book, this information, to chance-discovery. What if the bureau had been given to Goodwill, or sold at a yard sale or – then it dawned on her. Uncle Gus knew she wouldn't do that. She might refinish the bureau, or paint it, but she would never give away or sell a piece of Cloud Cottage history.

"Uncle Gus," she said aloud, "you addressed that letter to Clan MacLeod, but you knew that I would find it, didn't you? I'll bet you even knew that I would move upstairs for the summer. You knew I would clean from top to bottom, that's why you put it upstairs. Downstairs someone else could happen upon it. Still, Uncle Gus, you did take a chance, or at least a calculated risk." Katherine closed her eyes and drifted off to sleep.

11

Morning seemed to arrive way too early the next day. The first noise she was aware of was the sound of light footsteps outside her bedroom door. Oh, the twins, she groaned inwardly. She wanted to roll over for another thirty minutes, but that was winter behavior. She stretched and got up. She found her young guests in the living room looking at the bookshelves.

"Good morning. Are you finding anything of interest?"

"Oh, we're just counting how many different topics we can find, Aunt Katie."

"Keep counting, let me know what you decide. I'll see about something for us to eat."

After breakfast Katherine had already planned to start the day with a roundtable discussion to establish a daily routine, define expectations, propose projects, and create a wish list of activities. All went well, and they were soon out and about for the day. A stint of weeding in the garden followed by an exploration of deer paths in the woods, lunch, and an afternoon on the beach made for a very full day.

The twins had been disappointed that there were no kite boarders about the Point, but the calmer winds made it safe for water sports. Katherine had invested in two kayaks and a standup paddleboard. The water was chilly but fine for splashing or brief dips, and the new 'toys' were a hit. The twins were delighted that Aunt Katie kayaked too. They must think I am ancient, Katherine thought. Why not? I always thought Uncle Gus was old.

All day Katherine had managed to focus on the current activities and not dwell on the book. She knew how special it was to have the twins with her and intended to appreciate and enjoy them. As she sat on the beach to dry off and watched the two kayaks circling around each other, her thoughts drifted to Uncle Gus and what she had learned the night before. One thing had finally made sense to her – why all the books on the Civil War? The collection really did go beyond an immigrant's casual interest. Clearly Ancestor Aonghus had been searching for information.

"Watch this, Aunt Katie," Connor called, as he and Caitlin raced their kayaks to shore. "I win."

Caitlin grinned, "I let you win," she teased.

"I'll race you again."

"Tomorrow," Katherine interrupted the rivalry, then added, "maybe I'll win."

The twins pulled the water toys high up on the beach for safekeeping. Katherine gathered up the towels and other beach paraphernalia. Together they climbed up the path to Cloud Cottage.

As they climbed, Connor asked, "Did Ancestor Aonghus name his house 'Cloud Cottage' because it is so high?"

"Connor!" Caitlin exclaimed. "It's called 'Cloud Cottage' because of our name 'MacLeod.'" She then turned to Katherine for backup, "Isn't it, Aunt Katie?"

"Yes, but we don't know everything that Ancestor Aonghus was thinking. Perhaps he had meant it to have multiple meanings. I wouldn't be surprised if he didn't feel like his house was in the clouds."

"You mean," Connor asked, "like Caitlin is a name in Gaelic but it means Katherine in English?"

"That's not a multiple meaning, that difference is due to another language, and is a translation," she explained.

They had reached the top of the hill.

"Okay everybody, outdoor shower, dry off in the mudroom before you go upstairs to change."

Each twin took a turn. Installing the outdoor shower had been another innovation of Uncle Gus. It had definitely cut down on the amount of sand that made it into Cloud Cottage. As Katherine rinsed off, she reflected on her comment to the kids about Ancestor Aonghus, perhaps using multiple meanings when he named Cloud Cottage. She should keep that in mind.

"What's for dinner, Aunt Katie?" The twins were already dressed and back downstairs.

Katherine laughed, "Give me a few minutes, I'm not even in the house yet. While I get dressed you two check out the freezer and choose a couple options for dinner, everything is labeled. I'll make the final decision."

On rainy days during the spring Katherine had filled the freezer with entrees for days such as this.

"Great," was the response.

Katherine didn't hurry, she knew the twins would be fine and were engaged in long negotiations about the choices. While she was getting dressed the phone rang.

"Hi, Aunt Katie, how's it going?" Dano asked.

"Wonderful, we have just come up from the beach. How was your day?"

"Interesting!"

"Hmmmm, that's non-committal. The kids are downstairs. I'll call to them in a minute. I want to check to see if you are still planning on this weekend?"

"Absolutely, I'll be up Saturday morning."

"Do you remember that Sunday is Father's Day, and your dad, sister and family are coming this weekend too?"

"Yes, I remember – and I promise to be on good behavior."

"You're incorrigible!"

"Of course."

Katherine had walked downstairs as they talked. She found the twins in the kitchen as she expected, and handed them the phone. An aluminum tray of frozen lasagna was on the counter and a store-bought frozen pizza. Katherine chose the quicker of the two options, and put the lasagna back in the freezer. She would add toppings to the pizza and fix a salad. Thirty minutes later they sat down to eat. Katherine watched as Connor and Caitlin attacked the pizza. Aside from a minor conflict about sliced tomatoes on the pizza it had been a very easy day. A side salad with no tomatoes was the compromise. Katherine mused, BLT's for dinner might not be an option later in the summer.

"Do you know what Sunday is?" she asked.

"Father's Day," Caitlin responded. "We went shopping with Mommy last Saturday. We have a package all wrapped."

Connor interjected. "We have to make cards, Caitlin."

"Yeah, we didn't find a card we liked, so we each have to make a card. I brought paper, stickers, markers, and stuff."

"Good idea," Katherine answered. Pleased, that despite issues, their mother had prepared them for Father's Day. "Your grandpa will be here too. Do you think you have enough supplies to make him a card?"

"Sure," Connor answered.

Katherine continued, "Do you know Aunt Jennifer and Uncle John are coming?"

"JJ and Megan are coming?"

"Yes, your cousins will be here too."

"Cool, are they bringing their dog?" Connor asked.

"I don't know. You'll just have to wait and see."

It would be a good diversion for the twins to have other children to play with for the weekend. John Jr. was nine and Megan was seven, so they were younger, but Katherine was confident they would blend well. Summer places and Christmas holidays were the time and place for cousin bonding.

"You can work here on the kitchen table and make your cards this evening. I have a project on the computer in the den I need to do."

While Caitlin went to get the supplies, Connor asked, "Aunt Katie, aren't we going to have an Ancestor Aonghus story tonight?"

Katherine impulsively hugged the child. "Connor, I want to share all the MacLeod stories with you, but we have many nights this summer. Tomorrow I have an adventure in mind, and Friday night your cousins will be here. Wouldn't it be a good idea to have your cards ready? Besides, maybe JJ and Megan would like to hear about Ancestor Aonghus."

"What kind of an adventure?" Katherine had roused his curiosity, and for the moment Ancestor Aonghus was forgotten.

"Later, first let's all do our projects."

Caitlin had produced her supplies for card making and the twins started to create.

Katherine headed for the den. Although she had not allowed the book to dominate her thoughts all day, she had considered several issues and had come to some conclusions. One, this information, at least for now, she would keep 100% to herself. Two, she needed to do some research to understand what she had read the night before. Three, she had to protect the book. Her mission tonight was to research scanners, laptops, and tablets. She needed to have some portable computer capability for her oasis under the eaves. She would need privacy when she worked on the book during the summer. That would not exist anywhere downstairs. Also she needed to protect the information until the time came to share it. Katherine hoped she could encrypt a file that a younger, computer-savvy family member might not hack.

53

To protect the book itself she intended to scan the pages. She could then put the book safely away and not handle it every night. The scanned pages would be her worksheets. She didn't think she would even print them, at least not yet. For now a computer was the tool she needed. She had already planned on replacing her older computer and had done some preliminary research. She thought she knew what she wanted. It was scanners or photo printers she had not researched. That's what she needed to do tonight. The timing was perfect. She was confident Jennifer's husband, John, would set everything up for her this weekend.

Katherine parked herself in front of the computer and went to work. She was so intent that she didn't hear the twins until they were at her elbow.

"Are you going to buy a new computer, Aunt Katie?" Connor asked.

"That's the plan."

"Is that the adventure for tomorrow?" he continued.

"Yes, Connor, at least in part. Shall we go buy a new computer and scanner tomorrow?"

"Cool," was the response.

"Good, I've got a little more research to do. Why don't you play a game?"

"We haven't finished our cards yet, Aunt Katie," Caitlin said. "We just came to check on you."

Katherine shook her head as they headed back to the kitchen. The twins had just confirmed her concerns about privacy. If she had been working on pages of the book right now there was no doubt in her mind that Connor's eyes would have focused right in on certain words. Katherine was also amused that they checked on her. She wondered what their father had told them.

Katherine finished her research, but before she shut down the computer she checked hours and facilities at several parks near the computer stores she planned to visit. She knew one had a fine interpretive center on dune formation and wonderful trails. It would be a great follow-up to this morning's hike.

"Katherine," she said out loud, "you just can't help yourself. You will always be a teacher." She slipped her research notes into a folder just as the twins reappeared.

"Done?" she asked, "May I see?" The twins looked at each other, reluctance on their faces. "Ah," Katherine continued. "You want them to be a surprise?"

"If that's okay?" Caitlin asked.

These two were so intent on pleasing her it was almost as if they were walking on eggshells. Katherine wondered if it wasn't a carryover from the troubled household of their parents. She didn't believe for a minute that Connor and Caitlin hadn't picked up vibes.

"Of course it's okay."

"We made one for Uncle John too, one from both of us." Caitlin continued, "I only had supplies enough for one more card. Do you think that will be okay?"

"Caitlin, I'm sure Uncle John will be pleased you thought to make him a card."

"Where can we put them, Aunt Katie? I don't want anyone to find them before Sunday.

"Let's see, how about in a file folder in the back of this cabinet?" Katherine handed Caitlin the folder and Connor concealed it in a drawer.

12

The sun was setting and the den was filled with all the wonderful colors of day's end. Katherine watched Connor look at the colors as they splashed against the light walls of the room. She suspected he was as intuitive and artistic as Caitlin was factual and organized. He would notice the wide variety of topics covered by the books in Ancestor Aonghus's library. Caitlin would want to count them. So they had. She led, he followed. She listened, he absorbed. She competed, he triumphed.

"Connor," Katherine asked, "What name shall we give the colors of tonight's sunset?"

"Oh," he responded. "How about *Laughing Rose* for this one, and *Lemonade Delight* for here?" as he pointed to the wall. He had understood immediately. Caitlin for once was quiet, "and *Sassy Salmon*," he continued.

"*Pink Grapefruit*," Caitlin's voice was hesitant.

"That's a good one," Connor assured her. "You name one, Aunt Katie."

"I think *Purple Mist* for this color in the corner," Katherine answered.

"That's a good one too."

The last stages of deep purple had begun to take over the clouds as they gathered at the window to watch.

"That was cool, Aunt Katie," Connor concluded. Katherine made a note to encourage his imagination and artistry.

"Was this room always a den?" Caitlin asked as she plopped down on the sofa.

"No."

"It wasn't?" Connor asked, surprised. "What was it?"

"I don't know for sure what it was used for when Cloud Cottage was first built," Aunt Katie began. "I think a bedroom. At least when I was a little girl it was a bedroom. After Ancestor Aonghus's son Daniel married and his wife moved into Cloud Cottage, Ancestor Aonghus used this as a bedroom. The family slept upstairs, Ancestor Aonghus slept downstairs."

"Except when he went to the attic in the summer," said Caitlin.

"Right," agreed Katherine.

"When did it become a den?"

"About forty years ago Uncle Gus made it an office/den, after his father, my grandfather, passed away. You see, my grandfather Daniel, used it for his bedroom too. It was hard for him to climb the stairs in his later years, so he used this room and Uncle Gus slept upstairs. All the other family members had married and moved away. It was just Uncle Gus and Grandfather Daniel who lived here then."

"After Grandfather Daniel died, Uncle Gus lived here all by himself?"

"For many years, do you remember Uncle Gus?" Katherine asked. "Perhaps you might remember a very old, tall, thin man."

"With lots of white hair?" Caitlin asked.

"I remember him sitting in here," Connor said.

"You would have been six, almost seven the last year Uncle Gus lived here at Cloud Cottage."

"Is that his picture?" Caitlin asked, pointing to a photo on the wall.

"Yes, but it is a three-generation photo. It was taken about 1920. Uncle Gus is the little boy. He would have been about ten years old. This is his father Daniel, and this is Ancestor Aonghus."

"Wow," was the unanimous response.

"I didn't know there was a picture of him," Connor said.

"How old is he in this picture?" Caitlin asked.

"Let's see," Katherine did some quick arithmetic, "about 72 years old."

Silence descended on the room as the uniqueness of the photo sunk in.

"I like this room," announced Connor.

"I like, I LOVE Cloud Cottage," Caitlin said.

"Well, yeah, everybody loves Cloud Cottage," Connor retorted.

Caitlin ignored him, then addressed Katherine, "I have a question. Wasn't Cloud Cottage built before they had bathrooms?"

Katherine, once again, was amused, little Miss Factual was putting events in sequence.

"Yes it was, Caitlin. You know the stone building I use as a garden shed? That was the original outhouse."

"When did they put in the bathrooms?"

"I don't know, but I think about 75 or 80 years ago. It was after Ancestor Aonghus died, I'm sure. It was the first major remodel of Cloud Cottage. I was told that the old wood stove was taken out of the kitchen and replaced with an electric range. The kitchen became smaller, and that extra footage along with three or four feet of this room was used to make space for two bathrooms. A full bath off the den, and a half bath off the front hall were added. Okay, enough for tonight, off to bed." Katherine had wanted to do some historical research on the computer, but she followed the twins upstairs.

13

The next two days passed quickly. The shopping trip had been successful. New equipment was waiting in the back room to be installed. The twins had been kept busy helping Katherine get ready for the family, and were now anxiously awaiting the arrival of their cousins.

"They're here, they're here," Connor and Caitlin called out as they raced out the front door.

Katherine watched as they bounced up and down waiting for JJ and Megan to get out of the car. Katherine chose to wait on the porch and let the young ones bond on their own. She had grown up with first and second cousins coming and going all summer. Some of her fondest memories were sharing secrets, giggling long into the night, playing volleyball and softball, singing songs around a beach fire, and the older cousins helping the sleepy young ones back up the hill. She remembered one older cousin had actually carried her up when she was five or six. He had held that over her for future payback. Never once had she ever told him that she hadn't been asleep, that she was pretending. Oh well, he probably knows now, Katherine sighed. He had been the first cousin of her generation to pass away. It had been just last autumn and Katherine would miss him this summer.

"Hi, Aunt Katie." Jennifer dropped her suitcase to give Katherine a big hug.

"I am so glad to see you," Katherine responded, returning her hug. "You too, John, welcome."

Katherine looked around and asked, "No dog?" Jennifer and John looked at each other.

"No, Aunt Katie," Jennifer answered. "John wanted to bring him, but I discouraged it. Would it have been okay?"

Katherine suspected bringing the dog had been a big bone of contention. "Of course," Katherine said. "Connor was looking forward to it. Feel free to bring him for the 4th of July."

The children bounded up behind them and asked the perennial question, "May we go to the beach?"

Katherine hesitated and glanced at Jennifer. Now the dynamics would change. She went out on a limb and answered, "I propose we have dinner right away, and all go down for a sunset walk together. How does that sound to you, Jennifer, John?"

"Great," Jennifer answered, looking relieved. Katherine was well aware it was one thing to allow two ten, almost-eleven, year olds to go alone to the beach. It was quite another to have four children from seven to ten down there alone.

"Okay, suitcases inside. Connor and Caitlin, you help JJ and Megan. Jennifer and John, you will be in the master across the hall from the children."

Jennifer stopped as she headed up the stairs behind the children.

"Aunt Katie, isn't that your room?"

"Not during the summer, I've moved upstairs."

"The attic? Aunt Katie…"

"I'm already settled up there, and as I told Daniel it is my oasis under the eaves. No argument – go. I'll get dinner out of the oven."

The kitchen table had been extended to seat seven and it was a boisterous group that gathered around it. Katherine listened to the conversations. Sometimes it was nice to just sit back and be a spectator. Jennifer may have sensed Katherine was in a 'rest' mode, because she insisted on cleaning up after dinner. The twins had still cleared the table and loaded the dishwasher with help from JJ and Megan, but Jennifer put away the leftovers and finished up.

"Do you know what time your dad is arriving Jennifer?" Katherine asked.

"No, how about if I call him?" A moment later she came back. "Dad is about an hour away. The children are so anxious to go down to the beach I told him we wouldn't wait for him."

"I agree," Katherine was quiet for a moment. "Jennifer, would you mind if I waited here for your dad and didn't go to the beach?"

"Not at all, I think that's a great idea."

"You're okay having Connor and Caitlin with you?" Katherine asked.

"Of course, Aunt Katie, and I love that they are so good with JJ and Megan."

"Alright then, I will see you all off to the path."

As the prattle of voices grew faint in the woods, Katherine strolled back to the house. "Ahhhh," she exclaimed as she settled in the porch swing. She hadn't sat here all week. She closed her eyes and allowed the gentle motion of the swing to soothe her. Katherine hadn't realized the level of alert her being had shifted to since the twins arrived. Only now that she had relinquished that responsibility to Jennifer did she relax. Katherine sat, eyes closed, comfortable, peaceful, at ease. She didn't even think about the book. She was still there when her brother Daniel arrived. She heard him drive up, but didn't move. She waited until the car door slammed and his feet hit the porch steps to open her eyes.

"Hi. Set your suitcase down and come sit," she said as she moved over to make room.

"Hi yourself. Do you spend all your time out here on the swing?"

"Jealous?" she asked.

"No, not of the swing. Maybe a little envious of your time with the twins."

"Don't be. You know you're welcome here too. This is good neutral ground to spend time with them. They are delightful children, just get to know them, Daniel."

"I'd like to."

"There's nothing here stopping you."

"I just don't relate to them like you, Kate."

"You don't have to have an in-depth conversation. Do something with them, create a happy moment, laugh with them, all four of them. They're your grandchildren; I'm only a great-aunt. I bought a couple of kayaks this spring and a standup paddleboard. Why don't you play on the beach with them tomorrow morning? The weather should be good and Dano probably won't be here until noon. Just be sure you clear it with Jennifer before you talk with the children."

"Sounds like a good idea. How has the week been?"

"Fine, busy, I just need to stay one step ahead of those two and that takes some planning."

Shrieks from the path announced the return of the beach walkers.

"Grandpa, Grandpa," was the excited cry.

"See, Daniel, they are happy to see you. Embrace their enthusiasm."

The porch was soon full of greetings and hugs. Caitlin climbed into the swing with Katherine.

"We came back to watch the sunset with you, Aunt Katie. It's about to go down."

Everyone turned to watch the yellow-orange disk sink below the horizon. As soon as it disappeared the question was asked, "Can we have strawberry pie now?"

"We waited for you, Dad," Jennifer said as she took his arm and headed for the kitchen. John grabbed Daniel's suitcase and looked at Katherine.

"The den," she acknowledged.

He nodded, dropped the suitcase in the den, then accompanied her to the kitchen. Eight around the table for dessert was very cozy, but they fit. Tomorrow, Katherine thought, we will need to use the dining room, then added, that's a good thing.

Katherine listened to the conversation, shared her thoughts, but at the first opportunity she hoped to excuse herself. She was ready for her oasis. The children were going to be allowed one quiet game before bedtime. Jennifer and John would be in charge; all would be well. Daniel, no doubt would retire to the den.

"Well then, goodnight all," Katherine proclaimed. "Sweet dreams."

Katherine prepared for bed in the family bathroom then headed upstairs. My first night up here, she thought. I wonder if I will dream of sinking ships, treasures, and desperate words of dying men. This night she wouldn't know what attic shadows might pervade her dreams. She was asleep almost at once.

It was the smell of coffee that awakened her. It took a minute for her to get her bearings. Oh, Daniel is here, she remembered. He is always up early and makes coffee. She was surprised the aroma carried to the attic. She wasn't anxious to start her day with lengthy discussions, so she closed her eyes again. She didn't even want to think about the book, yet it was in her thoughts. She needed to ask John to help her today. She hadn't mentioned it last night; probably this morning would be the best time. Jennifer, her dad, and the kids could play with the kayaks. Katherine had a feeling John would be more than happy to stay up at Cloud Cottage and work with the computer.

"Okay," Katherine said. "I have a mission now. I'd better get to it."

14

Katherine stood on the porch once again waving goodbye. How it had gotten to be Sunday night so fast amazed her. On Saturday they had spent the afternoon playing on the beach followed by an evening fire, with hot dogs and S'mores. On Sunday they celebrated Father's Day for three happy dads, and now everyone was leaving except Connor and Caitlin. The twins were exhausted from two hard days of playing with cousins. Katherine felt quite rested.

"Aunt Katie," Caitlin asked, "could we have an early snack for supper? I think I'd like to curl up on my bed and read."

"How about you, Connor?" Katherine asked.

"Yeah, I want to play one of my games. I haven't played one since I've been here."

"Sounds like a plan. Caitlin reads, Connor games, and I work on my new computer."

That's the secret. Katherine thought as she followed the twins upstairs a little later: wear them out! She would have to remember that. Katherine reminded the children she would be sleeping in the attic if they needed her, and said goodnight.

The sun was just touching the horizon as Katherine settled herself in the easy chair that faced the west windows of the attic. "My first sunset from my oasis, how delightful," she said. "The height of two floors increases the view so much up here. I love the expansive reflection on the water. When I watch a sunset from the front porch it really is only the horizon above the treetops that I can see."

She waited until the sun was down to open her computer. Tonight she wanted to familiarize herself with its processes.

In the morning a gentle rain pitter-pattered melodically on the roof. Katherine had always loved the sound of falling rain, but here in her oasis under the eaves she could detect variations of tone. Since there was no insulation overhead to deaden the sounds, it was as if she could hear each distinct raindrop's arrival on the roof. She wondered if large raindrops made a different sound than smaller raindrops. Katherine listened. She felt as if she were inside a drum. This is quite pleasant she thought, but I wonder what it is going to be like in a thunderstorm. I am sure I will find out. In the meantime I'd better see if the twins are stirring. She tiptoed downstairs; all was quiet. I suspect as tired as they were and as soothing as this rain is they may sleep until noon. Katherine left the stairway door open and went right back up. She would dress and then start scanning pages. She had worked quite late the night before, felt comfortable with everything, and even had scanned a sample page of another book as a test. It worked.

As Katherine began scanning, she committed to not stopping and reading anything until she had finished. One by one she carefully turned the pages and let technology do its thing. She only had a few left when she heard doors open and close downstairs. The house was quiet enough that she could hear the shower running. If she could just have ten more minutes she would finish. She listened to the sounds from below as she worked. She really could only go so fast. The scanner and the computer had to process. When she heard muffled conversation, she sighed and went downstairs. Connor and Caitlin were curled up on the cushioned seat in the leaded window alcove telling each other to be quiet.

"Why are you whispering?" Katherine asked from the hallway.

"Oh, Aunt Katie, we thought you were asleep."

"No, sleepyheads, I have been up and working on a project for a long time. I'm almost finished. Do you two think you can wait a few more minutes for breakfast?"

"Sure," was the response.

When she went back upstairs she checked the book – just four more pages. "Yes!" She exclaimed, a few minutes later. "I did it. Now I just need to name the file."

Hmmm, she thought, I need a name that will not pique curiosity if someone does access my computer. She typed a few letters then said "Ok, save, mission accomplished. Tonight I can start reading," then added, "I hope."

She looked at the time on the computer before she shut it down. It was 11:15, almost noon! Katherine collected Connor and Caitlin on the second floor and they all headed for the kitchen.

"I have a proposition," Katherine announced. " How about we have a brunch of waffles with fresh strawberries and either bacon or sausage links?"

"Yeah, with bacon."

"Okay, let's do it. Connor, you can hull the strawberries. Caitlin you can mix the batter. I'll get started on the bacon."

Connor hesitated. Katherine looked at him. "I want to make the waffles."

"You each will make your own waffles with my help," Katherine explained. "The strawberries are your preparation assignment." Satisfied, the young boy went to work in earnest on the berries.

During brunch the twins decided since it was still raining to watch a movie. Katherine was relieved they didn't seem to mind if she didn't join them. Once they were settled in the den with their movie, she brought her laptop down and set up to work in the living room. She resolved to start from scratch, going backwards chronologically. Katherine wanted to read every page again and to note what was known to be a fact. First was the letter in the envelope. This had been easy to read.

Fact: Uncle Gus wrote the letter.

Fact: Ancestor Aonghus had confessed something to him.

Fact: The book had belonged to Ancestor Aonghus.

Fact: Ancestor Aonghus wrote the first group of pages.

Fact: Uncle Gus wrote the second group of pages.

Fact: What Ancestor Aonghus wrote Uncle Gus did not understand.

Fact: Uncle Gus never found 'it.'

Fact: Uncle Gus had promised to find, value, and protect 'it.'

Katherine summarized: My mission is to decipher the pages, find 'it,' value and protect 'it.' She moved on to the pages from the book that was written by Uncle Gus when he was 25, at the time his grandfather Aonghus bared his soul on his deathbed. The writing was easy to read. The content was hard to believe. Katherine read the pages, then closed her eyes to retell them in her mind.

For Ancestor Aonghus the story began in November 1863. The night he was shipwrecked off Little Point Sable. The last man he found and the only one that made it to the beach alive had floated on a hatch cover torn from the ship. He demanded that Aonghus take the drawstrings of a sea bag he had wrapped around his body. With his last breath the man had looked into Aonghus' eyes and gasped, "For the cause, for the cause, lad, for the cause."

For a fourteen-year-old boy, who was already suffering some degree of shock, the experience was searing. The words, the look in the man's eyes, were to haunt him his whole life and on his deathbed. He had no clue what the "cause" was and couldn't grasp why this man had wrapped what appeared to be a very heavy bag around his body. It was possible he could have survived without the weight. When Aonghus undid the bag and looked inside he saw what appeared to be smallish gray bricks. He was even more puzzled when he realized why the other men had been so hard to drag ashore. They too had these bricks in their pockets or in a bag over their shoulder under their coats. Aonghus at this point was astounded that the men had weighed themselves down.

He couldn't fathom what was so important about the funny bricks that these men risked and lost their lives because of them.

What he did grasp was that they were valuable, and although he had not answered the dying man he felt bound to do something with them. After he buried the men, in a different spot, but close by, he buried the bricks. As he walked the beach looking for salvage from the wreck he was careful to watch for more of them. He didn't find any. He never knew if there were more, if they were in the wreckage or at the bottom of the lake. He didn't know what the "cause" was, what the bricks were, whether or not they might be stolen. What he did know was that he was alone, a foreigner on a strange shore, and if told, his story might not be believed. In short he was afraid. So he hid them. Every year he would revisit the spot to see that they were undisturbed.

By 1870, when land along the shore was for sale, Aonghus bought one hundred and sixty acres for farmland. He was just 21 years old, but he had worked hard and saved his money for seven years. At that time he moved his secret cache to his own property nearby. Over the years he had come to suspect that the men he had naively sailed with from Chicago were confederate agents or sympathizers. He knew that the funny looking bricks were silver ingots. He also realized their value, but for Aonghus they were tainted. He never did anything with even one ingot. He was content to work hard and prosper by his own means. In seven short years he had learned to read and write, grown to be a man, and purchased land with his own earnings. Never would that have been possible in Scotland.

He was too frugal to destroy something of value, so he hid the ingots again. He didn't know what else to do. He didn't know how he could explain their existence, and he certainly didn't know to whom they belonged. As he neared the end of his life he became tormented by fear. What would happen if someone found the ingots? What havoc would it wreak upon his family? What would his family think? Had he stolen them? What would he tell his Maker on Judgment Day? What sin had he committed by not understanding the desperate words of a dying man? What would he say to that man if he saw him on the 'other side?' The nightmare of his fears was endless and so intense that he often was delirious.

To piece this much of the story together, Uncle Gus had written that it took hours of listening for lucid moments. The actual location of the ingots Aonghus would not say in simple words. He insisted everything would be known when the book was read. Uncle Gus suspected Ancestor Aonghus feared others were listening, and he often lapsed into a paranoid rant. What Uncle Gus was sure of was that one phrase Aonghus repeated several times, both when he was and was not lucid, referred to the ingots, "hidden in plain view."

Katherine opened her eyes. "Hidden in plain view," she thought, that's not much to work with. No wonder Uncle Gus didn't find them – if he tried. She slumped back in the chair, contemplating and repeating details. She needed to chronicle the known facts just as she had done with the letter written by Uncle Gus.

"Hi, Aunt Katie, what are you doing?" The twins! She had forgotten all about them.

"Just working on a project," was her quick response. "How was the movie?"

"Good, we watched it twice."

"Twice, what time is it?"

"Six o'clock, Aunt Katie."

"Oh my goodness, I had no idea. Let me shut down this computer and we'll go see about something for dinner."

"Okay, but I'm not really very hungry," Caitlin said.

"Me either," added Connor. "I'm still full of waffles."

"Maybe Father's Day leftovers. How does that sound?"

"Good, because I want a 'story night,' Aunt Katie," Caitlin said.

"Yeah," Connor agreed. "You have to tell us more about Ancestor Aonghus."

"Leftovers, then story time – sounds like a perfect rainy evening," Katherine responded. Yet she wondered how she would ever tell the tales of Ancestor Aonghus without thinking of "hidden in plain view."

15

This night they all settled on the sofa together. The rain was really coming down hard, pounding against the windows. Katherine hoped it would let up before bedtime. She suspected it was downright noisy in the attic.

"I hope the sun shines tomorrow," Connor said. "I like rainy days, but I like sunny days better."

"Me too, but rainy days make great story nights," Caitlin contributed, then asked, "Aunt Katie, did Ancestor Aonghus learn to read?"

Oh good, Katherine thought, a starting point. I can do this.

"Yes he did," she answered. "He studied very hard all summer and fall. When the lumber camp opened again in late November, he moved back into the bunkhouse, but he kept studying whenever he had a few minutes. On Sunday afternoons he would meet the teacher at the foreman's house for tutoring and another week's lesson. Aonghus looked forward to those afternoons, and he appreciated the opportunity he had been given. There was another reason though, that he waited all week for those Sundays. The foreman had a daughter a couple years younger than Aonghus – and he was always invited to have supper with the family."

"Ahhhh," Caitlin knowingly rolled her eyes.

"Did he still have to peel potatoes everyday?" Connor asked.

"Yes. He still worked as the camp cookee that second winter. He also did more and more to assist the foreman, especially with the accounting and bookwork. Aonghus learned to read quickly, but he advanced through his arithmetic studies even more rapidly."

"Could he read the paper at night in the bunkhouse?"

"Yes, but the story goes that he would make a list of all the words he didn't know and that would be part of his lesson on Sunday."

"Was it a long list?" Connor wanted to know.

"I expect so, because he said in later years he read every word of every ad. If you'd like, you could read one of those same newspapers he read. The papers printed in Pentwater for that year are preserved and available online."

"Really? That would be cool," said Caitlin.

"On our next rainy day?" Connor asked.

"That would be a good idea."

"I wonder what he liked to read best?" Connor pondered.

"My grandfather said that Ancestor Aonghus read and reread everything about the Civil War. Remember this was now the winter of 1864-65, the last few months of that war. One of the topics in the paper and the subject of conversation in the bunkhouse was the draft, also the bounties that were being paid men who enlisted, and how much some men were paid to go as a substitute. Bounty and substitute fees were often several hundred dollars, an amount that seemed huge to a man working for $25.00 to $35.00 a month in the woods. It must have seemed like a fortune to Ancestor Aonghus. By the time the snow melted in March, and logging ended for the season, he had decided to enlist."

"But," Caitlin interrupted, "it had only been two years since he ran away from Scotland. He was fourteen then, so he was only sixteen."

Katherine couldn't help smiling again; her grandniece did keep track of details.

"You're right, Caitlin. One was supposed to be eighteen to enlist, but many boys under eighteen lied about their age and did serve in the war. By 1864 there was a shortage of men to fill the ranks in the army. It was the fourth year of the war, people knew terrible war stories, and had heard of the horror of the battlefield. To get men to enlist they were offered money, and the recruiters, anxious to fill their quotas, often didn't ask questions."

"Did Ancestor Aonghus get money?"

"Yes, he did, and with the help of his friend, the foreman, he invested it along with all the wages he had saved, in a bond sold by the government that yielded a very high rate of interest, from seven to ten percent. It really was a shrewd financial decision – if he survived the war."

"But wasn't he sad to leave his foreman, and teacher, and what about the foreman's daughter?" Caitlin wanted to know.

"I expect he was, but according to the story his foreman was even sadder. He didn't want Ancestor Aonghus to leave. He also understood, so he helped him as much as he could. He not only assisted him with the investment bond, but saw that he had what he needed to go to war, and advised him on an important deception."

"What's a deception?" Connor wanted to know.

"It's a form of lying."

"Ancestor Aonghus lied?" Caitlin asked.

"He had to," Katherine explained, "he wasn't eighteen. All men, when they went into the army, had to take an oath that stated they were over eighteen."

"But he was only sixteen."

"That's right, but there was a trick that a God-fearing man did, so he would not lie under oath. Before he went in to swear his age and allegiance to the Union, he would write the number eighteen on a piece of paper and stick it to the bottom of his shoe. When the officer in charge asked him to swear if he was over eighteen, the individual could honestly answer, "Yes, I am."

"That's what Ancestor Aonghus did?"

"Yes, and that's what his foreman told him he could do." Katherine wondered what seed for oblique deceptions she had planted with this part of the story.

"So did he go to war?"

"Well, no. He did enlist, but by the time he got to Detroit the war was over. General Lee surrendered to General Grant at Appomattox on April 9, 1865."

"So did he just come back home to Stony Creek?"

"No, once you enlist you belong to the army. You can't just come and go as you please. Some men who enlisted in the spring of '65 served their entire one to three year enlistments. Once again, fate smiled upon Ancestor Aonghus. The officer he reported to in Detroit took one look at him and knew he wasn't eighteen. He began to fill out a discharge paper stating 'underage.' The story goes Ancestor Aonghus refused to accept the discharge on the grounds that he had accepted money and was bound to serve. According to the legend the officer kept Aonghus standing at attention for a long time as he studied him. He finally asked Aonghus what he was good at. His answer was of course 'ciphering' – working with numbers. The officer must have liked what he saw and heard because he had Ancestor Aonghus attached to his office at Fort Wayne in Detroit."

"Did he stay in the army for three years?"

"No, but he did serve just over nine months, until December of '65. By that time most of the men from the war had been mustered out and the post-war activity at Fort Wayne had decreased. The officer was being reassigned. Just before Christmas he called Ancestor Aonghus into his office and asked to see the bottom of his shoes. Alarmed, he showed them, and knew he was in trouble because the number eighteen had worn off. The officer asked how old he was, and Ancestor Aonghus had to answer he was still sixteen. He would not be seventeen until March. The officer shook his head and told Aonghus he didn't have a choice but to discharge him. He did grant him an Honorable Discharge because he had served well. The officer explained that he was being transferred west and it was time for Aonghus to go home, at least until he turned eighteen.

"Aonghus didn't mind the idea of going home to Stony Creek. It was logging season and he missed the camp. He just was worried about the money he had accepted for serving. The officer assured him that many men were already home who had received bounty and subscription monies. Aonghus thanked the officer and collected his things. If he left right away he could be home by Christmas. The day Aonghus arrived at the station was one of three days a week a train ran westbound to Grand Haven. It took some creative traveling on his part to get from Grand Haven to Stony Creek because the snow was already deep. He got a ride on a mail stage, he walked, and hitched rides with passing sleighs, but he did arrive in Stony Creek on December 24th."

"Christmas Eve?" exclaimed Caitlin.

"That's right. The story goes that from Grand Haven he carried a bag of white flour for the foreman's family."

"A bag of flour was a present?" Connor asked.

"Absolutely! You see, white flour was a treat. They usually had just cornmeal and always ate johnnycake. For you, because you seldom have it, johnnycake is a treat."

"It's really good!"

"I agree, but sometimes, what you don't have often tastes even better." Katherine paused as the children absorbed this concept, then continued, "Aonghus went to the foreman's office first to see about a job and to deliver the flour. The foreman was happy to see Aonghus, hired him back, and invited him to his house for Christmas Day."

"Was the foreman's daughter happy to see him?" Caitlin asked.

"I'm sure she was."

"Did he work as a cookee and peel potatoes again?" Connor asked.

"No, this winter he was old enough to work in the woods, but he also helped the foreman with the bookwork."

"Did he still study on Sundays?"

"Yes, he went right back to his studies again. Actually, he never stopped. He kept up his studies when he was in the army at Fort Wayne too."

Connor yawned.

"I agree, Connor, this is a good place to end our Ancestor Aonghus story tonight. Let's go to bed."

That night Katherine went to sleep with thoughts of silver ingots, and dreamed of future wealth. She, like Ancestor Aonghus and Uncle Gus, had everything she needed for the meat and potatoes of life and then some, but the possibility of having an extra dessert now and then was exciting. Her mind was full of possibilities, flat screen TVs for Cloud Cottage, a new car, travel…such sweet dreams!

16

The next morning was clear, bright and fresh. Katherine had hoped to catch up on weeding, but even on the sandy ground it was too wet. Perhaps by afternoon she could weed. She also needed to clean because a friend was coming to visit for a couple days this week. It was too pretty a day to clean, but the day before, when it was raining, she had rationalized it was too dark to clean.

"I better just do it and be ready. Besides, I can think while I clean, and maybe I'll find something 'hidden in plain view.'"

She was working in the master bedroom when the twins appeared.

"Good morning, you two."

"Good morning, Aunt Katie, did you sleep here last night?"

"No, I'm just getting this room ready for our next visitor. My good friend Ellen is coming tomorrow."

"Do you need any help?"

"Not at the moment, thank you, maybe after breakfast. Let's go down."

As Katherine scrambled eggs she noticed there was some nudging going on between the twins. She wondered what was up, but thought she would wait for it to unfold. Sure enough Connor spoke up.

"Aunt Katie, Caitlin and I were wondering if we could do something from our Summer Wish List today?"

"Maybe," she answered. "Let's look at your list and see." Connor and Caitlin watched as she read down the list.

"Climb the dunes, miniature golf, bumper boats, go to the top of the lighthouse, tube down Stony Creek, go on a dune ride, eat lots of ice cream." Katherine laughed, "I think we definitely should get started on that one. Go fishing, and …did you have something particular in mind?" Katherine asked.

Again the nudging, Caitlin spoke up this time.

"We would like to go on a dune ride!"

"I see," Katherine thought for a minute. "How about if we wait a day and take my friend on a dune ride when she is here? Perhaps today after we do a little more cleaning we could pack a picnic lunch and take a long walk on the beach to the north."

"Yaaaay."

"Then when we come back we need to weed the garden."

"Sure, Aunt Katie."

Katherine loved the gusto with which the twins entered into projects. In no time they both had completed their chores, the house was ready for company, and they were on their way. Caitlin's backpack held lunch; Connor's backpack had their beverages. Every day was an adventure.

That evening it was six tired legs that rested in various poses in the living room.

"Can you tell us an Ancestor Aonghus story tonight, Aunt Katie?"

"Tonight, are you sure?"

"Yeah, tomorrow your friend will be here."

"Okay. Well, let's see, where did we leave off?" Aunt Katie asked.

"Ancestor Aonghus had just come back to Stony Creek on Christmas Eve," Connor said.

"That's right. Well, for the next four years Ancestor Aonghus continued to work for the lumber camp, the sawmill, and depending on the season, other businesses in the area. He worked hard and saved his money. In the spring of 1870 he turned twenty-one, he bought his first land, and asked his sweetheart to marry him."

"Was it the foreman's daughter?" asked Caitlin.

"Yes, it was. Her name was Moira, and she became your great-great-grandmother." Katherine went on to explain how Ancestor Aonghus had collected stones and built Cloud Cottage.

"How many children did they have?" Caitlin asked.

"They had five children, four girls and finally a boy named Daniel."

"Was that Grandpa?" Connor asked perplexed.

"No, silly." Caitlin interrupted. "This Daniel has to be much older."

Katherine explained, "The first Daniel MacLeod to live in this house was your grandfather's grandfather. Your father is Daniel MacLeod IV."

"What were the girl's names?"

"They were all Gaelic names, Annella, Annis, Glynnis, and Davina."

"Is Daniel a Gaelic name too?"

"It's a biblical name that's spelled the same in Gaelic as in English," Katherine responded.

The children were quiet for a few moments. Finally Caitlin asked, "They were all born here in Cloud Cottage?"

"Yes," Katherine answered, "as well as all of the first Daniel's children, Uncle Gus, his three sisters and my father."

"What kind of work did Ancestor Aonghus do after he married and lived here at Cloud Cottage?"

"That's a very good question, Connor," Katherine said. "He bought more land, he farmed, he had an orchard, raised peaches, and other fruit.

He also kept sheep and helped some of the other farmers on the Ridge who had flocks of sheep."

"What Ridge," Connor asked.

"Blackberry Ridge. That was the name of the closest settlement to Cloud Cottage in the late 1800's."

"Was it a town?"

"Not really, it was the name of the post office, there was also a church and a school. The buildings are all gone now, but they stood on the corner across from Cherry Point Farm & Market."

"Is that where the sheep were too?" Caitlin asked.

"Yes, the farm on that corner had sheep, but there were others too. I know there aren't any sheep being raised here now, but there were in the late 1800's. Ancestor Aonghus understood sheep because he had grown up working with them on the Isle of Skye with his father."

"Did Ancestor Aonghus live in Cloud Cottage the rest of his life?"

"Yes, he did."

"Awesome."

"What happened to his daughters?"

"Oh, they married, moved away, and had families of their own. Their grandchildren are my second cousins. Some live here in Michigan, some live in other states. Several of them are coming to our family reunion."

"A MacLeod family reunion?" Connor asked.

"The last weekend in July, there will be so many cousins here we'll all need nametags," Katherine laughed.

"May we make the nametags?" Caitlin asked.

"That's a wonderful idea, thank you. We should get some supplies so you could get started. I have another idea for a project for you too. How would you like to design a tee-shirt for the reunion?"

"Everyone would get a special tee-shirt?"

"Every member of the Clan."

"Awesome. Can we really design the tee-shirt, Aunt Katie?"

"Why not? How about you work together and come up with five designs, then we'll choose one together."

"Okay," was the enthusiastic response.

"You can dream about it tonight – off you go. I'll be up to say goodnight in a few minutes."

Well, Katie Ann MacLeod, she thought, that was a moment of inspiration, a tee-shirt design. They will want to start designing tomorrow; it will be a great project for them while Ellen is here.

17

Katherine turned out the lights and went up to her oasis. Two months ago, when she and Ellen had planned this visit, Katherine had no idea how busy her life would become. Still, she was looking forward to non-family adult conversations. She just wished she could share the story of the book with her friend. It was not an option. She was on her own in this mission. As she fell asleep the words "hidden in plain view" echoed in her dreams.

It was just after two a.m. when Katherine awoke with a start. The idea that had awakened her was pretty bizarre. It didn't really fit with what she thought "hidden in plain view" meant. But she knew she wouldn't sleep unless she looked.

She crept downstairs, found the stepstool, and carried it to the living room. She set it down in front of the fireplace bookshelves, climbed up, and reached for a book. The top shelf books were all very thick volumes on world history. Katherine suspected they had been purchased in the early 1900's through a peddler like an encyclopedia salesman. She looked at the book in her hand. It looked normal, it was heavy, but then it was a big book. She took a deep breath and opened it. Pages of print, she thumbed through it, just pages. She put that book back, and pulled down the next one, same result. She worked her way across the top shelf, opening one book at a time. She finished the shelf on one side of the fireplace and shifted to the other. She repeated the procedure. Finally she put the last book back, no dice!

The books were thick enough to have had a section in the middle cut out and ingots hidden inside, but there were no ingots. She knew it was doubtful Ancestor Aonghus would have destroyed a book to make a hiding place even for the ingots, but she had to look. She was confident now; she need not look at any more books.

Katherine put the stepstool back and returned to bed, yet she couldn't sleep. She contemplated purchasing a metal detector. They had been around for thirty to forty years, but Uncle Gus might not have thought of using one. If she understood how they worked, they had to be pointed at the object, and there was always the issue of background 'noise,' all the other metal content of the area that had to be accounted for. Katherine didn't need to be told where the pipes ran connecting the well to Cloud Cottage. Besides, the ingots are "hidden in plain view." She wasn't looking for a buried treasure, and with everyone coming and going, what if she did find something suspect? How could she be discreet? Katherine sighed. She could still see an argument for trying a metal detector, but if she ever did try one it would have to be in the fall, when she was alone. For now, her best option was still to focus on deciphering the handwritten pages of Ancestor Aonghus. He told Uncle Gus the information was there. She would just have to find it. The gray light of dawn was already filtering in the east window of the oasis when Katherine fell asleep.

She awoke with a start. It was late; she had overslept. Horrified, she glanced at her clock. The big red digital numbers glared accusingly as she read "9:30." Oh, she gasped, the twins. Katherine threw on her clothes and charged down the steps. She was glad that it wasn't an arthritic morning and her one bad knee complied with her urgency. No twins on the second floor; concerned, she went downstairs. She heard their voices in the kitchen. She heaved a sigh of relief. They weren't supposed to leave the house without asking permission, but if she was sleeping, and wasn't available – well, you never know. She would have to speak with them about that.

"Good morning, sleepyhead," Connor said with a grin, as she appeared in the doorway.

"Sleepyhead is right! I'm so sorry, guys."

"It's okay, Aunt Katie," Caitlin spoke up. "We're working on the reunion tee-shirts. Do you want to see?"

Katherine thought for a moment, "No, I don't think so. Not unless you have a question or need my help."

"No," Connor answered, "Caitlin and I have got this."

"I just bet you do, and I'd like to wait and see what you come up with."

"Cool," Connor gave her one of his special grins that was so reminiscent of Dano.

"How about some breakfast?" she asked.

Both children were silent. It was Caitlin who spoke. "We hope it's okay, we both had some cereal. Was that alright?"

Katherine looked at them with a stern face and asked, "Did you have the cereal Aunt Jennifer left here last weekend? The sugar – honey something or others?"

"Yeah," was the meek response.

"Did you eat all the cereal?"

"No," was the even quieter response.

Katherine couldn't maintain her act any longer. She laughed and said, "Good, then you left some for me."

"Aunt Katie, you tricked us."

"Just teasing, just teasing. Of course it was fine you had some cereal. Just never turn on the stove or oven if I'm not here, agreed?"

Two heads nodded, smiling.

18

Later that afternoon Katherine welcomed her friend Ellen to Cloud Cottage. They walked together on the beach, as the twins raced back and forth, playing a game of tag with the waves. The waves were big, and every time one crashed on to the sand, stretching its watery fringes around their toes, they shrieked. The lake had tagged them.

"You enjoy the twins, don't you, Katherine?" Ellen asked.

"Yes! I wasn't sure how it would work out, but if they are having half as much fun as I am, it will be a summer to remember for all."

"How about retirement, does it suit you?"

"You know, I have been so busy with the house, family, and now the twins, that I haven't felt the effects of retirement. Perhaps this fall it may be a challenge when I don't return to school. I will admit that the last few days I have been looking forward to your arrival. I haven't made friends in this community yet, so going to lunch in Pentwater and poking in shops just sounds so good."

"Terrific! We have a plan for tomorrow."

"We do."

"What about the twins?"

"They go with us. But I have signed them up for an art class at one of the galleries. Connor has a very artistic side that he needs to explore. This will be a good opportunity. While they are in the studio, we will have at least some time to ourselves. The children are easy. I just wasn't sure about shopping with them."

"Sounds good."

"Oh, one more thing. They go with us to Pentwater. Then one day while you are here we go with them on a dune ride. It is on their Summer Wish List and I promised them we could go when you came."

"No argument from me. A dune ride sounds like fun."

"They always are!"

The two women continued to walk and talk. The twins were the ones who suggested they return to Cloud Cottage. Dinner was a non-stop conversational delight, followed by a game marathon. Ellen had also been an educator, and related well with the children. It was past their normal bedtime when the twins laughed their way upstairs. Katherine and Ellen left the straight chairs of the game table in the den and relaxed into the cushions of the living room sofa.

"This is such a lovely room, Katherine. I think I am beginning to understand the hold Cloud Cottage has always had upon your heart."

Katherine nodded. "But it's more than a structure, a home. It is continuity, connection, a sense of place and an understanding of belonging. In our mobile society few people today still have an ancestral home. Grandpa's farm isn't there for children to visit. Sociologically, what has replaced agrarian roots is the 'summer place.' All up and down the shores of the Great Lakes, on every river and inland lake there are places like Cloud Cottage where families gather. They come back from all over the world for one or two weeks every year to spend time together in that place. It is the one constant in their lives and it's where they return to reconnect and restore. Cloud Cottage is very special, but it's not unique in the role it plays in the lives of my family."

"I never thought of that. I get it," Ellen said. "The only thing I still question, and this is just me, your good friend talking, is the isolation. Don't you feel like you're in the middle of nowhere?"

Katherine smiled. She understood. This response was common among first-time visitors. One had to learn to shed the habit of going to get something, anything on impulse. One learned to plan trips to town, or the city. It was a matter of conservation, both of gas and time. It was a change of lifestyle.

"I haven't yet felt isolated. I think there has been a realization that I don't need to always be on the go, that I can be content discovering each day some new thing around me. Every day here is different, the lake changes, the sand, the development of the plants. Nor do I need a choice of one hundred stores in which to shop. My needs are simpler. Perhaps it would be different without the Internet. The world is still at my fingertips. I'm just sitting at a computer overlooking Lake Michigan, instead of in an office. I do hope this fall to integrate into the community through church or volunteering. I will not dry up like an old prune. I will not become an eccentric hermit, I promise! I'll always enjoy having people visit.

Ellen and Katherine both laughed.

"I'll hold you to that, Katherine, and sometime in the coming months I hope to see you on my doorstep. Travel on the highways, even here, goes both directions."

The women said goodnight outside the master bedroom and Katherine went up to her oasis.

Exhausted from the long day with her friend, and her sleuthing from the night before, she relaxed into a deep sleep.

19

It was a weekday in June but the main street in Pentwater was busy. Katherine turned onto a side street to find a parking spot.

"Okay, everybody out, it's time to have fun in Pentwater."

Together they walked to the gallery. Katherine was glad to see three other children were there for the same class, two girls and another boy, all about the same age as the twins. This is good, she thought. This class will be large enough to allow Caitlin and Connor interaction with others yet small enough for individual instruction. The twins were excited and after meeting the teacher joined the other children exploring the studio. As Katherine watched, Connor went right to the painting easels. Caitlin was intrigued by the potter's wheel.

Ellen leaned close and whispered, "I think this was a capital idea Kate, look at them."

"I hope so." Katherine confirmed the time for picking up the twins. She and Ellen had three hours to enjoy. "Okay, Ellen, what shall we do first?" she asked.

"Lunch! I'm starving." Before they left Cloud Cottage the twins had been fed peanut butter and jelly sandwiches. Ellen and Kate had opted to have lunch in Pentwater.

"Me too. Let's eat."

A short time later they were seated in a local eatery ordering Chicken Salad a la Oceana County. Katherine assured Ellen she would love it because dried cherries made everything better. She also insisted that because they were having a healthy lunch, they should indulge in another Oceana County specialty for an appetizer, deep-fried beer-battered asparagus.

"Katherine, you've got to be kidding."

"No, it is a 'must have.' Besides I haven't had any yet this year and the season is almost over." When the crispy-coated steaming spears arrived at the table, Ellen, with some hesitation, took a bite. The expression on her face changed from doubtful to delighted.

"Oh my God, this is so good."

Katherine laughed as her friend reached for another spear. "I told you, and here, try some dip on your next one." Together they devoured the entire order. As they savored the last bites their entrees arrived. Ellen was equally delighted with her cherry chicken salad.

"Kate," she said. "This lunch has been fabulous. What else have you been keeping from me?"

"Ellen, Oceana County is the best kept secret in West Michigan. You'll just have to wait and see. Right now I feel like shopping, and I need a style consultant. When I got dressed this morning, I couldn't find anything I wanted to wear. Everything I put on made me feel frumpy."

"You always look "smart," Kate, today too. There is nothing wrong with khaki capris and a blue top with that striped India scarf."

Katherine shrugged. "Maybe, but sometimes it's more about how one feels than how one looks."

"Hmmm, got it. Well, how about your sandals?" she asked as she peeked under the table. "Maybe something more fun, less functional? I know, let's get manicures and pedicures."

Katherine laughed at her friend. "Whoa! I said 'style consultant,' not 'make-over artist.' Let's just check out the shops and see what we find."

"Okay, but I warn you, when I get started, there's no stopping me."

For almost two hours the women poked through the delightful shops of main street Pentwater. They modeled hats, looked at dangly earrings, tried on sandals, sunglasses, and worked their way through racks of clothes. In each store Katherine gravitated toward the sales rack. An exasperated Ellen directed her to the new arrivals.

"How about this jacket, Kate? It has nice detail, it's lightweight, reversible," and she added, "it's packable. It would be a great travel garment."

Katherine was intrigued, so she tried it on.

"It looks great. How about this blouse to go with it?" Ellen asked.

Katherine looked, but still wearing the jacket, walked back to the sales rack, and pulled out several tops. One-by-one she tucked them under the front edge of the jacket to show Ellen.

"They're nice too. Why don't you reverse the jacket and see if they still blend. Looks good, Kate. I vote you take the jacket and these three tops. Now we need to find slacks or a skirt to go with them."

In the next shop they found both, and a cute pair of flats.

"Enough!" Katherine said. "This is great fun, but we have to stop."

"Not quite, this triple strand of beads is the perfect necklace for your outfit. See how it has the same teal as the jacket? Do you like it?"

"It's lovely." Kate answered, as she pulled the jacket and one top out of her shopping bag to check color. "You have a good eye, Ellen. See the bronze in this bead is the same as in this top, and on the reverse side of the jacket."

Necklace in hand, Ellen smiled at Kate as she headed to the checkout. "I'm getting this for you, a thank-you token." Kate started to object. "No, I want to do this."

"Thank you, Ellen, that's very kind of you, and thanks for helping me pick things out. I appreciate your help. It's so much more fun to shop with someone."

"You're welcome. Now there are a couple more stores across the street."

"Ellen!"

"I warned you, there was no stopping me."

The parcels in their hands multiplied after each store until it was time to pick up Connor and Caitlin.

"Let's drop these bags off in your car," Ellen said. "I would like to treat everyone to ice cream cones. We'll need our hands free."

"Great," Kate responded. "You will be the twins' favorite Ellen."

Between licks of Butter Pecan, Chocolate Mousse, Blue Moon, and Raspberry Truffle, two children chattered while two adults listened. Both children were thrilled with their adventure in the studio. Each one had brought home a project. Katherine had been right about Connor.

On the ride home, Caitlin asked, "Aunt Katie, do we have plans for tonight?"

Katherine glanced at Ellen. The tone in the little girl's voice indicated a proposal. "Not yet. We haven't even gotten home."

"I know, but, well, Connor and I wondered if we could have a beach fire?"

"Ah, ice cream and S'mores in the same day?"

"We didn't know we were going to have ice cream when we got the idea."

"What do you think, Ellen? Can we handle deep-fried asparagus, ice cream, and S'mores on the same day?"

"Only in Oceana County, and I'm here, so I'm in."

"Then it is official. A beach fire it is. Ellen, may I assume you have your old friend in the trunk of your car?"

"Never leave home without her, and she always enjoys a good fire."

The two friends looked at each other, aware of silence in the back seat. They suppressed any laughter and waited. The twins were looking at each other. Katherine wondered who would be the spokesperson.

Caitlin addressed Ellen, "What kind of a friend do you have in your trunk?"

Kate and Ellen both burst into laughter.

"I travel with a musical friend. She has strings and when she sits in my lap...."

"A guitar?"

"Yes," Ellen answered, still laughing. "My friend is a guitar."

"Cool."

"I met Ellen," Katherine explained to the twins, "when she came to my school to perform concerts and conduct musical programs. She's a singer, songwriter, speaker and performs all over the state."

"Will you bring your guitar friend to the beach fire?"

"Would you like that, you guys?"

"Yes!"

"Me too," Katherine said. "Connor and Caitlin, you're in for a special treat."

Katherine drove up the driveway to Cloud Cottage. It was just after five. She proposed there would be time if Ellen, Connor, and Caitlin would like to go for a swim. She would get the fire supplies together and join them. Katherine worked fast.

Hot dogs and buns, catsup, mustard, relish, potato chips, marshmallows, graham crackers, chocolate bars, roasting forks all went into the beach basket. She grabbed some extra towels and a couple blankets. She picked up the basket and headed for the door. On the porch, Katherine stopped. She had forgotten the matches and old paper for starting the fire.

"Some Girl Scout you are, Katie Ann MacLeod!" She collected what she had forgotten and headed for the beach.

Ellen was already out of the water.

"I did it, I got under," she called to Katherine, "but it is a little too cold for me."

"Good, then you can help me build the fire."

"Okay, it will be a good way to dry off too."

The twins stayed in the water until they saw smoke rising. They grabbed their beach towels and raced up the beach giggling as they ran.

Ellen commented, "They are best friends, aren't they?"

Katherine handed each child a fresh towel to wrap up in and laid the damp ones to dry on the beach grass.

The fire wasn't quite ready to cook on yet, so the twins asked Ellen if she would play her guitar.

"Sure," she replied. "What would you like to sing?"

Connor and Caitlin hesitated.

"We'll find something we all know," Ellen said, as she tuned up. A few minutes later they were all singing *Row Row Row Your Boat*. "Now let me teach you a new one. This is the chorus."

When the last notes died away, Connor asked, "Did you write that one?"

"Yes."

"Awesome."

"And many more," Katherine added. "But I think it is time for our first intermission – and dinner."

"Yay!"

They sang after hot dogs, took another intermission for S'mores, then sang some more.

As the fire burned lower, the song choices seemed to become more mellow.

"How about one from the old days, Kate?" Ellen asked, as she started to sing *Where Have All The Flowers Gone.*

"Connor and Caitlin, you can join in on the chorus." She continued with *Michael Row Your Boat Ashore.* While they watched the sun set, Ellen strummed *Kum Bah Ya*, and as the last sliver of orange disappeared she began to sing softly. Katherine joined in and by the third chorus, the twins were singing too. When the last note faded into the evening air Ellen whispered, "Good night beach, good night lake, good night world."

No one around the campfire spoke for a long time. The moment was too magical to mar with spoken words. It was Katherine who finally got up and started to pack the beach supplies.

Later as the twins said goodnight they each gave Ellen a big hug.

20

Katherine had always been an early riser, but at Cloud Cottage she was learning to enjoy sleeping in. Perhaps it was the place, her stage in life, or just moments of complete contentment and relaxation that allowed deep healing sleep. Bright yellow sunshine filled the attic the next morning when Katherine surfaced from her slumber. She stretched, aware that it was late, not even caring enough to look at the clock. The day before had been such fun. She had participated in hundreds of beach fires, but last night had been sublime. The sharing of Ellen's talent, the joy of blending voices in songs that were fun, that had a message, the delight on the children's faces, the sound of the waves lapping on the shore, the light breeze that had brushed their cheeks, even in the memory, a special energy coursed through Katherine's being. It had been one moment in time but what was it that had made it so unique? The setting, for one, she thought. In this place there is a special quality, an energy that enhances positive thoughts and emotions. People become their best here. Another factor, she decided, that made it special, was the sharing. Ellen brought her music and love for new experiences, the twins their innocence, their enthusiasm, and she, well, she had brought the food. When each one brings their best to a gathering it can be an amazing experience.

Katherine heard voices from the floors below and glanced at the clock. It was even later than she thought.

"Up and at'em, Katie Ann MacLeod," she said. "If your theory is right, today will be wonderful too."

She found Ellen, Connor and Caitlin on the front porch, sharing a special moment of their own.

"Good morning, may I join you?" she asked.

"About time," Ellen answered.

"I slept so well. It must have been your music."

"Yeah," Connor and Caitlin agreed. "We did too."

Ellen smiled. "I hope you don't mind, Kate, but the twins and I have been planning my last day with you."

"Fine. How many hours of weeding did you schedule?"

"Aunt Katie!"

"Don't you remember, Aunt Katie, today is our dune ride?"

"Oh, that's what you want to do today?"

"YES!" both twins exclaimed.

Ellen and Katherine laughed.

"We thought we would like to go on our ride this morning and this afternoon spend our time on the beach."

"Great, my only suggestion is that we visit the dunes on foot in the pedestrian area too. If we leave soon we will have plenty of time and the sand won't be hot."

"Sounds good," Ellen answered.

"Have you three had breakfast?"

"We waited for you, Aunt Katie," Connor said.

"Okay, then let's all have something to eat. We need to fuel up in order to climb those sand dunes."

Katherine, the twins, and Ellen had all been on a dune ride before, but it didn't matter, every ride is great fun. The bumps, the turns, the driver's narrative and his humor, the sweeping expanse of shifting sand, and the laughter all make a fun-packed half hour. Four happy riders were still laughing and brushing off sand when they climbed out of the scooter.

"That was fun," Caitlin said.

"Yeah, even more than last year, I liked this driver better," Connor added.

"Aunt Katie, why don't you have a dune buggy?" Caitlin asked.

"I'm happy to let someone else do the driving."

"When I'm old enough I want to drive," Connor said.

"Me too." Caitlin added.

The twin's future dreams of driving were displaced by the sheer joy of rolling down a sand dune. Katherine and Ellen climbed slowly and watched as the twins raced ahead up the dune, rolled down to them, jumped up, and raced to the top to do it again.

"Such energy," Ellen said.

"Such exuberance," Katherine answered.

At the top they stopped to wait for the twins and absorbed the beauty of the landscape.

"I don't think I have ever walked up here, Kate."

"One can walk all the way across the dunes to Lake Michigan if one chooses. There is a little lake, half buried trees, tree trunks sand-blasted into sculptures, and the dunes are different every time."

"Spectacular."

"Yes. I don't think I even realized how spectacular until this spring. I walked up here before the dunes opened for motor vehicles. It was pristine, and the patterns and sculptured formations in the sand took my breath away."

"Aunt Katie, may we walk over there and watch the private buggies?"

"Sure, but stay on the pedestrian side. We will be right behind you."

The twins took off on a run, but soon slowed to a walk. Ellen and Kate joined them, and they watched the show together.

"Whoa, did you see that, Aunt Katie?" Connor asked.

"He almost flipped over," Caitlin said.

"One does have to be careful driving on the dunes," Kate answered. "It can be dangerous."

They watched a few minutes longer until Katherine said, "I think I hear the beach calling."

The twins turned to go, but kept watching over their shoulders until they started down the last dune, then they both rolled to the bottom.

Ellen looked at Katherine. On impulse she said, "Shall we try it?"

"Race you," Katherine answered.

The twins watched in disbelief as their two favorite adults of the moment rolled down the dune.

"Aunt Katie, Miss Ellen," they greeted them with giggles.

"I won!" Kate said.

"Yeah, well, remember the laws of physics about mass and speed."

"Ohhhhhhh, that's hitting below the belt," Kate laughed. It was a true statement, Ellen was petite, she wasn't.

"Sorry, just couldn't help myself. I'm a sore loser."

"Forgiven, because you're right."

"What are you talking about?" Caitlin asked.

"Come on, we will have a physics lesson in the car on the way home."

"Kate, before class begins, may I make a suggestion? Given the pounds of sand we are wearing, how about we pick up something for lunch here, and picnic on the porch, my treat?"

"Good idea."

Katherine had been right about it being another wonderful day. Beautiful weather, laughter, and good energy prevailed throughout the afternoon. The wind did pick up late in the day, and dashed the children's hopes of another fire on the beach. Katherine was glad. She was happy to preserve the magic of the night before as a unique moment. Instead, after dinner they gathered on the porch, watched the clouds roll in, and sang.

Rain was coming. But it could not dampen the high spirits of the group. Their voices blended with the rhythm of the first raindrops and the low rumble of distant thunder. They continued to sing until a final whoosh of wind blew through the trees and a loud crack announced the arrival of a hard driving rain. All scurried inside.

It was bedtime for the twins, and once again they said goodnight with hugs. Katherine and Ellen sat down to visit in the living room.

"The other night this room was comfortable," Ellen said. "Tonight it is cozy."

"There's something about a rainy night at Cloud Cottage that defines 'cozy' and for me, usually demands a book," Katherine answered. "Tonight I'm happy for conversation. Thank you, for coming Ellen, and thanks for being so good with Connor and Caitlin. It's been a fun three days."

"For me too, thank you for having me. We've done so much and I enjoyed every minute. There has, however, been one obvious omission."

"What's that?"

"Kate, not once have you mentioned school, favorite places, activities, friends, anything from down state. Have you, can you, so completely leave that life behind?"

Kate thought for a moment before answering. "I am living in the present. I am where I want to be. I'm in a good place in my life. I'll go back to visit sometime and I will keep in touch with a few friends, but, yes, I've left that life behind."

"And Tom?" Ellen asked.

"And Tom! We had become comfortable old friends. We were for each other a safe, convenient companion. There wasn't anything more there for us. He has his life and I have mine. I always knew that."

"A comfortable old friend can be a good thing."

"Yes, and it was. And that's a wrap. Shall we call it a night?"

Ellen nodded. It was obvious this conversation was over. She had hoped Katherine was as happy as she seemed to be. Ellen concluded she was.

"Sleep fast, sleep well," Katherine said, as the good friends said goodnight.

21

Once again Katherine stood on the porch, waving goodbye. I do this a lot, she decided. It had been a good visit with Ellen; she hoped she would see her again soon.

"I liked your friend Ellen," Caitlin said.

"Me too," Connor added. "She was fun, and I liked her friend the guitar."

"We did have a good time, didn't we," Katherine said. It was a statement, not a question.

"Yeah," said Connor, "she even bought us ice cream cones."

Katherine listened to their comments. They had been good days, but now it was ten o'clock in the morning of another day, and a cousin's family was due to arrive the next evening.

"Okay, you two, front and center! We have had play days, today is a work day." Katherine went down a list of assignments for each child. "Let's see how much we can finish by lunchtime. Go!"

She was anxious to get things done fast so she could have some computer time. The words of Ancestor Aonghus were waiting.

Lunch was late, but all the chores had been finished. Cloud Cottage was once again ready for guests. The twins had headed for the beach; Katherine had an hour for the computer. She chose a chair in the living room where she could watch the beach path and got started.

It was just as frustrating as it had been the first time she had tried to read them. This time she had no choice. She had already finished the pages by Uncle Gus. She had to make sense of these pages by Ancestor Aonghus. Part of the problem was the handwriting was hard to read, the ink faint—then Katherine had an idea. What if she treated each page like a photo and cleaned it up in a photo program by adjusting the lightness and darkness, tweaking the contrast, and enlarging? It just might work. Katherine was an amateur photographer and was familiar with photo editing. She and John had installed photo software on her laptop last weekend. She could do this. With renewed energy, Katherine went to work.

Again, she resolved to edit all the pages before she tried to read them. She chose a couple words on each page to focus on, to see if she was gaining legibility as she manipulated the program. She was excited. Letters and many words were much easier to distinguish. She really was on a roll when she heard the twin's voices. Glancing at her watch the hour was up, and they were on time. She would have to quit. At least it was easier to stop when one knew where to start in again. She was not discouraged this time. She saved her work and shut down the computer.

She glanced out the window again. Connor and Caitlin were closer now, and were making a beeline for the back of the house. Katherine drew in a quick breath. The twins were covered in sand from head to toe —and wet. She pressed her lips together and marched to the back porch. When the twins rounded the corner of Cloud Cottage, Aunt Katie stood in 'teacher mode' to greet them. Their expressions of urgency changed to tension. Silence hung in the air as feet shuffled.

Caitlin spoke first. "It was an accident, Aunt Katie."

"There was a huge log," Connor added. "We wanted it to sit on for our beach fires."

"A big wave came and started to pull it back out again." Caitlin picked up telling the story. "I was holding the log but I fell. Connor grabbed me and fell too."

Katherine did not respond. The twins glanced at each other as they realized they were really in trouble. Lower lips began to quiver from bowed heads.

"I'm sorry, Aunt Katie."

"I'm sorry too, Aunt Katie."

Katherine watched her grandniece and grandnephew. She knew every moment she waited to speak they were in agony. Sometimes that was the most effective punishment, but these weren't her children, and she hadn't established the beach rules. In a low thoughtful voice Katherine addressed the twins. "What were your father's instructions for the beach?"

Connor replied, also in a soft low voice, "Stay out of the water, stay together, be back in an hour."

Caitlin nodded in agreement.

Another silence enveloped the back porch at Cloud Cottage. "It appears to me," Katherine began, "the rules you have broken were established by your father. When he comes for the 4th of July, you will explain to him what you have done. Until then your privilege of going to the beach alone is suspended. Understood?"

Two heads nodded.

"Aunt Katie," Caitlin asked, "how long till the 4th?"

"Eight days."

The twins looked at each other horrified. Eight days was an eternity.

Connor swallowed hard and said, "We are very sorry, Aunt Katie."

"Me too," Katherine answered. "I am also very thankful you are okay. Now both of you shower off that sand, and I'll go get towels."

It was a quiet threesome that shared dinner that evening. Katherine knew the twins were overwhelmed with remorse. In their enthusiasm for securing the prized log, they had simply forgotten the rules. She understood the exuberance of youth, but also the consequences of throwing caution to the wind in a moment of perceived invincibility. How much danger the twins' situation had been, Katherine didn't know, but the lake had been very rough. The presence of a strong undertow was probable. She did not want to make light of their transgressions, yet the somber sad faces across from her were heartbreaking. She wondered what activity would be appropriate for the evening. She opted for a movie. It was something they could do together without talking too much. She also suspected a group cuddle on the couch would be reassuring.

"Connor, Caitlin, I have an idea. Instead of dessert tonight, let's have popcorn – and a movie." Katherine's suggestion resulted in timid, hesitant smiles.

"What movie would you like to watch, Aunt Katie?" Caitlin asked.

"I'll enjoy whatever you choose." Katherine hesitated, "as long as it is not a scary one."

"Aunt Katie," Connor said. "Dad told us you think the *Wizard of Oz* is scary. Do you?"

"Guilty," Katherine answered. "I don't do witches and flying monkeys." She smiled and allowed herself to wink at them.

"For real, Aunt Katie? They aren't that scary," Caitlin said.

"They are to me. Always have been, and always will be," she replied.

"Come on, Caitlin, let's go pick out a Disney movie," Connor said.

"Good idea. I'll microwave popcorn and be there in a few minuets." Katherine wondered what they would choose. It didn't matter. The first step towards neutralizing the somber atmosphere had been taken. Learning to live after a transgression was part of growing up.

22

In the morning the twins were still subdued. They stayed close and were attentive. By lunchtime they wanted to know who was coming this weekend and did they have any children. Katherine explained that it was one of her first cousins and her husband, and their four grandchildren. She didn't know their ages. Connor and Caitlin would share their rooms again, just like they had with JJ and Megan the weekend before.

Katherine wondered how best to spend the afternoon. She considered going to the beach, but that didn't seem quite right, not yet. She opted for Plan B.

"Connor, Caitlin," she asked, "would you like strawberry shortcake for dessert tonight?"

"With whipping cream?" Connor wanted to know.

"Of course."

"Aunt Katie," Caitlin interrupted, "We don't have any strawberries."

"Let's go pick some."

"Can we?"

"I called the U-pick farm earlier this week and they said they still had berries. So let's go."

A short time later all three were bent over a row of strawberries. Connor and Caitlin were in front picking the biggest berries they could find. Katherine followed and picked all the berries they missed.

After about a half-hour Caitlin asked, "Aunt Katie, how big of a short cake are we going to make?"

"I want a big one," Connor said.

"We know, Connor, and with lots of whipping cream."

Katherine laughed. "We have enough strawberries for several big shortcakes, Connor, but let's pick three or four more quarts. These berries are so nice I would like to put some in the freezer for next winter."

On the way home Katherine surprised the twins by pulling into a pizza place.

"Aunt Katie?"

"Pizza?"

"Does that sound good for dinner tonight?"

"Yaaay!"

"I agree. We'll take it home and have a pizza picnic on the porch."

It was a pleasant evening so they stayed outside to await the arrival of their guests. Katherine weeded her flowers. Connor and Caitlin were kicking around their soccer ball.

"I hear someone coming," Connor called.

One can always hear the rev of the engine as a car started up the hill to Cloud Cottage. It was like a 'Guest Alert' notice. Katherine removed her gardening gloves, disposed of her handful of weeds, and was ready to greet her guests by the time their car was visible. It had no sooner pulled to a stop when a young boy about thirteen or fourteen bounded out. He headed straight for the soccer ball that was being passed between Connor and Caitlin. He intercepted it, showed off his moves, then passed it back to Connor.

"Cool," Connor shouted, as he kicked it back.

Well, it looks like the twins will have at least one playmate this weekend, Katherine thought. She waved to the rest of the family climbing out of the car. There were three girls, maybe twelve to seventeen years of age. Hopefully Caitlin would enjoy them. In a flurry of suitcases, greetings, and hugs everyone converged on the porch. Accommodations were allocated, and the question was asked as always, "May we go to the beach?" The twins looked at Katherine, their eyes beseeching her to give permission to accompany their guests to the beach. Neither one dared to ask. Katherine hesitated, then nodded 'yes.' Their punishment was suspension of solo trips to the beach. Connor and Caitlin, and the band of cousins, old and young, sans Katherine, headed down the path to the lake. In some ways life was easier, she realized, when a family arrived to visit. It was a diversion and a never-ending supply of new playmates for Connor and Caitlin. It was computer time for Katherine.

Her favorite workplace had become the chair by the living room window. Its position allowed her the visual advance notice she needed to shut down the computer when beach walkers returned. Katherine went to work. She had a system now, and one-by-one worked her way through the remaining pages. She now had two files of Ancestor Aonghus pages, one of the original pages, and one of enhanced photo-corrected pages. She knew time was running short, but she hoped she could read a few pages. She began again on the first page. The words were now legible, but not always comprehensible. The letters often didn't spell a word she recognized. Had Ancestor Aonghus written in code? Had he deliberately written these lines to appear nonsensical? Regardless, without a meaning for the words she didn't recognize, it was impossible to sequence into a cohesive thought. To complicate it further, sometimes there were numbers.

Stumped, Katherine sat for a few minutes staring at the page on the screen. As she became lost in thought and stopped focusing, the words on the page blurred a little in front of her eyes. She became aware of faint lines under some words. Katherine jerked back to attention. They were very faint, but only a few words had them. Curious she opened the file of the original pages. The lines were there, but she never would have seen them. The bleed of the ink over time almost obscured them. Katherine brought both open files up on her screen, side-by-side. She wanted now to look at both for cross-reference. She reached for a pen and paper to write down the words that were underlined. In the distance she heard voices. NO! She thought, not now, go back to the beach. She couldn't stop now!

The first word she wrote down that had been underlined was 'silver.' Clearly she was on to something. The second word was 'and,' the third 'statehood.' Katherine was perplexed, but she kept writing down everything that had a line under it as fast as she could. Then the lines stopped. The voices were getting louder as her eyes scanned two…three pages more. There were no lines. Was she missing them? With a huge sigh Katherine powered off her computer. She had to quit for now.

The Clan MacLeod cousins encircled her in the living room, talking and laughing all at once.

"Who's ready for dessert?" Katherine managed to ask in between the chatter.

A chorus of 'Meeees' was her answer. The group started to move toward the kitchen, freeing Katherine from her chair.

"Aunt Katie?"

"Yes, Caitlin," the little girl was still by her side.

"Would you like me to get your book for you?"

"My book?"

"Un huh, 'Silver and Statehood – The History of Nevada,' the title you wrote on your paper. I know where it is."

Stunned, Katherine could only nod yes. She watched as the little girl went over to the Ancestor Aonghus bookshelves, ran her finger along the shelf until she pulled a large volume out.

"Here it is, Aunt Katie. May I help you dish up the strawberries now?"

Katherine incredulously received the book into her hands.

"Thank you, Caitlin," she whispered as she hugged the little girl, and marveled at the child's retention of facts. "You are the best helper, of course you may help me with the strawberries."

Katherine stood for a moment, the book clutched tight in her arms as she watched the child skip off to the kitchen. She still held in her hand the paper with the underlined words she had printed. She reread them, and the numbers she had also written down. Could they be page numbers, she questioned? Incredible! She inserted the paper inside the book, set it on top of her computer, and went to celebrate this triumph with strawberry shortcake.

23

It was a very pleasant gathering she joined in the kitchen. Connor and Caitlin had taken charge and were setting out bowls and spoons. In just a few minutes everyone was seated, feasting on fresh strawberry shortcake. The twins had bonded well with the older second cousins, and there were plans for kayak races in the morning, weather permitting.

As the young people finished and headed to the den to watch a movie, Katherine fixed tea for the adults. As anxious as she was now to read the book, she also would relish a few quiet moments of conversation with her cousin and her husband.

"Your grandchildren are so grown-up," she began.

"So are Connor and Caitlin," her cousin answered. "Katherine," she continued, "I want to thank you for what you are doing here at Cloud Cottage. There is no place else that I could bring my grandchildren to enjoy and experience their heritage."

"It's your ancestral home too," Katherine answered. "Ancestor Aonghus and Uncle Gus always welcomed everyone here. It's important the 'welcome' continues."

"I agree, and share your understanding of family, but I also appreciate the commitment it takes for you as a person to make it happen. I don't know if the other cousins will say this, but we all are grateful for the opportunity to spend time at Cloud Cottage with our families – and we're looking forward to the reunion."

"Thank you for your kind words," Katherine acknowledged, then added, "I'm looking forward to our reunion too."

Her cousin's husband then spoke up, "My family doesn't have anything like Cloud Cottage to offer the children. This is truly unique. Now I think I'll catch the last half of the movie with the kids. If you'd like, I'll turn out the lights and herd everyone to bed when it's finished."

"That would be wonderful," Katherine said, "I would appreciate turning in early tonight."

Together they headed for the den. Katherine motioned "good night" to the group, then collected her computer and the book from the living room, reminding herself that she must not leave anything related to the ingots lying about.

At last, Katherine thought, as she settled herself in bed. She plumped pillows behind her, adjusted the comforter, and laid the book in her lap. She felt like a child about to open a present. She verified the first number on her note sheet. Assuming it was a page number, she opened the book, turned pages until she found the one she wanted, nothing fell out. Well, she thought, it doesn't look like Ancestor Aonghus hid anything here. I guess I read.

Two hours later Katherine finally finished. She had read every one of the page numbers she had written down, and many of the pages in between. She sat, the book still open in her lap. What had she learned? She itemized facts in her mind. In 1859 the Comstock Lode was discovered in Nevada, the largest discovery of silver deposits at that time. In the first years after the discovery, there were many small mines, and smelting the silver ore was done in small batches often using modified techniques of Native Americans. During the Civil War the price of silver rose sharply. Although the Federal government attempted to buy all production, many miners stopped selling their silver to the US government and sold instead to other buyers for higher prices. Nevada was a territory, but not yet a state during the early years of the war and Washington's control was limited.

Anxious to exercise as much influence as possible, the Lincoln administration filled Territorial positions with appointees that held

Republican and Anti-slavery views. In many ways this was an offensive move. Nevada was dominated by Republican, pro-union politics, but there were more Southern sympathizers in the state than any other in the west. Reports of Confederate conspiracies and other activities in the mining towns were frequent. It was essential to the Northern war effort not to allow silver or gold to flow from Nevada to the Confederacy. In order to maintain control, a state of martial law was in effect throughout the territory for most of the war. Unofficial instances of punishment against Southern sympathizers were often perpetrated by pro-union activists. Yet some Confederate activity did continue throughout the war years.

This information was contained on the page numbers designated by Ancestor Aonghus in his book. So what does this have to do with the ingots, Katherine wondered? Is Ancestor Aonghus trying to tell us that the ingots came from Nevada, from some small mine operated discreetly by a Southern sympathizer? It's plausible. Katherine had found these pages very interesting, and read on to learn on September 7, 1864, three and a half years after becoming a Territory, the people of Nevada voted to approve a State Constitution. One draft was sent to Washington by sea, one overland. When neither one arrived, Secretary of State Seward informed the Territorial Governor, who then telegraphed the document. At that time the 16,543-word constitution was the largest telegram ever sent, and cost $4303.27. Katherine wondered at the expense until she read more. President Lincoln, in October of '64, was concerned about his re-election. The war had dragged on; voters were weary of the conflict. He was confident that if Nevada were a state, the three electoral votes it possessed would be cast to support him. It might make the difference between winning and losing the presidency. Therefore, Seward's communication to the Territory resulted in a telegram, and on October 31, 1864, just days before the election, Lincoln declared Nevada a state.

The Union needed Nevada's silver, but as a Territory it already controlled most of it. It was Lincoln who needed, or thought he needed, Nevada for re-election, and to support the 13th Amendment abolishing slavery. Katherine read on. Nevada did support Lincoln that November, but Lincoln would have won anyway. He defeated McClellan in a landslide. Nevada's ultimate support of the 13th Amendment, however, did prove essential.

Fascinating, Katherine thought. I want to remember this book for a January read, but right now it's time to get some sleep. Once again Katherine's dreams were dominated by silver ingots and Southern sympathizers. Imaginative ideas also began to take form about how Ancestor Aonghus' ingots may have crossed the continent to Little Point Sable.

24

There was little time in the next few days for any Ancestor Aonghus research. Katherine's thoughts often returned to what she had learned about Nevada and silver during the war, but any additional investigation had to wait. In some ways Katherine was glad the arrival of guests interrupted her time with Ancestor Aonghus' book. She realized hunting for a supposed treasure could become an obsession. The last thing she wanted was for the ingots to preempt spending time with family. Besides, it was good 'steeping time' for her thoughts. With this mindset Katherine joined in beach walks and all the other Cloud Cottage activities with her cousin's family.

On Sunday evening, as she stood with Connor and Caitlin on the porch for their 'Wave Away,' she thought what delightful young people her cousin's grandchildren were. She extended her arms around the twins and continued her thought, Ancestor Aonghus, this generation is your real treasure.

"Aunt Katie, who's coming to visit next?"

"Yeah, next weekend is the Fourth of July, who's going to be here?"

"Well," Aunt Katie answered, "the Fourth of July is on Thursday. So on Wednesday evening we will have a house-full: your grandpa, Aunt Jennifer, Uncle John, Megan, JJ, Aunt Gillian and Uncle Steve, and maybe three or four of their grandchildren. Oh, and of course your dad."

"Where are we all going to sleep?"

"Oh, we have room, Gillian and Steve will have the master bedroom, Jennifer and John will use the den. That means Connor, your dad, grandpa, and JJ will all be in the boy's room."

"That also means," said Caitlin, "that Aunt Gillian's grandchildren better be girls, because the only beds left are with Megan and me."

Katherine laughed. "That's true, Miss Factual. But if there are more boys, it won't be the first time sleeping bags have been used at Cloud Cottage. Now, we have three days to spend together. How shall we use them?"

Her question elicited excited responses. After some discussion it was decided that Tuesday would be their go-to-town day. Groceries and everything for the weekend needed to be procured. Katherine then added that on the same trip they should go to the screen-printing shop and order the reunion shirts. She suggested finishing their designs would be a good project for tomorrow – and weeding the garden.

The twins agreed, with less enthusiasm, about weeding, but they agreed. They asked if she would choose the design for the tee-shirt the next evening.

"Yes," Katherine answered. "It will have to be. I'm concerned if we don't get them ordered soon we won't have them in time for the reunion."

"Caitlin and I will have our designs ready," Connor assured her, then continued, "May we have our Ancestor Aonghus story tonight then?"

"Oh, I guess so," answered Katherine. She wondered what she would tell them this time.

Later that evening Katherine seated herself in the porch swing. Connor and Caitlin dragged cushions off the other porch chairs and plopped down on top of them at her feet. Katherine looked down at their tanned faces. Caitlin's sprinkling of freckles had become more pronounced in the sun. Strands of her shoulder-length strawberry blonde hair had escaped her ponytail and hung loose around her face. Her greenish-blue eyes looked up in expectation. Katherine smiled as she shifted her glance to Connor. His eyes were bluish-gray and were also fixed intently upon her. She wished she knew what was going on inside their heads. Not once in her whole explanation about who was coming for the holiday weekend had they asked about their mom. She supposed they had been told, during one of the almost daily phone calls that she wasn't coming. Still it seemed odd they never spoke of her, but they didn't talk about their dad either. Katherine sighed. Maybe that was a sign that they were content. They looked it as they lounged in front of her.

"On the Fourth of July," Katherine began, "in 1866 a big celebration was planned in Pentwater. There was to be a parade, and each township was to be represented by a unit, and of course all the returned soldiers were invited to march. Ancestor Aonghus joined the group that represented Benona, which was the real name of the community at Stony Creek. He and his traveling companions sailed to Pentwater on a new side-wheeled steamer that made a round trip from Grand Haven to Pentwater three times a week. It stopped at Stony Creek, among other places, to pick up passengers and freight.

"This was a huge event for Aonghus. It may well have been the first outing he had ever taken just for pleasure. The Fourth of July activities in Pentwater included not only the parade but also orations, a community dinner, hot-air balloon ascension, and fireworks. That Fourth of July was a turning point for Aonghus. He was very proud to wear his military uniform and march in a parade. It was the first time he had ever seen a hot-air balloon or fireworks, but most importantly Ancestor Aonghus said it was the first time he felt like an American. It was the day he decided to become a citizen. Every Fourth of July for the rest of his life, Ancestor Aonghus told his family the story of that Fourth of July excursion to Pentwater."

"What is an 'oration?'" Connor asked.

"An 'oration' is a formal public speech, given at special ceremonies."

"Ohhhh."

"Did Ancestor Aonghus become a citizen?" Caitlin asked.

"Absolutely, and he made a point to vote in every election."

"Are we going to have fireworks on the Fourth, Aunt Katie?"

"Not here at Cloud Cottage, but we can go to Silver Lake and watch the fireworks over the dunes if you like."

"That would be cool."

"Okay, maybe we could do that."

The sun was very low in the sky when Katherine finished. In silence the three MacLeods watched the day to its close. When the last sliver of red had disappeared Caitlin exclaimed, "We forgot to name colors."

"I didn't," Connor said. "Tonight there was *Peaceful Pink, Resting Red, Purple Pleasure, Majestic Magenta*, and *Quiet Orange*."

"Oh," Caitlin said, obviously feeling left out.

"You can name one now, Caitlin."

"May I name one too?" Katherine asked, feeling it would be a good idea to mediate.

"Sure," Connor agreed. "Every second there's a new color, I can't name all of them."

Bless this child, Katherine said silently, then said out loud "I see *Insightful Indigo*."

"Come on, Caitlin, name one."

The little girl was studying the horizon.

"I see two new colors, *Evening Rose* and *Forever Pink*"

"I like those," Connor affirmed.

"I chose them because I want evenings like this to last forever."

"Me too," Katherine said, as she hugged both children.

25

The next morning Katherine was up early. She knew the children would rest this morning after the busy weekend and she wanted to get a head start on the weeding while it was cool. She was pleased to see she would have fresh radishes for the weekend, and she suspected she could dig some potatoes if she wanted to. Katherine weeded, her hands working together in a subconscious rhythm while her thoughts traveled into the realm of silver ingots. Why couldn't Ancestor Aonghus just write about silver and Confederate sympathizers in Nevada? Why did he resort to obscure clues? Was he afraid? Was he paranoid? Was there something there in the history book she was missing? Or was there something still on the Ancestor Aonghus pages that she had missed? She decided her next step was to go back to the enhanced pages on the computer and try to decipher a few more.

Katherine stood up. She had finished weeding one row. She stepped over a few more rows and picked a big handful of strawberries that had now ripened. The season was always later along the lakeshore. There, she thought, just enough for the children's cereal.

She hadn't been back inside the house long when Connor and Caitlin appeared in the kitchen. Both children had sheets of paper in their hands.

"Have you been working on your designs already this morning?" she asked.

"I have." Connor answered, "I got a great idea last night and I wanted to see how it looked."

"Terrific. Do you have time for breakfast?"

"Of course, Aunt Katie!" They all laughed.

After eating, the twins worked on their designs, Katherine opted for Ancestor Aonghus. She informed the children she would be in the den if they needed her. She resolved to assume she knew what Ancestor Aonghus had wanted her to know about silver and Nevada from the first three pages he had written. If she hit a brick wall she would go back and start over, but for now she would look at the next pages.

There seemed to be groups of pages. The first group she had just finished had three. The next one was only two. She started to read. Once again the sentences rambled and did not always form complete thoughts. There was one pattern of letters however, that repeated, did not comprise a word, and clearly had significance. It always appeared after the word 'MISS.' A girl's name perhaps? The letters were 'G D F C.' I guess I need to learn how to write and decipher codes, Katherine thought. The unit 'MISSGDFC' appeared in phrases like 'MISSGDFC changed everything.' 'MISSGDFC made it impossible.' 'MISSGDFC suffered.' 'MISSGDFC was very sad.' 'MISSGDFC changed plans.' 'MISSGDFC closed the door.' I wonder who she is? The rest of the words before and after these clauses appeared nonsensical. Was there a woman aboard the schooner that grounded off Little Point Sable? Did Ancestor Aonghus discover, when he went to bury the men, that one was a woman? What difference would it had made if one of the sailors was female? Could 'MISSGDFC' have been in Chicago? Nevada? Oh, Ancestor Aonghus, she wondered, what is it you want me to know?

Katherine went over the two pages one more time. Nothing else caught her attention. She read the previous page and the following page just to be sure. The phrase 'MISSGDFC' only appeared on these two pages. That was all she could do for now. She would have to think about this – and maybe research codes! Katherine shut down and secured her computer.

Back in the kitchen the twins were still hard at work. Katherine was amused and pleased.

"How's it going?" she asked.

"Good."

"Well, I'm going to go outside and start weeding. When you finish come help, okay?"

"Okay, Aunt Katie."

As she went out the door, Katherine chastised herself for her choice of words. She wondered if they would ever "finish" and come out. She might be weeding the garden alone today. Well, it was her garden. It took a while, but lo and behold, there were four more hands pulling weeds in the rows next to hers.

"Hi," Katherine said.

"We got them all done, Aunt Katie."

"Terrific! I'm anxious to see them."

"Can we look at them together right after dinner?" Connor asked.

"Sounds good to me."

Almost an hour had gone by when Katherine finished weeding the row she was on. She stood up and said, "I declare a moratorium on weeding." Connor and Caitlin stopped and looked at each other.

"Aunt Katie," Connor said with a sigh. "That's another one of your big words."

Katherine looked surprised. "Yes, it is a big word. Do you think I use a lot of big words?"

"Yes!" was the resounding response from the twins.

"Oh, okay, sorry. Moratorium means 'no more.'"

"So you mean we can stop pulling weeds?" Caitlin asked.

"You can stop pulling weeds."

"Yaaay!" the little girl exclaimed.

"Caitlin," Connor addressed his sister, "before we quit help me finish my row, I only have a few more feet."

"Thank you, Connor, that's a very good idea, I'll help too." Katherine said.

"I just started a new row," Caitlin said.

"I know. We'll finish Connor's today and yours another day."

In a few minutes they were finished.

"Alright," Katherine said. "It's time for ice cream. Everyone to the kitchen."

"Yay," Connor and Caitlin exclaimed as they raced to the house. Katherine followed. There was no bounce in her step, she had weeded about one row too many. She had pushed the limits because she doubted she would get back to weed any more during the holiday week.

Katherine rested while the twins enjoyed their ice cream, but when they went outside to play she went upstairs to start preparing for guests. Connor and Caitlin were responsible for their rooms, but with all the extra people involved, Katherine would help. Her cousin had stripped all the beds and had done the laundry before she left yesterday. Everything was clean, so Katherine started making beds. Dinner, by popular demand, was lasagna. It was in the oven and would be ready when the twins returned. She had an hour to work, if she hustled she could get everything done.

As she made each bed, 'MISSGDFC' kept going through her mind. She couldn't help wondering about this mysterious woman and what she had to do with the ingots. The beds were made and Katherine had just finished cleaning the master bath when she heard the twins' voices.

26

During dinner Connor and Caitlin's excitement and anticipation was demonstrated in non-stop chatter. They had both worked hard on their designs and were anxious to show them off. As soon as the table was cleared five pieces of paper were laid out. Katherine finished wiping the counters and dried her hands.

"Is it time? May I see them now?" she asked.

As she approached the table she watched the twins. They were both beaming. They had fun with this project and were proud of their work. Katherine hoped she didn't offend either one as she looked at the designs. At first glance, she was captivated. How was she going to choose? They were creative and quite wonderful. She knew the children were watching her.

"I don't know which one to choose," she said. "Do you have a favorite?"

"I like this one best," Caitlin answered. "Connor likes this one."

"How about if you tell me about them."

"Well, I did this one, mostly," Caitlin said. "I didn't draw it all out, but it's the MacLeod Crest. See, here are the bull's head, two red flags, and the words "Hold Fast." Isn't that what Cloud Cottage is all about, Aunt Katie? Holding fast to family and clan?"

"Yes, Caitlin, it is. I love it. How did you know about the crest? I haven't told you?"

"Daddy did, Aunt Katie. I have a copy at home that he printed off the computer for me. I just don't have it here. So we'd have to print another copy. Connor tell Aunt Katie about your favorite now."

"My favorite has to be a blue shirt. On one side of the front I like this big puffy white cloud. I printed our name 'MacLeod' so that the 'Mac' would be in white letters on the blue and 'Leod' is in blue letters on the white cloud. Aunt Katie, I'm tired of people mispronouncing our name. It's not 'Mac – Lee – Odd.' When we wear this shirt people should get the idea it's spelled 'MacLeod' but pronounced like 'Cloud.' I am proud to be a MacLeod, so I printed 'Proud' in white letters underneath the cloud. See, it reads 'MacLeod Proud.'"

"It is very clever, Connor, and a striking design. I like the other three designs too. I would wear any one of these shirts. However, if these two are your favorites then I think we should decide between them. But how, any ideas?"

"Aunt Katie, you said you would choose."

"I know, but I'm asking for help."

"Well," Caitlin began, "blue shirts don't get dirty as fast as white. Do they cost more than white?"

"I don't think so, Caitlin," Katherine answered. "If they did, it wouldn't be much different. One consideration is on the 'MacLeod Proud' shirt there is only one color ink, white. On the family crest there are three or four colors of ink. That might cost more."

"Because the crest shirt has more colors, it's brighter," Connor spoke up. "Some cousins might like it better than dark blue."

Katherine was amused that each twin championed the other's favorite in the decision process. Finally she spoke.

"How about if we take both designs with us tomorrow and we'll see what the screen printer says? He'll understand what will look best when it's printed."

"Good idea," Caitlin said. Connor nodded in agreement.

A light rain had started to fall, so there would be no sunset to watch that evening.

"I propose we call it an early night," Katherine said. "Rain makes for great sleeping."

"I like to read myself to sleep when it's raining," Caitlin said.

"Me too," Katherine responded. "Shall we go up to bed then?" Connor was already half way up the stairs. She knew his answer.

Katherine checked the windows and doors, retrieved her computer, said goodnight to the twins, and went upstairs.

The light rain on the roof was so soothing she would love to curl up with a book and read herself to sleep. Not tonight. She had some research to do and a code to crack. She doubted it was very sophisticated, but even so she knew nothing about codes. Maybe she should challenge the twins with the code assignment. They probably would solve it in a heartbeat.

Tuesday morning dawned bright and sunny. Katherine awoke with her laptop still on the bed.

"I guess I fell asleep to the sound of the rain after all. Lucky I didn't dump my laptop on the floor." She remembered reading websites on codes but assumed she hadn't cracked hers, at least she didn't remember it. "Another day," she said, as she put the computer on to charge.

It was to be a busy day. They departed from Cloud Cottage before nine. Their first stop was the screen-printer. After a lengthy discussion of pros and cons, 'MacLeod Proud' on a unisex shade of blue, was chosen for the reunion shirt. The crest design was to be held for another year. Stamps were purchased at the post office, a visit to a Dollar Store yielded some additional and much coveted beach toys, and lunch at a local coffee shop was a special treat before the trip to the grocery store.

Each family coming for the weekend was responsible for either lunch or dinner every day. Katherine, both Daniels, and the twins were to cover breakfast. Katherine's brother's solution to his responsibility was to give her money to buy groceries. It wasn't a bad arrangement. Daniel III financed, Katherine planned and shopped, Dano prepared. The twins and their father had a good system. They could flip pancakes and scramble eggs like pros. Katherine, on most meals, hovered in the background if she was needed, but usually she was shooed away.

Katherine also needed to replenish some staples and general groceries for herself and the twins, although the last two weeks they had eaten very well on weekend leftovers.

"Okay," she said, as she checked her list, "from this aisle we need peanut butter – extra crunchy."

"Got it."

"Caitlin, you're in charge of coupons. Do we have one for a cereal you and Connor like?"

Item by item they went down their list. They were almost finished when they passed the bakery counter. Two heads pivoted as their eyes stayed glued to the baked goods.

Katherine stopped, "Alright, what is it that has your attention?"

Caitlin pointed to a raspberry jelly Bismarck. Three were requested and packaged for smiling faces.

"Are we done? Let's check out."

27

Twenty-four hours later all the prep for the long holiday weekend had been completed. While they waited for arrivals Connor and Caitlin, with Katherine's help, had set up the badminton net and were now trying hard to perfect their skill at the game. Katherine wasn't sure which person they would be happiest to see, their father, their grandpa, their cousins, or the dog that for sure was coming this weekend.

The first car that arrived brought Jennifer and John with JJ, Megan, and the dog. This is a good choice for first arrivals, Katherine thought as she went out to the porch. Connor and Caitlin were already outfitting JJ and Megan with badminton rackets. That's interesting, Katherine observed. She had thought the dog would be the biggest attraction. Connor had asked several times about this dog coming to visit. Katherine started down the steps as an energetic Blue Heeler came bounding up the path.

She liked dogs, but she didn't love them and was often unsure around them. One thing she knew, she wasn't going to be jumped on. Jennifer and John were busy unloading the car and no one was watching the dog. She stood tall and as the dog came closer, in a strong voice, said, "Stop." The dog did. So she tried, "Sit." It sat. Well, Katherine thought, this is good. So she said "Good dog," and held out her hand for it to sniff.

The dog wagged its tail.

"Do I smell okay?" she asked. "May I scratch your ears?" With some hesitation she scratched, petted, and repeated, "Good dog."

She thought she should help Jennifer and John, so she started down the path to their car. She stopped and turned around. The dog was still sitting.

"Come along," Katherine said, and they walked together down the path.

"Hi, Aunt Katie," Jennifer called out.

"I see you have made friends with Blue," John added.

"Blue?" Katherine said. The dog's ears went up.

"Yes, his name is 'Blue.'"

Katherine looked down at the sturdy face with a dark patch over one eye that looked back up at her.

"Good dog, Blue," she said again as she scratched his ears once more.

" Blue, carry," John commanded, as he held a large tote bag towards the dog. Blue took the handles in his mouth and trotted along side as they carried suitcases to the house. John explained that as a working dog breed, Blue was happiest when he had a job to do.

"Are we the first ones here?" Jennifer asked.

"Yes"

"Where are we quartered this time, Aunt Katie?" Jennifer asked laughing. "Cloud Cottage is going to be full to the rafters."

"As it should be," Katherine responded. "Will the den be okay this time for you and John?"

"Of course, Aunt Katie. A hammock on the porch would be okay."

"Hmmm, a hammock on the porch."

"Careful, Jennifer," John teased, " We might get reassigned." They all laughed together.

Another car arrived; Gillian and Steven were here. Katherine had been watching for them. She hadn't seen her sister since before Christmas and a lot had happened since then. This time she walked right down to greet them. About half way she realized she was being followed. She had forgotten the dog was on the front porch.

"Come, Blue," she said. The dog bounded to her and walked by her side. Not sure Gillian liked dogs any more than she did, she stopped a little way from the car and said in the same strong voice, "Sit, Blue. Stay."

By that time Gillian was out of the car embracing Katherine. Steven, three granddaughters, and one grandson made up their party.

"I'm so glad you're here. I was afraid at the last minute you wouldn't be able to come."

"Wild horses weren't going to keep me away this weekend," Gillian answered.

"I'll swear to that," Steve confirmed. "We're all very glad to be here."

"Good," Katherine responded. "Let's go introduce the young people, and then we will get you settled."

Connor, Caitlin, JJ, and Megan had shifted from badminton to croquet. Gillian's grandchildren ranged from nine to sixteen in age, but Katherine was confident that the group would meld, MacLeod cousins always did. It was Caitlin who suggested they start a new game of croquet playing as four teams of two. In just a moment the eight children were paired and challenges issued.

As the adults returned to the car for a load of suitcases, Gillian said, "Kate, you used to play a mean game of croquet."

"Still do." At that point Katherine became aware Blue was still sitting by the car.

"Good dog, Blue," she praised. "Good sit." She petted the dog's head. He was appreciative of her attention, but he kept turning his head toward the children.

"Hmmm," thought Katherine. This could be problematic, but JJ and Megan should know how to command their dog.

"Okay, Blue," she said, "go play." With a bound he was off. Katherine wondered how many croquet balls would have teeth marks by the end of the game. There were several squeals and laughter as Blue dashed from one child to the next, but everything seemed to be under control.

"Kate, I didn't know you had gotten a dog," Steve said.

"Me, a dog? No!" Katherine answered. "Blue has just arrived with Jennifer and John. He seems to be a nice dog, and I think we have become friends. Now, I have considered adopting a kitty, maybe this fall. Do you think the spirit of Uncle Gus's cat could tolerate another little feline roaming around Cloud Cottage?"

"I wouldn't take that chance," Gillian laughed. "That cat didn't like anybody or anything invading its turf. She terrified me as a child, always hissing from behind doors and pretending she was going to pounce."

"I remember. Uncle Gus ended up keeping her in the attic when we all came."

"What's this about you moving into the attic for the summer?" Steve asked.

"It just made sense, Steve, and I am very cozy up there. I have come to call it 'my oasis under the eaves,' and so far there have been no sightings of cat ghosts." They all entered the house laughing.

Katherine directed them to the master bedroom and suggested the children's bags be placed in the appropriate boys' or girls' rooms.

"Remember what fun it was to pick out our bed?" Kate asked Gillian.

"Of course I remember. It's nice you have organized it so this generation can too."

"It's a Cloud Cottage tradition," Katherine answered, "besides it just makes sense. However, in the boys' room, someone will be on an air mattress this weekend. We may have to make that decision if there is too much discussion."

At that point Jennifer and John appeared in the hallway. Another round of greetings and hugs were exchanged. Katherine excused herself and went back outside. She thought she had heard a car, her brother Daniel had just pulled up.

"Hi, Grandpa," Connor and Caitlin left the game long enough to hug him. How wonderful, thought Katherine, that's huge. Dano's own barriers with his father had prevented much of a relationship between grandfather and grandchildren.

"Work your magic, Cloud Cottage," she whispered. "Work your magic."

The children returned to take their turns playing croquet and Daniel started up the path towards Katherine, Blue following at his heels.

"Good dog, Blue," Katherine laughed. "You brought me another guest."

"Hi, Kate, what's with the mutt? I had the distinct feeling I was being herded."

"You were," Katherine answered. "He is Jennifer and John's Blue Heeler."

"Gillian's here?" Daniel asked, looking serious again.

"She just arrived too. Everybody is inside."

"How is she?" he continued.

"If I didn't know, I wouldn't know," Katherine responded. "Daniel, let it be her conversation when she is ready."

He nodded. For the moment, at least, Daniel seemed compassionate.

Well, Katherine thought, that just leaves Dano to arrive. I hope he was able to leave the office on time. The children are so anxious for him to get here. I doubt we should hold dinner. I think it's Gillian's turn tonight; I better go see if I can help.

It was a memorable evening at Cloud Cottage. Dano arrived in time to join them at the table for dessert. Almost all of Katherine's immediate family was together at Cloud Cottage. The only ones missing were Gillian and Steve's two sons, their wives, and Caroline. She would miss them, but at least all eight of her grandnieces and grandnephews were there. The second generation, even if they couldn't come, sent the third generation. It confirmed for Katherine that even in their absence, they valued the traditions of Cloud Cottage, and she knew they did plan to come for the reunion. Katherine understood that young people had to make choices about vacation days, and when the Fourth of July fell on a Thursday, Friday wasn't a holiday. They had to work. Now, Katherine thought to herself, if only they had been teachers like me they could have been here.

That evening everyone went to the beach for the traditional sunset walk except Katherine and Gillian. They sat together on the porch swing, enjoying the quiet sounds of the summer evening. There were moments when the breeze would crescendo through the trees, but mostly it was still.

"How is it I seem to forget how peaceful it is here?" Gillian asked.

"Perhaps because you don't come often enough."

"Cloud Cottage, a mecca for the family, a monument for the clan, a haven of peace for everyone," Gillian whispered.

Katherine answered softly, not wanting her voice to disturb the serenity of the moment. "It is where we have always come to restore ourselves, Gillian. We restore with nights of deep healing sleep, with peaceful moments like this, but we also restore with laughter and play, with walks and talks with family. Here we shed the layers of everyday life that encapsulate our emotions and thoughts and we breathe freely. Here the toxins of society are expelled, we become whole."

"Such articulation, Katherine. I have always envied your ability to summarize in a few words the entire essence of what I was feeling."

"And I, Gillian, have always envied your voice. I would so much love to be able to sing."

"Oh, Kate, you can sing."

"Gillian, be honest, I croak at best." They laughed the hard deep laugh of siblings who know each other well.

"That felt good," Gillian said.

"That's why they say 'laughter' is the best medicine." Katherine answered.

"Well, then I guess I need to do a lot of laughing."

"What do you know, Gillian?" Katherine asked, her voice subdued and concerned.

"Not much, the results of the biopsy are still pending. When they come back then a course of action will be defined."

"How are you feeling?"

"Physically fine," Gillian stopped, then added, "emotionally panicked. At first it felt like someone – some thing – had my throat in a tight grasp and I was choking. It's that 'C' word thing. Then the information begins to pour in from the doctors, families, other people, the Internet, it is overwhelming. But I think I have come to the point where I can put everything in perspective. Put all that data in the appropriate columns, like useless, important, medical, emotional, psychological, survivor, non-survivor. I think I am at a point where I can accept and fight even if I am still angry some days."

"Good, Gillian, fight it, and breathe in all the healing energy of this place to help you." Katherine was silent for a moment then asked," How may I help you?"

"I don't know, Kate, just answer when I call."

"Count on it. I am sorry you have to make this journey, Gillian."

"Yeah, me too."

"Daniel asked about you as soon as he got here. He may not say much, but he is concerned about you too."

Just as Katherine had finished her sentence their favorite brother came around the corner.

"Hey, is this a private party?"

"Yes, it is," answered Gillian, "and you're late."

The three siblings were still laughing and talking on the porch when the rest of the family finally returned from the beach.

28

The Fourth of July was a perfect summer day. A light breeze, 80 degrees, Lake Michigan was calm, and a bountiful feast of summer was spread outside Cloud Cottage. The family engaged in endless rounds of water sports on the beach, yard games at Cloud Cottage, and feasted on potato salad, ham, baked beans, deviled eggs, watermelon, and a host of other favorites. It didn't seem possible that anyone would have any energy left when Caitlin asked, "Aunt Katie, what time are we going to Silver Lake?"

The rest of the family looked at Kate in surprise.

"Okay, Caitlin," Katherine said. "You may now share our plans for the evening."

"Aunt Katie rented a pontoon boat so we can all watch the fireworks from the middle of the lake. They shoot them off the dunes at dark."

There were exclamations of "Oh," "Wow," and "Cool" from various members of the family.

"Well then we better get going," Dano said. "We don't want to be late, not when we have the best seats in the house."

With renewed energy everyone piled into cars and drove the three miles to Silver Lake.

As they were standing in line to board the boat, Katherine found herself next to Daniel, who leaned over and whispered in her ear, "This was a fantastic idea, Kate, thank you."

Katherine gave him a quick wink and stepped aboard.

The evening was even more perfect than the day. Later, Katherine climbed the stairs to her oasis, pleased that all had gone so well. Everyone had enjoyed each other, and the fireworks from the pontoon – they were the icing on the cake. This was the kind of day that once lived, made memories for life, the kind of memories that Ancestor Aonghus had kept with him his whole life from his first Fourth of July in Pentwater. Connor and Caitlin had insisted Katherine share that story with the family while they cruised Silver Lake waiting for the fireworks.

"Ancestor Aonghus, I had fun today," Katherine said. "Your whole family had fun – together! I think, I hope, this day will be remembered for a long time."

All three families had made plans to climb the dunes the following morning. Katherine, Gillian, and Daniel excused themselves, and each one was looking forward to a few quiet hours. Gillian and Daniel both opted for post-breakfast naps. Katherine retreated to her attic oasis and considered a nap but opened her computer instead.

It had now been three or four days since her foray into the pages of Ancestor Aonghus. Let's see, she contemplated, the issue at hand is to understand what 'MISSGDFC' means. She assumed the key was the group of four letters, GDFC, but she didn't have a clue what they meant. Perhaps she should consider MISS. Her first thought had been 'MISSGDFC' was a woman. What if the meaning of MISS was not a feminine title, but as a verb? Did someone or something miss GDFC? Did they fail to reach or make contact with GDFC? However, that usage didn't make as much sense in the context of the clauses in which 'MISSGDFC' appeared, as did the feminine title. Katherine further considered that perhaps this was a regret by someone that they weren't with GDFC, but if so, who? And it still didn't fit the clauses well. Stumped, Katherine shifted her attention back to GDFC and the idea of codes. She assumed that only GDFC was a code because M-I-S-S spells a word that was recognizable. All eight letters could be a code for something.

She reached for her computer to start researching codes, since she had fallen asleep the last time she had tried. Then she stopped, and turned her computer off. Ancestor Aonghus didn't have a computer. She needed to think like Ancestor Aonghus. As far as she knew he didn't have any life experience that would have exposed him to codes, unless it was the nine months in the army, but that was unlikely. He was young, a private, and the war was over. Katherine thought if I were sitting here in this attic, one hundred years ago, agonizing about how to conceal yet reveal the existence of these ingots in a code, what would I do?

After a few minutes Katherine reached for a piece of paper and wrote out the alphabet in block letters. The first thing that came to mind would be to shift the letters. She thought if I were to shift all the letters, one letter 'MISSGDFC' would become 'NJTTHEGD,' that's no help. So she tried shifting two letters, it became 'OKUUIFHE.'

"Hmmm," Katherine said, as she studied the letters in front of her. "What am I missing?"

She didn't know what else to try, so she resumed rewriting 'MISSGDFC' in additional patterns of letter shifts. She was interrupted by the sound of footsteps on the attic stairs. On guard, alert, she shoved her work papers inside a book and moved to the stairway. She met her brother on the top step.

"Hi, Kate."

"What are you doing up here?"

"I couldn't sleep, so I came up to visit."

"The attic is off limits, you know that."

"Hey, we're not kids anymore, and you're not Uncle Gus." With a bold step he moved around Katherine and walked about the attic. "I heard you call this your 'oasis.' I can see why, it's nice up here."

"Daniel, this is my space, please go."

Instead he settled down in one of the easy chairs, "Why, Kate, you're angry. Glad to see it. You're not so perfect after all."

Katherine was more than angry – she was livid. She glared at her brother, thankful for one thing – he had sat down by the west window. She had been working by the east window, so the book with her notes was out of his sight and reach. She needed to get a grip and get him to leave without walking around any further. Yet, somehow she couldn't help herself, she slipped into sibling mode.

"I never said I was perfect."

"You didn't have to, everybody else did – and does. Saint Katherine of Cloud Cottage."

"Sounds to me like you're the one with anger issues."

"Don't go being self-righteous, Kate, you might tarnish your halo."

Katherine sighed, finally gaining control of herself. "Daniel," she addressed her brother, "neither of our lives has turned out the way we anticipated, or perhaps would have chosen. I can't change that. All I'm trying to do here is welcome everyone who is a descendant of Ancestor Aonghus, to encourage family bonding, to foster tradition, and celebrate the clan. I'm sorry I snapped at you but think about the meaning of oasis. I call this my oasis not just because it is a pleasant space, but because it's my refuge, my quiet, calm space amidst all the company. It's off limits to protect the tranquility. When you came barging up the stairs, uninvited, and unannounced, you intruded, Daniel. What if I'd been getting dressed?"

"I would have looked away."

"You are missing the point. On those weekends you have stayed in the den, I didn't go in that room, even to use the computer. For that interval of time it was your space. This is mine. Now I would enjoy visiting with you, but not here. Let's go downstairs, I'll fix some coffee for you and tea for me."

Daniel stood up, "I've already had enough coffee, I'm going to go for a drive."

Katherine sighed. "Daniel, I'm sorry, but please try to understand and don't leave. When the twins get back they will be disappointed that you're not here to go to the beach with them. Haven't we both learned that walking away is just another way to close a door? We're at a point in our lives when we need to be opening doors, not closing them any more."

"Dammit, Kate, why do you always have to be right?"

"Daniel, you were also right, we're not kids anymore, and it's not about who's right, it is about understanding."

"Yeah, yeah. You have any lemonade?"

Kate nodded affirmatively.

Daniel walked to the stairs, but turned before he headed down. "I get what you're saying, and I should have at least knocked, but, Kate, I know you, and the way you reacted when I came up the stairs, there's something you didn't want me to see. You're hiding something." He fixed his gaze upon her. "You don't have to answer, I know I'm right. Oh, sorry, I 'understand.'"

"Daniel, you're crazy, impossible, and always want to have the last word."

He shrugged and went down the stairs, Katherine followed behind him.

29

The rest of the day passed without incident. Katherine was thankful, that for the moment, the confrontation with her brother seemed to be defused. Yet it had been a reminder of how close to the surface some emotions were harbored, and that old wounds still festered. She was glad when she could say goodnight to the family and go upstairs. She had no interest in codes this night, and went right to bed. Of course her dreams were inhabited by her brother, cross words, ingots, codes, and deceptions.

When she awoke at daylight, she was still tired. "I need to work this dark mood out of my thoughts," she decided.

Katherine tiptoed while she dressed, then slipped out of the house. Outside she stood still and took in some deep cleansing breaths.

"Ahhhh," she said, "I have been neglecting my yoga."

She took time for a few stretches, then headed for the garden. She wanted to weed. It felt good to bend down and connect with plant life and earth.

"Sorry Bindweed, sorry Quack grass, sorry Plantain," she whispered, "you are part of creation but you are not welcome in my garden."

She started down a row of beans, her hands finding their familiar rhythm. There is something about working with one's hands, she thought, it is almost spiritual.

"I'd knock, if there was a door."

"Good morning, Daniel," Katherine addressed her brother, choosing to avoid his inference. She was feeling better and did not want any confrontational energy to reenter her thoughts. "You're up early."

"Always am. Do you remember what our Mother would do when she was upset?"

"Clean drawers!" Katherine answered laughing.

"She always cleaned drawers." Daniel said as he continued to study her.

"What?" she answered.

"Oh, you reminded me of her just now. You were weeding the same way she sorted."

"Daniel, you do know me well, but everything is fine. Let's go in. We should help Dano and the twins with breakfast at least one morning."

Saturday's morning activity was to climb the lighthouse. Once again Katherine excused herself and stayed at Cloud Cottage. This time as she settled into her favorite workstation in the living room, she didn't open the Ancestor Aonghus files. If someone surprised her, she didn't want to have to lie, not answer, or hide anything. She was still bothered by her brother's visit to the attic. Instead there was a project for the twins she wanted to research. There would be just over three weeks before the reunion weekend and Katherine wanted to have some activities ready if she needed them.

It wasn't long before she saw movement by the beach path. This didn't look good, she thought. What happened? Connor and Caitlin were walking, no, marching, in front of their father. As they approached the house it seemed like their steps started to drag a little and there was a slight slump to their shoulders. The party of three entered the house, went upstairs, and never looked in her direction. Katherine heard doors close, muffled conversation, and one pair of footsteps on the stairs walking down. Dano was almost past the living room door, their eyes met. He put his finger to his lips and motioned for her to come outside.

What in the world did the twins do, she wondered. It must be serious if they are being denied the much-anticipated climb of the lighthouse. She studied Dano's face but waited for him to speak.

"Connor and Caitlin need some time to think about things this morning." Dano began, his voice low. "They asked one thing that I agreed to, and that was that I not tell Aunt Katie. This is between the children and me."

"Oh. Alright," Katherine responded. "Although I guess I didn't know they were afraid of me."

"Not afraid, Aunt Katie, adore. They, like me, never want to disappoint you."

Katherine was quiet for a moment. "May I ask if anyone else was involved so I might be prepared for any subsequent issues?"

"No one. Again, this is between Connor, Caitlin and me."

"And the lighthouse?"

"I will do that with them at another time." Dano then gave Katherine one of his special smiles. "Maybe we will do it as a family."

"I haven't asked, Dano, and it really hasn't even been a month yet, but are you encouraged?"

"Hopeful, Aunt Katie, we are making progress. Enough so, that I would like to talk with you about what week would be best for Caroline to come." Together they decided on the third week of August. That was two weeks after the reunion. Then after their family week, there would still be one week left before the twins needed to return home.

"Caroline and I talked schedules before I came this weekend. This was her first choice of when to come in August."

"I'm glad, Dano."

"Me too, Aunt Katie. Now what are you working on all the time on your computer?"

"Hmmm," Katherine thought. She needed to be very careful if even Dano was starting to ask questions. She was glad her morning's research provided a rational explanation and a good alibi.

"I want the twins to be busy and happy," Aunt Katie said. "It has been great to have a revolving door of cousins for them to play with. I would also like them to explore and be challenged. I'm not real familiar with it, but I have been researching the concept of geocaching."

"Geocaching?" Dano asked. "Maybe I've spent so many years studying that I have missed life. What is 'geocaching?'"

Katherine smiled. "I had to learn about it, Dano. I guess I would summarize it as an Internet-based hunt for hidden objects. There are caches hidden all over the world, but there are many close by. I thought it might be fun for the twins. They could go online, chose a cache location, then go find it. They might walk to one or two, but most would be reached by car."

"Aunt Katie, this sounds really good for Connor and Caitlin, but would you mind if we did it as a family instead? I think it would be something Caroline could embrace. You know, Aunt Katie, the twins and I are very settled in here. When Caroline comes for that week I don't want her to feel 'odd man out.' This geocache thing is new to all of us. It is interactive, and we can all participate equally."

"Dano, if you think it would help you, you're welcome to it." Then with a dramatic sigh, Katherine added, "The twins and I will just play more games of Old Maid."

"Aunt Katie," Dano hugged her, "you're the best – and just for the record, I have never understood why you didn't marry."

"Ah yes," Katherine laughed. "The secrets of past years, old loves, and roads not taken. I will never tell!"

"Dano," she said, changing the subject. "There is something we do need to address before you leave: beach rules for Connor and Caitlin. What have you decided?"

Dano looked away and hesitated. "I have been postponing the decision. I hate feeling that it is not safe for two ten-year olds to be on the beach alone at Cloud Cottage. We always were, but if anything happened to Connor and Caitlin I would never forgive myself nor would you. I don't want to put you in that position." Dano heaved a big sigh. "So the suspension stands, no alone beach time."

Katherine studied her nephew. "It won't be so bad for them. We will go together. Other guests include them, and it is only three weeks until the reunion, and then another two until you are here as a family."

"I know, and I will explain to Connor and Caitlin, again, the issue of safety. I will be the bad guy."

"You're a good dad, Dano."

30

The grand finale of the Fourth of July holiday at Cloud Cottage was to be a beach fire. Hot dogs, hamburgers, S'mores, and all the trimmings were willingly transported down the beach path by young legs. The men had started a fire, and everyone staked his claim on a hot dog fork or a hamburger fryer as they waited for the fire to be just right for roasting. This was Jennifer and John's meal to organize. Katherine and Gillian seated themselves on the sand, their backs against a log, their feet extended to the fire. Blue, tired from all the activity, came to sit by Katherine, no doubt anticipating a hot dog at the end of the evening.

"How many times have we done this, Kate?" Gillian asked.

"I don't know," Katherine answered, "but not enough."

"I look around the fire and I see Mother's brow, Father's nose, Uncle Gus's chin. I hear Grandpa's laugh, and sometimes I think they all have the same smile. I wonder if fifty years from now this generation will sit here with their backs against a log. What will they see in the faces gathered around the fire?"

"Gillian, don't you remember Grandpa and Grandma sitting as we are? It's a natural cycle. There is a time to be young on the beach, there's a time to sit with one's back against a log, and there will be a time to watch all this from the horizon."

They sat in silence; the lapping of the waves on the shore was a melodic background to the excited voices of the children and the snap of the fire. It was as it always was around the fire on the beach, a moment one wanted to last forever.

"Ladies," Dano asked, "are you roasting or would you like to be served? One of these young people would be more than happy to burn a hot dog for you."

"I'm roasting," Katherine said, "as soon as there is a free fork."

"Me too," Gillian agreed. "Some day you may have to wait on me, but not yet."

Gillian found a place near the fire to cook the hot dog that Dano handed her on a fork. Katherine opted for a hamburger. Every time she flipped her fryer over meat juice dripped out onto the coals, sizzled, and emitted a tantalizing aroma. She could almost taste it. After a few more minutes, she checked it. Perfect! She turned to stand up and realized there was a hand extended in front of her.

"A pull-up, Aunt Katie?" Dano must have been watching her and was at the ready.

"Thanks, wouldn't want to stumble and have this perfectly cooked hamburger land in the sand."

"Oh you would eat it anyway, sand is always part of a beach picnic."

"That it is."

Katherine ate her burger standing, savoring its flavor, and crunching on occasional grains of sand. How was it, she wondered, that sand gets in even when she is so careful? Dano was right, at a beach picnic, sand is a given.

"I shouldn't, but I'm going to," Katherine announced to the night air. "I'm going to have a hot dog too. One of those like Mother always fixed, with the cheese slice and wrapped in bacon."

She returned to the prep station and speared a special hot dog. As she held it over the dying flames to cook, she thought about how many of these fun traditions like sparklers on the beach and bacon wrapped hot dogs were really her mother's contribution to the clan. She had loved gatherings like this, and always made them fun.

One of Gillian's grandchildren sat next to Katherine ready to roast a marshmallow. Other young people already held their forks over the flames.

"Wow!" one exclaimed, as their marshmallow burst into flame.

"Let's wait a few more minutes before we do S'mores," John suggested, as he redirected JJ, "Let's watch the sunset first."

Everyone's attention focused on the flaming orb in another picture-perfect end-of-day moment. Katherine had to divide her attention between nature's show and cooking her hot dog. She turned her fork over to make sure the bacon on that side was cooked through.

When she glanced back, the colors of 'going-down' were being softened by those of 'afterglow.' She could hear enthusiastic voices calling out names of colors. This tradition, she thought, is my contribution to the clan. She knew it was one Connor would never forget.

"Okay, my hot dog is done and Dano is not here to help me. I'm on my own, UP!"

Jennifer had left a bun and all the condiments out for Katherine. The rest of the table had been taken over with the preparation for S'mores. Forks with marshmallows were ready for the sunset-watchers to roast in the now glowing coals.

"Aunt Katie, did you see it?" Caitlin called as she ran towards her.

"See what?"

"The green flash. I finally saw one."

"I missed it," Katherine answered, then asked, "but you really did see it?"

"Yes, so did Daddy."

"Pretty cool, isn't it?"

"Yeah, way cool," Caitlin agreed as she reached for a fork and found a place by the fire. Katherine watched with envy and remembrance the easy drop to the knees as the little girl knelt.

146

"I think I'll go sit on the log," she said with a sigh.

Daniel, Gillian and Steve were in the middle of a conversation, so she addressed Blue. The dog had followed the sunset watchers back, and had plopped down next to her.

"Well, Blue, did you see the green flash?"

"Aunt Katie, dogs don't see color," Connor corrected, as he came over to sit beside her and enjoy his S'more.

"Oh, I guess I did know that."

"Aunt Katie, you're not feeding Blue are you?" Jennifer called out.

"No, I'm not sharing my hot dog. Sorry, Blue. Connor, how is that S'more?"

"Awesome, but I burned my marshmallow. I'm going to roast another one."

Katherine looked around, then tore a little piece of bacon off her hot dog.

"Here, Blue, good dog. I didn't say I wouldn't give you bacon."

The group around the fire had settled into poses of post-S'mores indulgence when John announced, "Time for sparklers, everybody down by the water. Dan, are you in?"

"I've got your back. I'll distribute the sparklers, you bring a burning stick."

A short distance away the children were soon waving their sparklers in the twilight, giggling at the iridescent patterns they momentarily created. A couple of the teenagers were managing one in each hand. Dano and John were kept busy lighting and handing off sparklers.

How many boxes of sparklers do they have, Katherine wondered. What a fun way to end the evening.

Daniel, Gillian, and Steve, still conversing, rose to watch the activity. Katherine went to help Jennifer pack up, but she could hear the children a short distance away.

147

"Thanks for helping, Aunt Katie."

"I haven't done anything. I've just been enjoying myself. I didn't even check to see if you had a chance to eat."

"Oh I ate, too much!"

"That's part of the tradition," they both laughed.

By the time the last glitter of the sparklers had faded, everything was packed up for the trip up the hill.

"Well," the question was asked. "Do we throw another log on the fire or call it a night?"

Gillian spoke up. "It's so pleasant, let's add to the fire and stay down a while longer."

"Great," Dano agreed. "Dad, Uncle Steve, can you take care of the fire while John and I go up the hill with one load of gear? We still have a little daylight to see by without using flashlights."

"We got it. Go and hurry back."

The new logs on the fire ignited and as the fire grew brighter the group seemed to become quieter.

"Aunt Katie, tell us a story," Connor spoke up.

"Oh, Connor, I think someone else should tell a story tonight. Daniel, why don't you tell the young people about the summer you lived with Uncle Gus and worked on a cherry shaking crew?" Daniel looked startled. "I'm sure they'd love to hear about cherry fights, pit spitting contests, getting dunked in tanks of cold water and ..."

"Hey, stop! If I'm going to tell the story, let me tell it," Daniel interrupted, and he began.

Gillian squeezed Katherine's arm and whispered in her ear, "Good job, that was smooth."

Katherine winked back. She was glad Daniel had taken the suggestion. It was important his grandchildren learn about him too, not just Ancestor Aonghus.

Dano and John joined the group around the fire listening to Daniel's adventures in the cherry orchard. Katherine let her mind wander. The stars were now visible, and the night skies seemed huge. It always amazed her how on nights like this, one could stand on the beach, look up, feel so insignificant, and yet so connected.

Sunday morning it was raining. It had been absolutely calm and gorgeous when they had finally come up from the beach the night before. Not a cloud in the sky, and now it was raining. Many at Cloud Cottage slept in. Those who were up, mostly the adults, were gathered around the kitchen table, enjoying coffee, tea, and conversation. After four days together you'd think we'd be 'talked out,' Katherine thought as she listened to the lively discussion. By eleven o'clock most of the children were watching a movie in the den. Even though it was still raining, John had gone out for a quick run accompanied by Blue. They both returned drenched. Katherine had seen them coming and met them at the back door with towels.

"Blue, you are a sorry sight, but I think you're smiling,"

The dog looked up at her and wagged a happy tail as she dried him off in the mudroom. John had already gone in to shower.

"Alright, Blue, that's all I can do. Place!" She pointed to his bed in the corner of the room. He looked up at Katherine, gave his tail another happy hopeful wag. Katherine was firm and told him again 'place.' His head down, Blue padded to his cushion, circled until he had the perfect nest of blankets, then laid down. He watched Katherine throw the wet towels in the washer; by the time she went back into the kitchen he was asleep.

Jennifer was helping Gillian and her eldest granddaughter get lunch ready. Since it was rainy the families had decided to leave earlier than planned. Katherine pitched in to help. There was one more gathering around the kitchen table for the adults. The young people opted to eat in front of the TV. Then, in a flurry of laundry, suitcases, and hugs they were all gone.

Katherine had managed to have a few moments alone with Gillian, for which she was thankful. Her sister promised to call her with results as soon as she knew them. Interruptions were the norm with this many people together under one roof, and of course their conversation was cut short. This time it had been one of Gillian's granddaughters with a dust mop. Each one of the children had been given an age-appropriate cleaning assignment before they left. Cloud Cottage still needed a good once-over, but it was not trashed. Katherine sighed. She had enjoyed the weekend and everyone who had come, even Blue. The teapot whistled, and Katherine reached for a mug. She loved a full house, but she was looking forward to a quiet evening.

31

Connor and Caitlin were watching more movies. Katherine went to the living room. It was still raining and she closed her eyes to absorb the soothing sound of nature. It wasn't long however, until her thoughts were focused on 'MISSGDFC.' Every letter combination she had tried resulted in nothing recognizable. What else could she try? She just let her thoughts drift. Perhaps, replacing letters with numbers, but what would that yield – a multiple digit number. How could that help? Katherine had no idea, but she didn't have anything else to try, so she might as well see what it looked like. She retrieved some paper from the den, said a soft 'hi' to the twins, and retired to the living room. Once again she marked the letters of the alphabet on a piece of paper. This time she numbered one to twenty-six. Okay, let's see what we have: 'MISSGDFC' – becomes '13919197463.'

"I have no clue," Katherine said. So she reversed the numbering in sequence from 26 to 1: 'MISSGDFC' – becomes '14188820232124.'

Still no clue! Katherine tried adding each group of numbers together. She tried dividing them into groups of 2, 3, and 4, then added them to see if that would help. Wait a minute, she thought, I haven't tried a partial conversion. The first one she tried was GDFC, but not the MISS. This time the conversion 'MISSGDFC' became 'MISS7463,' and 'MISSGDFC' became '1391919GDFC.'

"I'm frustrated. I'm not seeing it."

At that moment her eyes shifted back to 'MISS7463' and something registered in her brain, 7/4/63, Vicksburg! Could the clue be 'Mississippi,

July 4, 1863?' The day Vicksburg fell? She remembered that date because Vicksburg and Gettysburg happened at the same time.

"My minor in history is certainly proving useful!"

Katherine looked at the clauses as they appeared in Ancestor Aonghus's writing; 'MISSGDFC became impossible,' 'MISSGDFC closed the door,' 'MISSGDFC changed plans.' After the fall of Vicksburg the Union controlled the Mississippi and the western front. It might indeed become impossible to travel with the ingots. The door was closed; access to the Confederate states would have been impossible.

Excited, Katherine folded the paper with the numbers and letters, put it her pocket for safekeeping and went to the bookshelf. She found what she was looking for – a book on the siege of Vicksburg, the battle for the Mississippi. She was still reading when the twins entered the room yawning. She closed the book; she had read enough to know she was right. Whoever brought the ingots east from Nevada, summer of '63, couldn't get through the Union lines to deliver the silver to the Confederacy. They could, however, cross the Mississippi into the northern states. Regardless of how they traveled, by November of '63, the ingots were in Chicago. Katherine thoughtfully replaced the book and followed the twins up to bed. They would all sleep well tonight.

Katherine turned out the light and relaxed against her pillows. She knew she would fall asleep soon, but she wanted to think through an idea that had come to her over the weekend. If and when she found the ingots would they be valuable enough to finance a trip to Scotland? She wanted to take her family, all of her father's branch of Ancestor Aonghus's family tree, to the Isle of Skye. How much would it cost? There were twenty-one of them now. She could just imagine Connor and Caitlin bounding over the Scottish highlands, asking questions of everyone they met. How awesome would it be to visit Dunvegan Castle, the ancestral home of the MacLeod Clan? Perhaps they could go at a time when there was a reunion, or a Clan Parliament. Katherine's mind was full of ideas and wonderful images, which soon became dreams as she drifted into sleep.

Bright sunlight was already streaming in the east window when Katherine surfaced from the dreams of a morning's half slumber. She stretched, then relaxed her muscles once more. She was too comfortable to get up. In her mind, the events of the holiday weekend ran like a video on replay. It had been a good gathering. She was looking forward to the reunion, but she knew it would be different. There would be many more people and less quality time with each. This weekend had been a mini-reunion with her immediate family. Her only regret was the incident with her brother. She knew she had overreacted and in doing so had triggered suspicion. She hoped her apology had soothed hurt feelings and diminished curiosity.

As for the ingots, Katherine was more confident than ever that they did exist and that they were hidden in 'plain view' on the premises. Ancestor Aonghus went through a great deal of effort to share their story, at least as far as he had been able to reconstruct it. What a journey those bars travelled, from a clandestine silver mine and smelter in Nevada, they crossed the mountains and plains. They would have had to avoid Indian war parties and Union patrols. Then as they approached the Mississippi, thinking they were home free, the "door" was closed. The risk of capture and confiscation of the silver ingots was too great. Katherine's imagination was on a roll. What if one dark night on the west bank of the Mississippi the group that transported the ingots split? One stayed on the bank, hidden, watching, while another climbed in a boat to try and cross. If they were successful, the second group would follow. What if, as they watched, flares were fired, the first group was captured, and their ingots were lost? To come so far with such commitment to their beliefs, how angry and bitter they must have felt.

Katherine couldn't help laughing at herself and her imagination. Stick to the facts she thought. A group of people did take great risks to smelt silver ore into bars, transport them across the western states to the Mississippi. To accomplish this did indeed require conviction and commitment. Individuals, who believed in a cause that strongly, when thwarted, would have resolved to find another way. That way involved a small schooner on Lake Michigan in November, but why? Perhaps the answer to that question was in the next group of pages in Ancestor Aonghus's book. You can tackle that piece of the puzzle tonight, Katherine thought, right now you'd better get up or the twins are going to call you sleepyhead again.

Downstairs all was still quiet. "Good, I am up first," Katherine announced to the kitchen, as she put the teakettle on to boil.

She needed to think through this next month's schedule. There are four weeks and three weekends before the reunion, Katherine reflected. Dano will be here on the middle weekend. The rest of the family will not be back until the reunion. This weekend, cousin Tim and his family will be here for five days. There will be playmates in that group for the twins. The next weekend will also be a group of first cousins, but just siblings and spouses, no children or grandchildren. That will work out well because Dano will be here and he and the twins haven't had a weekend together without other children since Memorial Day. The third weekend will be the third and last group of first cousins. They will also be here for five days and there will be grandchildren. Someone in that family has rented a cottage nearby for the week preceding the reunion. She needed to find out who would be staying for sure at Cloud Cottage. After this accounting Katherine realized there would only be a few weekdays free for twin activities in the whole month.

At that point, as if right on cue, the twins appeared. Katherine wondered at the fact that they always came down in the morning together. She wondered who woke up first and roused the other. She would have to be more observant.

"Good morning, Aunt Katie, what are you working on?"

"The schedule of all Cloud Cottage guests for this month."

The twins looked at each other. Katherine knew they must have a question, but was always amused at the choice of spokesperson. It seemed to depend on the topic, this time it was Caitlin, Miss Factual.

"Aunt Katie, on reunion weekend, there will be a lot of people here, right?"

"Yes, there are 327 descendants of Ancestor Aonghus. So far I have received confirmations that 163 are planning to attend."

"163! Aunt Katie!" Connor exclaimed. "There isn't room on the floor for that many air mattresses."

Ah, Katherine thought. Connor's room was a little crowded this weekend. I should have suspected, he is a child who needs space. I will have to remember that.

"Whoa, you two! No worries!" Katherine really did have to laugh at the concerned expressions on their faces. Miss Factual was struggling in her mind with the logistics of 163 people.

"During the reunion weekend the guests staying, sleeping, at Cloud Cottage will be the same as this last weekend." In her own mind she hoped that she was right and that Gillian would be able to return. She continued, "all the other members of the clan are staying in area hotels or have rented a cottage for the week before or the week after. Cloud Cottage will be full of people during the day on Saturday and Sunday and probably Friday evening too, but at night it will only be our family."

The twins looked much relieved and asked, "Are there any leftover cinnamon rolls?"

"There just happen to be two left. I think they have your names on them." Katherine laughed, happy that the more normal concern of what was for breakfast had displaced the weighty issues of the reunion.

"What are we going to do today, Aunt Katie?" was the next question.

"Connor," Caitlin interrupted him, "you know what we are going to have to do today – weed!"

Again Katherine laughed, "That's right – at least for a while. Are you ready to go out? It's already after ten."

Together they went to work. Katherine tried to make the stint in the garden fun by making up games as they worked. It was what her mother had done when she had been a child and the garden had to be weeded.

Sometimes Katherine could almost hear her mother's laughter blending with hers, Connor's and Caitlin's as they enjoyed some silliness together.

"Aunt Katie," Caitlin asked after about an hour, "isn't it time for a moratorium?"

"Almost, let's each finish our rows."

With renewed vigor the twins attacked the weeds with both hands. Katherine watched them out of the corner of her eye. She remembered the first day they weeded. They had worked lackadaisically with one hand. She showed them how to think ahead down the row, and work with two hands. They certainly had grasped the concept.

Katherine finished her row and moved over to the radish row. She pulled up several, until she had two big handfuls.

"Who would like a fresh radish sandwich for lunch?"

"A radish sandwich?"

That was less than an enthusiastic response, Katherine realized.

"Haven't you ever had a radish sandwich?" Two heads shook, no.

"Well, it is a garden treat I enjoyed with my grandmother MacLeod. Let's try it." Katherine stopped. "There is one difference though, she always had fresh homemade bread to make the sandwiches. How about if we make a quick trip to Cherry Point to get a fresh loaf of white?"

"Yeah," the twins agreed.

"Okay, rows finished?"

"Yes!"

"Then let's go in, wash hands, and go to Cherry Point."

Cherry Point was a farm market just a short drive from Cloud Cottage. It had been operated by the same family for decades. Katherine had stopped there with her family when she was a child. In that era her father had always bought a homemade cherry pie and quarts and quarts of sweet cherries.

As Katherine parked the car she announced, "Today we are only getting a loaf of white bread, no pie or strudels. We have left over sweets at Cloud Cottage." Her announcement was met by a silence that only meant disappointment.

"But, Aunt Katie, we don't have any more sweet cherries," Connor said.

Katherine, she thought, you are such an easy mark.

"Okay, Connor, I agree. Cloud Cottage cannot be without sweet cherries in July. You choose a quart, one quart," she emphasized. "Caitlin and I will get the bread."

Inside Caitlin asked if any white bread was still warm. In a moment a staff person returned from the kitchen carrying not a warm, but a hot loaf.

"Caitlin, our timing is perfect today." Katherine handed the loaf to the young girl. "Carry the bag by the top. Any pressure on the bread now will squish it."

They were a happy parade to the car, Caitlin holding the bread, Connor carrying his coveted cherries.

In just a short time they were all three sitting down to a sandwich of hot buttered bread with fresh sliced radishes. Katherine savored her first bite. It was always like a step back in time for her, a radish sandwich is ageless. As she enjoyed the textures of smooth and crunchy and the combination of slightly sweet creamy butter with the pleasant sharpness of the radishes, she watched the twins. Caitlin was relishing her sandwich with gusto. Connor was hesitant after the first bite.

"Connor," Katherine said, "If you would enjoy the bread more without the radishes, it's okay." She was rewarded with a smile as he scraped radishes off his bread.

The afternoon had become so pleasant and sunny Katherine suggested they go to the beach.

"Tomorrow morning we will have chores," she warned, "but this is a perfect beach day."

The water was warm and the waves choppy, it was great swimming. Katherine and the children swam, kayaked, played, and Katherine even tried the new boogie board. It was pure fun, just she and the children enjoying each other. They ended the day on the beach with a long walk to dry off. Actually Katherine walked, the boundless energy of the twins sent them running and chasing each other as much as walking by her side.

Bedtime was early that evening. Connor had requested an Ancestor Aonghus story. Katherine suggested a postponement until the next night. She had enjoyed the day, but was tired and anxious to start on the next pages of the book. Once the children were each settled in their rooms with books or gaming tablet, she said goodnight and went upstairs.

32

I'm ready for the next challenge, she thought. Her laptop was opened to the enhanced file of pages. She found the pages she was looking for and skimmed them. It was again, a group of three. Okay, what did Ancestor Aonghus have to say this time? She began reading. The first two groups of pages had been perplexing. This group seemed benign. There were no underlined words, no evidence of a code, nothing particular at all that stood out. At least I had an idea of what delineated the clue in the first two, she thought. The challenge there was to decipher the clue. Now, here it seems, I have to find the clue. I guess that gives new meaning to 'I haven't got a clue.'

Katherine read each sentence, then reread them. She read them as individual sentences. She read them in groups of two and three sentences, searching for implied meaning. Nothing! For the most part they appeared to be just more rantings of a troubled old man.

The sentences at least did seem to form cohesive thoughts. She gleaned some things that were helpful for her understanding. In the rambling sentences he mentioned that as an adult he remembered fragments of conversations he had heard on that ill-fated schooner. They had meant nothing at the time, but it was those remembered words that allowed him to piece together the origin and journey of the ingots. He had heard references to the Comstock Lode, to Nevada, to how long it took to smelt the ore in secret using the Patio Process. He thought men carrying the ingots left Nevada in groups as soon as the snow melted, and the passes opened in late June of '63. They rendez-voused in Denver then started east across the plains. Three of the men had spoken to the captain about four hard months on the trail and not being able to cross the Mississippi. The captain and the first mate appeared to be new acquaintances of the three men. They also were Confederate sympathizers or operatives. Aonghus heard them speak of the "Sons of Liberty."

Katherine did a quick Internet search and started to read about the degree of Confederate activity that prevailed in Illinois, Indiana, and Ohio during the last years of the war. Secret societies, most notably the "Sons of Liberty," had grown in size. Many of their members were anti-war Democrats, Copperheads, southern sympathizers, and some solid citizens as well as Confederate operatives. Their existence and prevalence in Chicago would have made discreet inquiries feasible for the bearer of the ingots. Assistance would have been available. It was unfortunate that the captain and his first mate, provided by the Confederate operatives, were inept Lake Michigan sailors.

"Oh, Ancestor Aonghus, what a coincidence that you were anxious to depart for Canada the same night as that schooner."

Well, this fills in the blanks for me, Katherine thought. It also raises more questions. Why did Ancestor Aonghus include these specific words he heard and his ideas here? Why didn't he just tell the story in the beginning? Katherine pondered this conundrum for a few minutes and considered two possibilities. One, if she hadn't already deciphered the clues in the first pages, these references would seem to be more ramblings of an addled old man. The second possibility was that he was indeed addled, confused, and not as coherent or cautious as he was in the first pages. In a way, it made sense to Katherine to have encountered the specific words and terms at this point. Ancestor Aonghus's words confirmed that she was on the right track without disclosing anything to a casual reader. Either way the question now became, was this the message of these pages, or was there more? Perhaps she should back up and try to make sense of the pages as a group.

Katherine read on. When she paused it seemed to her that Ancestor Aonghus turned philosophical in his ramblings. He wrote of how eerie it was that he had found his life in the Great Lakes. How eerie it was that one event in history so far removed from his place of birth could influence his future. Far from his clan on the Isle of Skye, he had found other islands, waves, and ships. How eerily the people involved were just as committed to their cause as he was to his clan. His last thoughts in the group of pages referred to how thankful he was for his life. How it troubled him that he had benefited from the loss of the schooner and six men's deaths. He wrote that an eerie connection always existed between him and those men.

Katherine shut down the computer and thought, these pages are going to have to steep in my subconscious for a while or perhaps in my dreams.

33

Somehow the hours of the next day flew by and it seemed before she knew it she was sitting down with the twins for the promised Ancestor Aonghus story. She had no idea what tale to tell them this evening, so she asked if they would like to hear about Uncle Gus.

"Sure," was the resounding response.

Katherine began the story of her favorite uncle. How he was the oldest in the family, and her father, Daniel, had been the youngest. How he and his siblings had walked from Cloud Cottage to a one-room schoolhouse not far from Cherry Point. Then, when he had finished eighth grade, he had gone to school in town. In the winter, because it was difficult to travel, he had boarded with a family in town and came home on weekends. She knew he had played football on the high school team, but when he wasn't in school or playing with the team, he worked. Katherine had a diary he had kept during those high school years. Page after page all that was written was "went to school, came home, worked." His father, Ancestor Aonghus, had become a farmer, but had also worked off the farm. Uncle Gus was needed to help with the MacLeod farm. He milked cows and sprayed the fruit trees with a horse-drawn tank and spray gun. Katherine shared that Uncle Gus always laughed and said he was a 'soaked bloke' when he finished spraying an orchard that way. It was a big day when the farm got a steel-wheeled tractor, and bigger still, years later, when the tractor had a cab on it to keep the chemicals off the driver.

"Uncle Gus got soaked with chemicals?" Conner asked.

"Yes, many many times."

"Didn't it kill him?" It was Caitlin who asked this time; the twins had a way of alternating questions.

"No, he lived a very long life."

"Did he go to college, Aunt Katie?"

"Yes, he did. He studied agriculture at Michigan State when it was a college before it became a university."

"Was he always a farmer?"

"Yes, but he did lots of other things too."

"Like what?"

"Oh, he liked to build and design."

"Like Ancestor Aonghus?"

"Yes, that's right, Caitlin, and often other people would hire him for a project. He taught school for a year or two and after he sold the orchards and retired, well, he did things just because they sounded fun. He volunteered at a National Park for one season, several winters he sailed on a big cruise ship for a month. In exchange for his fare he was to dance in the evening with all the single women onboard."

"You mean he sailed for free? All he had to do was dance?"

"That's right. It was a perfect job, because Uncle Gus loved to dance."

"Awesome."

"What else did he do?" Caitlin asked.

"Let's see. He was an avid reader."

"Those are his bookshelves right?" Caitlin motioned to the shelves opposite the fireplace.

"Yes they are. Oh, and he loved to play cribbage."

"What's that?" Connor asked.

"A card game."

"Can you teach us?"

"Of course, but another night. That's it for tonight. Time for bed! Tomorrow is 'go-to-town-day.' We should be off early."

"Okay, Aunt Katie, we'll set our alarms." Then diligently the two coordinated their watches.

"Goodnight, Aunt Katie. We'll see you at seven."

"Whoa, back here. What time did you set your alarms for?"

"Six-fifteen."

"Back it up an hour. Seven-fifteen will be fine."

"Aunt Katie, we just don't want you to wait for us."

"Thank you very much, but we'll be fine if we leave the house by eight-thirty."

She had told them an early start, that meant she better be ready too. As a precaution, she set an alarm and instead of working on Ancestor Aonghus pages she prepared the grocery list and identified all the stops she wanted to make the next day. Consolidating trips to town into one per week required planning. Katherine yawned, turned out the light, and went to sleep.

The next day went well. They had been organized, efficient, and completed their errands. They were almost home when Connor spoke up, "We are all out of sweet cherries."

"In other words, Connor, you think I should turn in here at Cherry Point?"

"Please. I love sweet cherries."

"Me too!" She handed him some money and reminded him just one quart. A few minutes later he returned to the car.

"These look so good, Aunt Katie. They're really big and dark!"

"It looks like you chose a very good quart, Conner. Every day now the cherries will be riper and sweeter. Have you and Caitlin had a pit-spitting contest yet?"

"No. What's a pit-spitting contest?"

"We'll have cherries for dessert tonight and I'll show you. Okay, groceries in the kitchen."

Katherine put away their purchases then sat down for a quiet moment. No, I'm not sitting here, she thought, I'm going to enjoy the swing. On the porch she rested her back against her favorite spot and extended her long legs. Her thoughts turned reflective. The turns our lives take can indeed seem uncanny, eerie, and almost supernatural. Not scary, just more than coincidental. Who could have predicted that the entire first summer she would spend at Cloud Cottage without other obligations, the twins would need to be here? There were so many details of this summer that had strangely fallen into place; she decided that Ancestor Aonghus was right. There was an eeriness to life sometimes, at least at Cloud Cottage.

That evening the entertainment for the twins became a full-blown pit-spitting contest. Katherine had washed the cherries and had prepared three equal cups. On the beach, they paced off markers, and with their backs to the breeze the competition began. Some shots went foul, others were lost to a giggle or fell short. No one really cared who won, it was just fun, and when the cherries were this good, everybody was a winner.

After the last pit was sent flying it appeared Caitlin had earned the title of Pit-Spitting Champion. Her award for winning was to clean up all the pits.

"This is soooo not fair," she protested, laughing, as Katherine and Connor cheered her on in her victory lap.

"You missed some over here," they chided her.

"Can we stay down and watch the sunset, Aunt Katie?" Connor asked. "I like watching the sunset from high up at Cloud Cottage, but on the beach the sky just seems bigger."

"I agree, and tonight there are some clouds low to the horizon that should show wonderful color. Caitlin, what do you say?"

"Yeah, let's."

The three took a short walk south so they could watch the sun as it sank lower on their return north. Other people were also out walking, enjoying the evening. Greetings were exchanged. Katherine and the twins were beginning to recognize familiar faces from their many walks. The timing was perfect and they returned to their beach as the red orb touched the horizon. They seated themselves on a dune to watch the show.

Connor spoke, "Let's each just name one color tonight, our favorite."

Katherine sighed. We have learned to go for quality, not quantity, she thought. No one spoke as they all watched and absorbed the beauty of the moment.

As the last red glimmer disappeared, Caitlin announced,

"*Marvelous Marigold.* I love the shade of yellow-orange before it turns red. What's yours, Connor?"

Connor just shook his head "no." He was still watching. The sunset for him wasn't over until the last shade of color faded to gray. Mother Nature was displaying her finest tonight, and Katherine waited for the young boy to speak. The low-lying clouds had indeed caught color. It might be a prolonged sunset.

At last Connor heaved a sigh, "That was awesome." Then added, "*Lavender Light* is my color tonight."

"*Light Lavender*, that's nice," Caitlin said. "I saw that too."

"Not *Light Lavender*," Connor corrected, "*Lavender Light*. It's the color of the underside of the clouds after the pink has gone."

"That's a perfect description of a beautiful shade, Connor."

Connor looked pleased. "What is your color tonight, Aunt Katie?"

Katherine paused, decided to change her color and said, "*Tangerine Tango*. I liked the intensity of the early colors tonight. They were so vibrant they almost danced."

Together they walked up to Cloud Cottage and a good night's sleep.

34

Their guests arrived the next day with an armload of pizza boxes for dinner. The twins were ecstatic. There was cheese pizza, pepperoni pizza, meat-lovers pizza, pineapple and ham, and …they were in pizza heaven. There were six children in this group, from eight to fifteen, one set of parents, and Katherine's cousin and his wife. During dinner Katherine observed behaviors that told her the ratio of adult supervision per child was too low. She would not send Connor and Caitlin along with them alone. She would need to go too. The entire weekend Katherine participated in all activities except one. They were going on a dune ride, and although Connor and Caitlin were invited and would have loved to go again, Katherine explained their previous participation and the three of them stayed home. She and the twins played a delightful game of croquet followed by lemonade on the porch while their guests were gone.

"This is nice, Aunt Katie," Connor said.

"Yeah," Caitlin concurred. "These cousins are always doing stuff."

"'Stuff?'" Katherine asked. "What kind of 'stuff?'"

"Just 'stuff.'" Connor said as he started to squirm. "Not bad 'stuff' just not nice 'stuff.'"

"Aunt Katie, when they go to the beach tonight do we have to go?" Caitlin asked.

"Not if you don't want to. Connor, what would you like to do?"

His answer was immediate and enthusiastic. "Learn to play cribbage like Uncle Gus."

"Yeah, can we?" Caitlin asked.

"Are you sure?" Katherine said. "I think they may have some sparklers on the beach tonight."

The twins looked at each other and in unison answered an emphatic, "NO!"

"Okay, we may only play part of a game, but it will be a first lesson."

Katherine should have known it wouldn't take the twins long to master the rules of cribbage. They not only played one game, but two. Her cousin's family didn't come up from the beach until well after dark, and even then, talked on the porch long after Katherine wanted to call it a night.

This group stayed until Monday. It was one day too long. Katherine enjoyed her cousins, but some of the family dynamics were trying. It was interesting that the twins had noticed it too. Their car was still in the driveway when the children asked if they should start weeding their rows in the garden. Surprised, Katherine couldn't help herself, she had to ask, "you want to go and weed?"

"Well it's Monday," Caitlin answered. "We always weed on Monday."

"And," Connor added, "it's quiet and peaceful in the garden."

"Yeah," Caitlin agreed. "Quiet."

Katherine had to laugh. "There wasn't much quiet here this weekend, was there?"

The twins both shook their heads "no."

"Let's go weed. It will feel good."

Katherine was very glad there were no children coming next weekend. The group would be four female cousins, two with spouses. The two single women would have to share Caitlin's bedroom, but that would mean it would only be Dano and Connor in the boys' room.

The twins were anxious to see their father. Katherine was a little concerned that perhaps they had been away from home long enough. They might want to go back with him. Her concerns deepened Friday when Caitlin asked if she could sleep in the boys' room with Connor and her daddy. Katherine's only response had been "let's ask your father when he comes."

Dano arrived late afternoon, and Caitlin moved before the other guests arrived. It was a good arrangement. The women had the girls' room to themselves, and Caitlin was where she wanted to be.

Dano spent wonderful one-on-one time with the children all weekend. They played, they walked, there was a constant chatter going on between them, and they climbed to the top of the lighthouse.

Katherine also had a delightful adult weekend. They walked, and talked, played some, and did not climb to the top of the lighthouse. They had met some interesting people on the beach and had even shared a glass of wine with them at their cottage. The whole weekend had been comfortable, casual, and very pleasant.

On Sunday afternoon the cousins left first, after not only stripping beds and doing laundry but remaking them as well. Dano and Caitlin's beds in the boys' room too. Katherine waved them an affectionate 'goodbye,' sorry that this was one group that was unable to return for the reunion. Upon hearing about the twin's tee shirt they all insisted they wanted one and prepaid on the spot. The twins now had an 'after reunion' project, shipping tee shirts…if they were here.

Dano joined Katherine on the porch. "You enjoyed this weekend, didn't you, Aunt Katie?"

"Very much, Dano. How about you?"

"It's been good."

"Connor and Caitlin? Have they had enough of Cloud Cottage?"

"Aunt Katie, are you kidding? I couldn't drag them away. Not when they have been promised the whole summer. Everything is fine, although I gather last weekend was interesting."

At that time the twins joined them and the conversation was redirected.

"I think I have time for one more walk on the beach before I go," Dano announced. "Will you join us, Aunt Katie, please?"

Katherine thought the swing looked inviting, but she joined them for the walk.

That evening, after two rousing games of cribbage the three MacLeods in residence at Cloud Cottage went to bed.

35

In the morning, as Katherine lay listening to the birdsong outside her window, she realized she hadn't even thought about Ancestor Aonghus and the ingots for several days. Good, she thought, I have not become obsessed with the hunt.

She was startled by the phone ringing. This is early, she thought, as she quickly answered it, so it wouldn't disturb the twins.

"Hello."

"Hi, Kate."

"Oh, Gillian, I'm so glad to hear from you. I have been waiting. Do you have news?"

"Yes, I do. I waited until after the weekend to call, Kate."

"Tell me."

"The biopsy showed malignancy. It's official. I have breast cancer. The doctors are recommending a lumpectomy followed by radiation and chemotherapy. The procedure is scheduled for tomorrow. It is the first step, and I'll know more as each step is completed. It may be a long journey. They say they are hopeful; it has been caught soon enough. The good news is, barring any complications I will be with you for the reunion. Any radiation or chemo would start after."

"How may I help you, Gillian?"

"I'll let you know. And, Kate, I will deal with this privately."

"Okay, I understand. Will you or Steve call me tomorrow?"

"Of course."

"Gillian, I don't know what to say except I'm sorry and I love you."

"That's all I need to hear, Kate. I love you too, and I intend to fight this and sit on the porch with you at Cloud Cottage."

They said goodbye and Katherine put down the phone. Damn, she thought, I wish she didn't have to go through this.

That morning, after their Monday weeding was completed, Katherine proposed a project. How would the twins like to help her put together a 'welcome bag' for each MacLeod family coming to the reunion? They would need between fifty and sixty bags. Each one would contain their tee shirts, a schedule of family activities, a map, and informational brochures for the area and anything else that might be useful and fun. She had ordered some clan plaid yellow and black double-handled bags.

"Connor, Caitlin," she asked. "What should we put in them? Any ideas?"

"How about a paper with the MacLeod crest on it that kids could color?" Connor suggested.

"Good idea," Katherine agreed. "We could easily print that off the computer, just like Caitlin had proposed for her tee shirt."

"If I got a bag I'd like there to be balloons," Caitlin said.

"I like that," Katherine responded. "I think we could do that. We'll research balloons on the computer next, and maybe we could add pens for the adults. These are all good ideas and I just got another one. How about if we put in a family tree chart that people can fill in as they meet cousins?"

"Doesn't everybody know everybody, Aunt Katie?" Caitlin asked.

"No, not everybody, and it has been twelve years since we have had a reunion. We used to have one every five years, so it's been a long time. That means there are a lot of new members of the clan."

"Like us," Connor said.

"Exactly!"

"Why did you stop having reunions?" Caitlin wanted to know.

"Well, Uncle Gus was very old, and the last scheduled reunion was cancelled because he was ill. Okay, we have work to do. Can you amuse yourselves while I do some research? In an hour come back and help me make decisions."

Katherine used the computer in the den and after a few searches found options. We can do this, she decided. We still have time to place an order, and I can afford the extra cost of balloons and pens. She was ready for the twins when they returned. She wanted them to have input on the colors and the wording. The decisions were made and the order placed.

"Good job, everybody!"

"What about the name tags?" Caitlin asked. "Are we going to make name tags?"

"I have thought about it, and I think it will be easier if each family makes their own name tag when they arrive. Now what would you like to do?"

"Go to the beach, we want to go swimming."

"That's the best idea we've had all day. Let's go to the beach."

That evening they had watched the sunset as usual then all turned in before ten. After late nights on the weekends, early nights during the week had become their routine. The twins didn't complain at all, and Katherine was grateful for the hour or two of quiet. Tonight she wanted to look at Ancestor Aonghus's pages again. She hadn't spent as much time with these because they hadn't presented her with a puzzle. Also she had been very busy. Puzzle or no puzzle there still was information there Ancestor Aonghus wanted to be known. She needed to be sure she hadn't missed something. Slowly and deliberately Katherine reread every sentence examining every word for markings. There just wasn't anything obvious. The sentences were long and rambling. They expressed regret, remorse, and anger about not understanding a dying man's words. So much so that later in life Ancestor Aonghus had been driven to reconstruct the events surrounding the ingots. For the most part all sentences were comprehensible. There were a few words she couldn't read, but unless she was way off on her assumptions of meaning, she thought she understood the content of the sentences. She really didn't feel the unintelligible words were key, or were they?

She looked again. They were indeed different words, and they appeared at various places in the sentence structure. They were illegible because of the handwriting and bleed of the ink, not unintelligible like a purposefully scrambled word. Just to be sure, however, she copied as precisely as she could discern all the words in question on to a piece of paper. She closed down her computer so she could study these without distraction. Nothing! All right words, tonight you are to float around in my dreams, and in the morning tell me something. Katherine laughed, and said out loud, "in your dreams Katherine, in your dreams." She turned out the light.

When she awoke the next morning her first thought was "the words." She searched her memory for any vestige of dream sleep. There were no word thoughts at all. Maybe she didn't dream last night, or perhaps the words didn't like being told to do something.

"Maybe I should have asked nicely, and said "please."" Katherine said, laughing. But at the same time, in her thoughts she rephrased her petition for help from the words into the form of a request. Katherine had always been open to other understandings, and accepted that there were other possibilities beyond accepted knowledge. She was a seeker and a thinker, not just a believer.

36

It wasn't the prettiest morning at Cloud Cottage, cloudy and windy with a threat of rain. Katherine decided it would be a good field trip day for the twins. Where should they go? She was contemplating the options over tea when they came into the kitchen.

"Top of the morning to you," she greeted them.

"Top of the morning?" Caitlin asked.

"It's an Irish greeting," Katherine explained. "Your family name is Scottish, but Irish blood flows in your veins too."

"Oh," they answered, as they reached for their cereal, milk, and bowls. They had become very comfortable and self-sufficient in many ways at Cloud Cottage.

"I have a proposition for you this morning," Katherine announced.

"A proposition for the reunion, like the welcome bags?"

"No, a proposition for a field trip. It looks a little like rain, so how would you like to go to the local museum, then have lunch at a local dairy and visit the cows? Or, we could go to Whitehall, visit the lighthouse there, and also have lunch."

Connor and Caitlin looked at each other. Katherine could see the mental telepathy between them. This time Connor was the spokesperson.

"Can we do both?"

"Not in one day. Choose one for today. If you would like, perhaps we could do the other option another day."

"Proposal One," Connor decided. "Right, Caitlin?"

"Right."

"Okay. After your rooms are tidied we'll be off on an Oceana adventure."

"Aunt Katie?"

"Yes, Connor?"

"You make everything fun."

"That's because it's fun for me to be with you."

They did have fun that day. The docents at the historical society answered endless questions from the twins as they toured the facilities. At every exhibit they were placing it on a timeline with Ancestor Aonghus and Uncle Gus. Both Katherine and the docent were amused.

"I think you have two young historians," he commented.

"What's an historian?" Caitlin asked.

"Someone who studies and is an authority on past events," Katherine explained.

"Oh, like you, Aunt Katie?"

"Not really. I'm not an authority, but I love history and more importantly I love sharing it."

The museum, lunch, and the whole day had been a success. It had been topped off with not one, not two, but three games of cribbage. The children seemed to have substituted the card game for Ancestor Aonghus stories. Katherine was glad. She had almost run out of stories, at least ones she could tell.

During the evening, rain did arrive and by mutual consent it was a "go to bed even earlier" night. Katherine was once again comfortable in her bed listening to the rain and looking at her computer screen. She was tempted to move on to the next group of pages, but refrained. Decipher each group as you go Katherine, they are stepping-stones. She hoped the words would coalesce in her dreams tonight because she felt like she was hitting a brick wall.

Mornings after an overnight rain are always remarkably fresh. Katherine stood on the porch; her hands wrapped around her mug of tea and inhaled clean air. She exhaled long slow breaths. She did need to get back to yoga. This fall, she promised herself. The winds of the night had whipped up the lake and she could hear the waves pounding on the shore. In summer she seldom heard the lake. Its roar was muffled by all the leaves between her hilltop and the beach. Today it sounded like it does during a November storm, she thought. If this wind kept up the kite boarders would be out this afternoon. The twins would love that. This morning however, was cleaning time, then tomorrow their usual go-to-town day, and guests would arrive the day after.

This weekend's guests would be easy. Part of the family had a cottage rented. The younger members of the family were at that cottage. The guests at Cloud Cottage were two couples and seven high school or college students. They were very good with Connor and Caitlin, but it was different, the age gap was too great. They were all at Cloud Cottage for breakfast, but lunch and dinner they were at the rental property with their families. They invited Katherine and the twins to join them for a beach picnic on Saturday evening. The children were enthusiastic participants and enjoyed the gathering. These were cousins that would be at the reunion next weekend, so there would be additional opportunities to interact. They left on Monday morning for an excursion to Mackinac Island, but they promised Connor a game of soccer when they returned on Friday.

The coming week would be a busy one. After the departure of their guests Katherine outlined for the twins a detailed schedule for the week; Monday weed and straighten, Tuesday go to town, pick up shirts and groceries, Wednesday pack welcome bags, Thursday clean. Friday morning early a tent would be set up in the yard, the porta potty trailer would be delivered, and by Friday afternoon she expected the first arrivals and in the evening the festivities would begin.

"Aunt Katie, you said a tent?"

"Yes, a big tent, with tables and chairs that will seat everybody."

"That explains it."

"Explains what?"

"We couldn't figure out where all these cousins were going to fit."

"It may be cozy, but we will all fit," Katherine explained. "Remember a lot of people will come and go, some will be on the beach. The only times I know for sure that everyone will be in one place at once will be for the group photo on Saturday at eleven and dinner at six. Okay, let's go to work."

The twins were troupers, but by four-thirty Katherine sent them to play before dinner. Once again, it was an early night for the happy trio at Cloud Cottage, and Katherine resolved to spend some time with Ancestor Aonghus.

All weekend she had hoped there would be an epiphany of the words. She had been waiting for a solution. Apparently, she was going to have to work for it. She started at the beginning, again, but she still didn't see anything obvious. Upon a full review she considered the repetition of the word "eerie." Katherine had wondered about its use before, but Ancestor Aonghus seemed so caught up in the coincidental phenomenon of his life's events, it fit his ramblings. Perhaps she needed to try thinking again like Ancestor Aonghus. What would it really have felt like for him to have his whole life pivot on one chance encounter? Could there have been religious connotations? Did he accept the premise of 'predestination?' If he believed that Little Point Sable and the ingots were his destiny and that he had failed, that would explain, at least in part, his torment. But doesn't "eerie" imply the element of the supernatural? Predestination doesn't coexist with the supernatural. Maybe I should check the definition of "eerie." Katherine looked up several online dictionaries. She confirmed "eerie" means "strange" and "mysterious." That fits his meaning and the concept of extraordinary coincidence. She also read that the word "eerie" had Scottish roots and implied "fear." That didn't fit. He was afraid he had failed and was afraid to meet the men he buried but not afraid of the circumstances that brought them together. Ancestor Aonghus had written he was thankful. Frustrated for the umpteenth time, Katherine closed the computer with a sigh.

"Good night, Ancestor Aonghus, you haven't made this easy."

37

Errands were the order of the day on Tuesday. The twins were excited because the first stop was the screen printer to pick up the reunion tee shirts. They had turned out very nicely, and Connor was particularly pleased. They wanted to put them on and wear them right then. On that point Katherine had held firm. The answer was "no." They would be worn for the first time on Saturday for the family photo.

One by one they checked off everything on their list of errands. It had been a long day, with just an uncharacteristic stop for a fast-food lunch. Finally on their drive home Katherine suggested 'Name Five.' It had always been a favorite car game. She went first and asked the twins to name five things road signs say. This first question was an easy one, and it would get the kids started. The kids quickly came back with stop, slow, railroad, speed limit, school.

"Name five things to wear in your hair," Caitlin asked.

"Scrunchie, hairclip," said Connor.

"Tiara," Katherine added.

"Two more," Caitlin demanded. Barrette and headband finally completed the list. "Your turn, Connor."

"Name five soccer moves," Connor asked laughing.

"Oh no, I'm in trouble," Katherine said. "Caitlin, what can you do?"

"Dribble, and scissors," she stopped to think. "Pull back, isn't that one?"

"Yes," Connor agreed, "you have three."

"Oh, oh," Katherine said. "I know there was a Dutch player. They named a move after him. He was always on the news. Chy...Cryuff."

"Good, Aunt Katie. "Now one more."

"How about a hook?" Katherine asked.

"Wellllll, what kind?"

"Let's see. Right, left, how about inside?"

"Got it, Aunt Katie, how did you know?"

"I think almost every sport has a hook play of some kind, so it was a lucky guess."

"Give us another one, Aunt Katie."

"How about naming the five great lakes."

"Lake Michigan, Lake Superior," the children paused, "Lake Huron, Ontario" they knew they were short one.

"Connor, remember the HOMES rule for the lakes? H for Huron, O for Ontario, M for Michigan, E for …"

"Erie," Connor interrupted, "that's the one we missed."

At the same time Katherine slapped the steering wheel. "Yes," she exclaimed. The children thought she was talking about the successful naming of the great lakes. But Katherine was miles away. Perhaps it had been something about the way Connor had exclaimed 'Erie' that penetrated her mental block. How could she have not seen it? Ancestor Aonghus could very well have been writing about Lake Erie, he just misspelled it to throw off the reader.

"Aunt Katie, are we still playing?"

"Oh, sorry, yes."

"Give us another one."

"How about five states that start with 'N?'"

"New York, New Jersey, New Mexico," the twins were on a roll, but it took them a couple minutes to name North Dakota and finally Nevada. By that time they were back at Cloud Cottage and Katherine's thoughts were on a different game, finding the ingots.

As they pulled up the driveway two boxes were visible on the front porch.

"Aunt Katie, look! Is it the balloons and pens?"

"I hope so."

"Can we start packing the welcome bags then?"

"Maybe, let's see what we have first."

Katherine loved that the children were so excited. She wanted to work on Ancestor Aonghus, but if everything they ordered was here, they would do welcome bags. Their orders had indeed arrived, so after dinner the evening was spent organizing and setting up a system for the bags. They filled one so they each knew their jobs, but Katherine decreed the actual project would take place in the morning. The twins went up to bed – after a discussion of whose turn it was to have the game tablet.

Katherine stayed downstairs. She had some reading to do and she was sure she would find it on Ancestor Aonghus's bookshelf. By title, she didn't see what she wanted, so she chose a general title 'Michigan In The War.' She had no doubt the information was there, but if she needed to, she could test her theory on the Internet. It didn't take her long at all to confirm her suspicions.

Katherine had never been aware that Detroit had felt threatened during the war, and had prepared for attack. She had never read about the Confederacy's failed attempt to capture the USS MICHIGAN and Johnson Island in Lake Erie, or the degree of supposed rebel activity in Ohio, Canada, and on Lake Erie in between.

Canada, along with England, was supposed to be neutral, but there was a partiality to the South; cotton was king. That made Canada a welcome place for Confederate operatives to work. In late 1863, after Gettysburg and Vicksburg, the South was desperate to achieve a victory, and replenish its army. In February 1864, the Confederate Congress established a secret fund to finance sabotage. A million US dollars were designated for use by agents in Canada. A headquarters in Toronto directed the mission known as The "Northwest Conspiracy." The commander in charge was intent on causing a revolution through insurrection that would turn the citizens of the north against the union. At that time forty percent of the population of Ohio, Indiana, and Illinois were estimated to have been born in the South. It was a fertile group for recruiting support. The ultimate objective was to affect a peace treaty on southern terms.

One plan was to free the Confederate POWs on Johnson Island, arm them, and then attack, burn, and disrupt strategic points in the Midwest. This was to be accomplished when operatives who booked passage on board Lake Erie steamers seized control of the vessels. The ships were to assist in the attack on the USS MICHIGAN where operatives were also on board. One steamer was commandeered in September 1864, however, the operatives on board the USS MICHIGAN were caught before they could take control of the ship. The whole scheme fell apart in failure.

A similar plan was in place to free the POWs at Camp Douglas in Chicago. It was delayed and rescheduled to occur on Election Day, November 8, 1864. That attempt was discovered just before its scheduled execution and never occurred. Most of the men involved dispersed throughout the Midwest, or back to Canada.

So Ancestor Aonghus, is that what you wanted me to know in these pages, Katherine wondered? That the Confederate sympathizers/agents were headed to Canada because they had information that there was activity and agents operating there? She marveled at how plausible it was. There was so much boat traffic on the lake one more small schooner wouldn't attract attention. During the war the whole Great Lakes were patrolled by one steam-powered warship, the USS MICHIGAN, and six revenue cutters. There was little chance of being caught by Union forces compared to crossing the Mississippi, and if the Confederacy did launch an attack on the northern states, the silver ingots would be needed there to finance that force as well. The only problem was one of geography. The sailors aboard that schooner did not know about Little Point Sable, where the Michigan shore bulges six miles out into the lake. They ran aground and the efforts of so many months ended on the beach in the hands of a bewildered Scottish lad.

What a story, Katherine thought. This was priceless history, an untold story of the Civil War. She needed to find the ingots to document it, but for tonight this was another piece of the puzzle solved. She now knew the 'how,' the 'why,' and the 'where to' of the ingots. Whatever else Ancestor Aonghus had to say in the book would have to wait until after the reunion.

Katherine was glad the next morning was rainy. It created the perfect ambience for filling welcome bags. They started right after breakfast. Katherine wrote a family's name on a bag and put in the correct sizes of tee shirts as indicated on their RSVP letters. She handed it to a waiting Connor or Caitlin with the slip of paper telling how many adults and children were included in that family. They in turn, would place in the bag the appropriate number of balloons, pens, and information pamphlets that was laid out on a table. The bags were organized in alphabetical groups by last name, except for MacLeod, which were all lined up in the front hall, alphabetical by first name. It sounded complicated, but it was a very simple system. Katherine had every confidence Connor and Caitlin were filling the bags as instructed.

38

The excitement of the twins reached an all-time high on Friday morning when the crew came to put up the tent. Their awe reminded Katherine of the stories her mother told about watching the circus tents go up when she was a child. Connor and Caitlin's father had arrived the night before, so he was in charge. Katherine was grateful; Dano would not only direct the twins but also help with other details. Jennifer and John were due by noon as well. The plan was John would take the children to the beach while Dano and Jennifer helped her. Katherine, however, was not sure the twins would agree to miss out on a single moment at Cloud Cottage. Gillian and Steve were coming too, but later. They had talked a couple times in the last ten days and Gillian seemed upbeat; still, Katherine was anxious for her arrival and a good talk.

"Aunt Katie," Dano called from the front door.

"Yes, I'm in the kitchen."

"Do you want the crew to set up the tables and chairs?"

"They might as well, Dano, we have a good weather forecast, so I don't see any reason not to get as much done as possible."

"Any particular arrangement?"

Katherine thought for a moment, "No, other than set up the buffet tables on the west end."

"Got it."

A little later Katherine joined him under the tent.

"It looks good, Dano."

"Hope so, what's next, Chief?"

"Signs and a few balloons. The helium tank and everything you need is in the mudroom. The sign locations are written in pencil on the back of each one. Dano, just a moment, Connor and Caitlin really want to help with the balloons."

"We're Team MacLeod. We're on it."

Katherine surveyed the tent. The arrangement of tables was fine for the moment. Tomorrow she was sure the caterer might move things, but that would be fine. The tables just needed to be cleaned and the centerpieces set out. They would need one table for registration, one for welcome bags, and one for nametags. She started to clean the tables. She was almost finished when Jennifer and John drove in.

"Hi, Aunt Katie, this looks great."

"Lunch has arrived," John announced, "shall we eat out here?"

"Why not?" Katherine answered. "We'll need the pitchers of lemonade from the fridge and a stack of paper plates and cups from the cupboard above it."

"I'll go and get them," John said. "You marshal the troops."

"Wait," Katherine said, "we're missing someone."

Perplexed, Jennifer said, "Who?"

"Blue."

John and Jennifer exchanged looks, then explained that Blue was feeling very left out. They had thought adding a dog to the reunion mix would be too much.

"Did I hear somebody call 'pizza?'" Dano asked as he joined them.

"Is there pepperoni?" Connor asked.

"We'll see, as soon as Uncle John gets back. Everybody have a seat."

It was a happy group that feasted on pizza under the tent.

"Thank you for bringing lunch, Jennifer, this was a big help."

"Yes, thanks," was echoed by the chorus.

"Absolutely, you're welcome. Now what's next?"

"Let's see. I have boxes to carry down from the house. Everything on the floor of the front hall comes here."

"Let's go, Team MacLeod," Dano announced. "Let's have a box parade."

In no time at all Jennifer was setting centerpieces on tables, Dano was organizing the welcome bags, and John and the children were bringing down the last group of boxes.

"Terrific," Katherine said. "We're almost ready and it is only two o'clock. John, are you spending the afternoon on the beach?"

"I hope to, anybody coming with me?"

Caitlin and Megan had come up alongside Katherine. The two girls set their boxes down. Caitlin looked at Connor. It was that twin thing again. This time the designated spokesman was Connor.

"Can we stay and help, Dad?"

Katherine looked at Dano. She had anticipated this. The children were vested in these preparations.

"Is that okay, Aunt Katie?"

"Of course."

"Okay," John said, "it's three for the beach, see you all later."

"Jennifer, may I share with you my thoughts for the nametags? I hope you will take charge of that table."

"Sure, what would you like?"

"A suggestion – when they write their name, if you would ask them, underneath in smaller letters, to write the name of their ancestor who was a child of Ancestor Aonghus. That will help correlate to the family tree we have set up over here."

"No problem, that's a great idea."

"That's good, because I think I hear the first car arriving. Oh, Caitlin, in addition to helping your daddy can you help me keep track of the refreshment table? If we run low on lemonade, fruit, or cookies, let me know." The little girl nodded, happy to have a role.

Friday night registration was to end at eight o'clock. Over half of the families checked in, stayed a while, sat and visited, or just listened to one cousin's acoustic guitar. It was a pleasant evening.

"Aunt Katie," Jennifer said as they packed up the remaining registration material, "if tonight is any indication this reunion will be a huge success, everyone was so happy."

"Certainly were, Aunt Katie," Dano agreed.

"I hope so. I just wished I had planned on more food. Tonight probably should have been a meal or at least heavy hors d'oeuvres."

"I disagree," Dano objected. "They are all going out to dinner now, it is still early enough. This was a 'meet and greet' hour. The fact that some people stayed and kept nibbling was a statement that they were comfortable and having a good time."

"Well said, Dano," John agreed. "But speaking of dinner those of us who played hard on the beach are hungry, do we have a plan?"

"I'm hungry too," Connor said.

"John," Dano answered, "this is Aunt Katie you're talking to, of course there is a plan."

"It's simple tonight," Katherine laughed. "BBQ sandwiches and potato salad, everything is ready."

"Look who's here just in time for dinner!"

Two cars had just driven up the lane.

"Grandpa!" was the exclamation of the children.

"Gillian and Steve!" Katherine announced with equal enthusiasm.

189

The newcomers were greeted and brought up to date on the activities by an endless chatter all through dinner. It was with particular pride that Connor and Caitlin modeled their 'MacLeod Proud' shirts. Their adult relatives were appropriately impressed and said so to the twin's great satisfaction. Katherine was a little concerned about JJ and Megan, but they took it all in stride. They had had a whole afternoon on the beach with their dad and were very happy too.

"How do you do it, Aunt Katie?" Dano asked.

"Do what?"

"Bring out the best in people."

"Dano, I …"

"I nothing, Aunt Katie, you do. Look at Dad tonight, he was engaged."

"Dano, it isn't me, it's this place, it's Cloud Cottage."

Jennifer was right in her prediction; the reunion was a huge success. Everyone visited, and joined in the activities on the beach and at Cloud Cottage. There was something for everyone. Croquet, badminton, music by family members in the tent, water sports, volleyball on the beach, becoming reacquainted with each other, finding their place on the family tree, and sometimes just sitting and enjoying each other's company.

Katherine had even been cajoled into joining a volleyball game. In her early teaching years she had coached girls volleyball and loved playing. It was during that game on the beach that Katherine had seen him. She was on the north side of the net; her line of sight was to the south. So many years had passed since she had sat on this beach, waiting and watching for him, yet she recognized his stride.

The ball was in play and her concentration was redirected to the volley, score for her team. It was Katherine's turn to serve. As she took her position and waited for the ball to reach her hands, she saw out of the corner of her eye that he had stopped. He was standing just twenty-five to thirty feet away, watching. Katherine tossed the ball in the air, through clenched teeth a quiet 'damn' escaped her lips, as she hit the ball hard, driving it across the net, point for her team! When she next glanced out of the corner of her eye, he had moved on. Katherine focused her attentions back on the game, but she couldn't deny she had been struck to the core. It was one moment in the day, and after the reunion maybe she would think about that brief visual encounter, but it was far from her thoughts the rest of the weekend.

There had been the caterers to meet, lunch and dinner to supervise, shirt sizes to exchange, and extra shirts to sell. Everyone loved the shirt and wanted to take one home to those that hadn't been able to come. Katherine would be surprised if she didn't have to order more!

Many cousins were unsure how to fill out their family tree chart in the welcome bag, so she had agreed to spend an hour in the tent both Saturday and Sunday, to help. Those one-hour sessions became two but she was pleased with the interest expressed.

39

Sunday had been a quieter day because some people only came for Saturday. However, those that were staying expressed an interest in brunch, so food was ordered, and many gathered for the third time to share a meal together. Overall, Katherine was very pleased, tired but pleased. She could not have done it better, nor could she have done it without her immediate family.

One family of cousins was still playing on the beach, but Katherine thought everyone else had departed. She was waiting on the porch, to say goodbye to Dano, Jennifer, John, Megan and JJ. Daniel, Gillian, and Steve would stay one more night. Jennifer and John came out first.

"Aunt Katie," Jennifer asked, "could we speak with you for a moment. Perhaps we could walk down to the tent."

Surprised, Katherine agreed. John commented how empty the tent looked, "It's positively forlorn, it looks like I feel. I am sorry this wonderful event is over."

"You put up with all this family business very well, John. Thanks for your help, yours too, Jennifer. I don't know what I would have done without you."

"Aunt Katie, we loved it. All four of us, every minute of the whole weekend." She stopped and became very quiet. "Perhaps because we have some news to share with you. We wanted to wait until the reunion was over." She looked at Katherine and saw concern in her face. " Oh, Aunt Katie, it isn't bad news, it's well…"

John interrupted, "I have received a job transfer at work, a promotion. It's rather exciting, but it will take us away from Cloud Cottage for two years. That makes us sad.

"Wherever you are going, Cloud Cottage will be here when you get back."

"Aunt Katie," Jennifer spoke again, "it's just that this has all happened so fast, we have to leave so soon, and Hong Kong seems so far away."

"Hong Kong! Wow! What an opportunity for you. I will miss you, but congratulations. Go experience it! We can always Skype. I'll learn how."

"It's not the same, Aunt Katie."

"I know. When do you leave?"

"In three weeks. This is our last weekend to come to Cloud Cottage."

"Are you sure?"

"There is a lot to do to pack. What will we need now, what do we want to have shipped to us when we find an apartment, what do we put in storage here?"

"I see. How long have you known?"

"Just a week."

"Everybody's been good at keeping your news."

"No, Aunt Katie, we just now told Dad and Dan. We will tell the children tomorrow. It was so important to us to have this weekend without any thoughts or emotions interfering."

"I understand. Oh my, this really is a big goodbye then, isn't it?"

Jennifer nodded, tears welling in her eyes.

"Aunt Katie," John spoke up, "we do have one question for you, and I will preface it by saying we will understand if you say no." He stopped, took a big breath then continued. "Would you consider keeping

Blue for us? We cannot take him and, even if we could, I wouldn't. An apartment is no place for a Blue Heeler."

"Well," Katherine hesitated. "I guess we did become good friends. It's just that I've never been much of a dog person."

It was Jennifer's turn to speak up, "Just think about it, Aunt Katie. We thought of you because Blue did bond with you. You know animals often choose their people. We think we choose them, but that is an illusion. Also, here at Cloud Cottage he would have the space he needs."

"I don't need to think about it," Katherine interrupted her, "I will keep Blue for you."

"Are you sure?" John asked.

"Yes, I'll have to think about the mechanics of having a dog, and I will want some guidance from you," she hesitated again. "I'll make up a list of questions as I think of them."

"Thank you, Aunt Katie," Jennifer hugged her aunt, then hugged her again. "That one is from Blue!"

"Okay, enough, you have miles to go and a future to prepare for. We'll need to talk soon and often." Jennifer, John, and Katherine returned to the house to say their goodbyes.

Dano was ready to say goodbye as well, and Katherine walked with him to the car.

"Big news about Jennifer and John," he commented.

"Yes, it is."

"How do you feel about having Blue?" Katherine looked surprised.

"You knew?"

"Jennifer asked me what I thought about the idea."

"And?"

"I told her you are a strong woman and if you didn't want Blue you would say so. And?"

"It will be another adjustment, but he seems to be a nice dog. He is part of the family, so we will 'hold fast!' "

"You're terrific, Aunt Katie. I dump my kids on you, my sister dumps her dog on you and you still love us."

"Absolutely."

"Caroline and I will see you in twelve days." He winked and was on his way.

It was a small tired group that stood on the porch to watch the sunset that night. The future of each one in the group held uncertainty. Gillian and Steve were facing a fight with breast cancer. The daughter Daniel was close to was moving half way around the world. Connor and Caitlin's parents were trying to avoid a divorce, and Katherine, well, all she had to do was learn how to live with a dog.

"Some news about Jennifer and John, isn't it?" Daniel said the next morning as he walked into the kitchen.

"Yes, but what an opportunity," answered Katherine. "I know you will miss her, but if you retire next year perhaps you could travel and spend some time with them in Hong Kong. By that time they will be settled."

"Maybe."

"You are still planning to retire next year, aren't you?"

"Yes, if I'm not terminated earlier."

"Daniel, that isn't going to happen."

"Oh yes it can, Kate. It's happening all around me in every division every day."

"Pretty stressful I presume!"

"You could say that. I have to go. I said I would be back in the office by noon. Great job on the reunion, Kate."

"Thanks. See you on Labor Day?"

"I'll be here. Say goodbye to Gillian for me."

"Say goodbye yourself, she's right behind you."

"Hey, little sister, take care you hear."

Gillian nodded, then impulsively gave Daniel a hug. After he was gone Katherine looked at her with raised eyebrows.

"Well, somebody has to be the first one to give a hug. I didn't figure I could wait forever for him." They both laughed and shared a long talk.

After everyone's departure Katherine and the twins straightened and put away the reunion paraphernalia. During a dinner of reunion leftovers, all three were yawning.

"That's it!" Katherine said when they had finished. "Books and bed, let's call it a night."

With a huge sigh, Katherine relaxed in her bed. She felt like watching some silly old rerun on TV, but she hadn't moved a TV into the attic, and she was too comfortable to move. No TV tonight, no Ancestor Aonghus, no reading, she just turned off the light.

40

When guests left on Monday it made the week very short. All of Monday and Tuesday projects needed to be done in one day. Gillian had insisted Steve strip the beds, but Katherine did the laundry, and then there was the garden. Of course there was the weeding, but now there was harvesting too. With all the catered food and leftovers, very little had been harvested this weekend. Jennifer had quickly picked some green beans, and Dano had taken some summer squash and zucchini, but Katherine suspected she would need to make zucchini bread today to utilize the overgrown ones. Whatever project she tackled she knew the twins would want to participate. She wondered where they were. At this point she happened to notice movement in the garden. Oh my goodness...

"Hi, Aunt Katie," Caitlin called as she approached. "We got up early."

"Yeah," Connor said, "we wanted to surprise you."

"You certainly did that. Good job, you two," Katherine said as she started to weed too.

That evening, still tired, the twins chose a movie, so Katherine curled up on the living room sofa. These are good days, she thought. She knew another weekend was coming, and there would be one last group of cousins. But it was all good.

Her laptop was in reach if she decided to spend some time with Ancestor Aonghus. It had already been a week since she had figured out that 'eerie' was an intentional misspelling of 'Erie,' and a double meaning. What the next group of pages held in store she didn't know. Well, she decided, no time like the present. With new resolve, she opened up the enhanced file. She scrolled through the pages. There seemed to be four this time. She began to read, and stopped at the first word. The letters were distinct but the spelling strange and the words completely unfamiliar. Not another code, Katherine groaned. Maybe I'll just get a metal detector after all. She strained to decipher any word anyplace in the four pages. Not one could she identify. Familiar now, a little, with the quirks of this book, she tried writing it backwards. She held it up to a mirror to see if she could read it. Frustrated, she was not in the mood for this tonight. She was tempted to put the file away; instead she sat staring at the pages letting her eyes lose their focus. That had helped before. By the time the twins came in to say goodnight the only thing she noticed that was odd or different was the spacing of the letters and a higher than normal use of a mark like an apostrophe.

"Ready for bed?" she asked. Her question was answered with yawns. "Me too."

The next morning Katherine watched the sun rise from her attic oasis. The large east window allowed the first colors of the day to pattern and tint the space around her. She wanted to absorb the energy of each light-bending shade and let it power her through the day. Ah, such vibrancy she thought. This is a 'rockin' red' morning. She continued to sit in the easy chair by the window; as she enjoyed the show on the horizon her thoughts shifted to the twins. What fun project could they do this week? They had been so good about helping with the reunion she wanted it to be something special. Of the things on their wish list, one that was left was tubing down Stony Creek. She would prefer their father took them tubing. Another thing on the list was fishing. Katherine didn't fish, and neither did Dano or Daniel. She guessed they were gatherers rather than hunter types. What could she do? She closed her eyes to think, as the first warmth of the sun penetrated through the glass panes. In a few moments she reached for her laptop and sent Dano an email. What did he think about taking the twins on a charter-fishing trip out of Pentwater or Ludington? Maybe they could just fish on an inland lake.

Dano's response came quickly, "Go for it! Neither Caroline nor I have a clue about fishing. Just tell me what it costs. I'm buying this fish dinner."

By the time the children appeared in the kitchen for breakfast Katherine had booked a boat willing to take rookies and children. The charter also had a relationship with a restaurant in town that would cook your catch. Dano would indeed be buying their fish dinner if they were lucky. The fishing trip was for the next day, which meant errands in town and cleaning for today. There was no argument from the twins. They were going fishing!

It was still dark the next morning when the sleepy but excited twins piled into the car. Katherine looked at the cloud-filled sky. She knew well the feel of the breeze that brushed her cheek.

"Please don't storm," she said, "not today."

Although she had heard of people fishing in the rain, she wasn't overly excited at the prospect. As they drove, it sprinkled off and on but nothing too hard. At the designated time Katherine and two excited twins marched down the dock. Katherine continued to watch the skies apprehensively.

"Don't worry, the fish don't mind getting wet," their captain joked.

Connor and Caitlin thought it was the funniest thing they had ever heard.

Katherine smiled, she was pleased that the captain did relate well with the children and in no time they were all best friends. Once out on the lake, Katherine started to relax and enjoy the outing too. There was a slight chop to the waves and it was overcast, but quite pleasant. Connor got the first bite. The captain moved over to help the boy bring in a trout. The exuberance in his voice as he held up his catch for Katherine to photograph was priceless.

Then she heard "Aunt Katie, you have a bite."

She secured her camera and followed the captain's instructions as to what to do. Ultimately she was smiling and also holding, with some hesitation, a trout, as the captain became photographer. Please let Caitlin catch a fish she prayed, but it was Connor's line that had the next hit. Then, the young girl had a bite too. Caitlin no sooner had re-baited her line when she had another bite.

"Cool."

"Awesome."

The captain looked at Katherine and winked as he moved back and forth between the children, helping them land their catch. Katherine caught three more fish too, but what she really caught was the enthusiasm for the sport. Fishing was fun.

After a couple hours the captain looked at the sky and announced it was time to head back to port. The children noticed the rock of the boat increased as they worked their way back. They encouraged the captain to hurry because they didn't want to shipwreck like Ancestor Aonghus, which prompted the telling of the story. Katherine listened. Their rendition was really quite spellbinding and accurate. The captain asked later, as they disembarked, if the Ancestor Aonghus story was true. He shook his head, incredulous. Katherine wondered what he would think if he knew the rest of the story.

"Fishermen, here's your catch." The captain held out the Styrofoam cooler.

Connor reached first, "I'll carry it."

"Captain," Katherine asked, "we have arranged at your suggestion, to have the restaurant cook them for us. Who cleans them?"

"They will do that too. Would you like me to clean one here as a demonstration for Connor and Caitlin? Cleaning your catch is part of the sport."

"Is it gross?" Caitlin asked.

"It's part of life. I'll do one. If you want to, you can look away."

Deftly the captain cleaned one fish. No one looked away, but no one volunteered to try a hand at cleaning another one. Katherine thanked him, Connor shook his hand, and Caitlin gave him a hug. Another boat captain on the dock took a group photo.

The twins never stopped talking all the way to the restaurant, during dinner, nor on their way home. Once back at Cloud Cottage, they asked to call their parents and their animated chatter began all over again. It had been a good day, a very good day.

The next weekend was also good. Their guests were three couples, one with an infant and a toddler. This was different for the twins; for once they were the big kids. To accommodate the families Caitlin moved in with Connor for the weekend. Katherine suspected they gamed very late those nights, but she wasn't too worried. She had revisited Ancestor Aonghus. It had been a great opportunity; with babies in the house everyone retired before sunset. It was so early she worked in the easy chair by the west windows instead of the bed.

With the laptop in front of her Katherine studied the pages. Such strange words she thought. The letter patterns are unusual. Upon closer examination she realized not all letters of the alphabet were being used. Could it be another kind of code? Katherine reached for a piece of paper. She began going through each word, starting with the first. She marked down each letter of the alphabet the first time it appeared. She searched and scrutinized all four pages. When she finished she reconstructed what she had. The writing – code – used eighteen letters, all five vowels but only thirteen consonants. There simply were no letters j, k, q, b, w, x, y, z. These omitted letters aren't the most commonly used, but it was strange to see four pages of writing without them.

"I guess I'm back to code cracking," she said. "At least I know more than when I sat down. I'll figure it all out another time, but not tonight."

41

Another Monday morning dawned. Our summer has developed a definite routine, Katherine thought, as she contemplated a tentative schedule for the week. The culmination of this week would not be the arrival of cousins but Caroline with Dano. The twins were excited. Nine weeks was a long time for ten, even almost eleven year olds to be without their mother. Katherine suspected Caroline's approach to motherhood was different, but it was still a long time to be apart.

Caroline was a career woman and her lifestyle did not lend itself to breaking a nail playing catch with the twins. She had combined a degree in art with an MBA. Her current position at the art institute involved contact with elite social circles, and required frequent weekend and evening commitments, both at the museum and in the city. Caroline was bright, stunning, charming, and capable. Katherine understood how Dano had been and was still smitten. She also understood and accepted that not all families function the same way. She just hoped for the twins' sake that Caroline and Dano could find their way.

I wonder where the twins are this morning, she thought. They are being very quiet. When Connor and Caitlin entered the kitchen they each held a handful of papers.

"Good morning," Katherine greeted them. "Looks like you have a project this morning too."

"We do," Connor answered.

"We want to make welcome signs for Mom. Kind of like the welcome to the reunion signs we helped Daddy put up," Caitlin explained.

"Isn't that a great idea?" Connor asked.

"It's a terrific idea."

"Aunt Katie, is there any helium left, and can we use it for some balloons?"

"Lavender ones, or at least purple," Connor said. "That's Mom's favorite color."

"We can look when we go to town. Do you want to make your signs now?" Katherine asked.

"We have already made some this morning, and we can finish them tonight." Caitlin explained. "We came down to help you weed."

"Okay," Katherine agreed. "Let's weed, and I think this afternoon will be a great beach day!"

That evening the twins lettered and drew signs. Katherine sat down to work on Ancestor Aonghus. She summarized what she knew. There were four pages of unrecognizable words. The words were spelled using eighteen letters; some letters of the alphabet were missing. The words were spelled using many apostrophes, but there were no other marks or symbols.

She decided to look one more time at the enhanced pages. Katherine scrutinized the pages line-by-line. If there was something else there, she couldn't see it now. She sat back in her chair to think. What if it is the missing letters that are the key, not the letters on the page? Katherine went back to her notes. The missing letters again were j, k, q, v, w, x, y, z. There were no vowels. They can't spell a word, what could I possibly do with them, she wondered? They could be converted to numbers, but then what? It is unlikely Ancestor Aonghus would use the same trick of disguise twice. It would be a waste of time to pursue that tack.

Katherine sighed. She did not relish starting to research codes again. There were so many possibilities and manipulations of the alphabet. Besides, Ancestor Aonghus was a simple person, and he never had access to the Internet. She couldn't help feeling there was a simple answer, a more obvious solution. She sat still contemplating, waiting for inspiration.

From the kitchen she could hear the twins' chatter, what a happy sound! They shared everything. When Dano had first asked her on Memorial Day if she would have the twins for the summer, she hadn't hesitated, but she had been apprehensive. All of which had proved unfounded. The whole summer there had not been one heated argument between them – at least not with her. She suspected that if they had been different-aged siblings it might have been different. Twins seemed to possess an unusual understanding of each other. They had their own way of communicating, their own language.

Katherine was going to be sorry when this summer was over. She realized what a unique moment in time it had been for her, Connor, and Caitlin. It would never come again. Oh, there would be other visits, but the combination of a whole summer in residence at Cloud Cottage with the wide-eyed curiosity of youth that was fresh, carefree, unprejudiced, willing, accepting, and still untainted in any way, would never come again. The memories of this summer were already very special.

Katherine changed positions as she continued to reflect on the past weeks. Then it came to her, twins had their own language, perhaps these pages had their own language. She searched the Internet. The question was what languages have eighteen letters in their alphabet. Bingo! Katherine could only sit back and laugh at herself. The first answer on the Internet page was the Scottish Gaelic language. She had stumbled upon the obvious. A silent presence invaded her space, Katherine looked up to find the twins staring at her.

"What were you laughing at, Aunt Katie?" Caitlin asked.

"Oh, I just realized I had been very silly."

"How?" Connor questioned.

"Well," Katherine stopped, scrambling for an explanation. "This evening I've been wondering what we should do tomorrow. I just realized I had forgotten one of the most important August traditions at Cloud Cottage."

"What is it?" Caitlin asked.

"We're going to make wild blackberry jam, just like I did with my grandmother."

"Cool! When?"

"How about tomorrow, if the weather is good?"

"Why does the weather have to be good?"

"We can't make wild blackberry jam without the berries. We have to pick them first."

"Ohhhh." The response was a little less enthusiastic.

"I propose this," Katherine said. "Tomorrow morning you come right down when you wake up, wearing shoes, socks, long pants, and your long-sleeved tee shirts. We will go berry picking first thing, then we will go to town in the afternoon. I'll make sure we have everything we need for making jam. We'll keep the berries in the fridge and make the actual jam the day after tomorrow."

Two heads nodded in agreement.

"May we go out for lunch, Aunt Katie?"

"Of course! That's our 'go-to-town-day' tradition."

"Yeah. Night night, Aunt Katie, see you in the morning."

Katherine was thankful the twin's curiosity was so easily satisfied, and that she had remembered blackberry jam. She climbed the stairs to her oasis hugging her computer. She knew tonight she would dream in eighteen letters.

42

"Where are we going, Aunt Katie?" Caitlin asked, as she and Connor followed along behind their aunt.

"To a clearing in the woods, Caitlin. It is just a short walk. Blackberries thrive on sandy soil in open clearings."

"Why?"

"They need sunlight. In the woods the big trees would shade them too much."

"Aunt Katie, may we eat the berries too?"

"Of course! That's half the fun. These are wild berries, so they have not been sprayed with chemicals. However you might want to check for any bugs before you pop them in your mouth."

"Yuck!" Caitlin said.

"We share our world with many creatures," Katherine reminded them.

She looked back at the two children behind her as they walked single file along the deer path. They had followed her direction for dress and were each carrying a four-quart pail. She had no illusions about their filling them, but it wouldn't matter, she would pick enough for jam. She hoped the mosquitos weren't too bad this morning. They arrived at the clearing and the bushes were laden with big succulent blackberries. Katherine had timed their expedition well.

"Wow! Look at all these berries," Connor said as he popped a couple in his mouth.

"Connor, you forgot to look for bugs."

"I don't care!"

Katherine instructed them on how to pick without squeezing the fruit, how to move around the outside edges of the bramble first, and how to reach to avoid getting scratched by the thorns.

It wasn't too long before she heard the first 'OW!'

"Are you okay, Caitlin?"

"Yeah, but that hurt!"

"Just be very careful."

Katherine picked as fast as she could. She wasn't sure how long their enthusiasm would last, nor did she want Caroline and Dano to be greeted by two wounded children. She was glad there had been enough rain for the berries to be large. It wouldn't take long to fill her bucket. When it was three-quarters full she stepped to the edge of the clearing and exchanged it for an empty one.

"Aunt Katie, is your bucket full?" Connor asked.

"No, I stopped before it was full so the berries on the bottoms don't get squished. How are you doing?"

Connor held up his bucket and looked at the mark on the side. "I have a quart."

"Me too!" added Caitlin.

"Well done!"

She was amused because from where she stood she could see Caitlin's pail had a very small quart in it. But she also knew this conversation had resulted in a challenge being issued. If Caitlin thought Connor had more berries in his bucket than she did, she would pick faster. Before long Katherine heard an "Ow" and then another one.

"Caitlin," Connor called to her, "reach from the bottom up to the berries. Don't reach through the thorny branches."

Couldn't have said it better, Katherine thought. She didn't tell them that, Connor figured it out by himself. In a short time Katherine had filled her second pail to the three-quarter mark. She proceeded to help each twin fill their pails to the same level.

"That's enough," she said, looking at her partners. "Let's go home."

Connor and Caitlin enjoyed the walk home through the woods more than the actual berry picking, but they were each intensely proud of their harvest and of their battle scars. Katherine instructed them to wash well in the mudroom while she took care of their berries.

"My right hand got really bloody, Aunt Katie," Caitlin announced. "One briar really got me."

"I only have three little scratches," Connor said.

Katherine inspected all four hands; none of the scratches were deep. She treated their badges of honor and her own with an herbal salve. She knew they would heal, but that there would still be evidence on Friday night to bear witness to the adventure.

The next morning Katherine was up early washing and cleaning the berries. She was glad she had calculated correctly, there were enough berries for three double batches, and breakfast. Everything was ready for the jam session when the twins made their appearance.

"Aunt Katie, you started without us!" Caitlin protested when she saw the kitchen staged for the event.

"Only the preparation, we're making the jam together. Have your breakfast, then we'll get started."

Katherine instructed Caitlin how and what to measure, and Connor how to stir and time with his fancy watch. Katherine supervised, filled and sealed the hot jars, and ran them through the hot water bath.

"This smells so good!" Connor exclaimed, as he carefully and slowly moved the long-handled wooden spoon through the mixture. "Is this a boil, Aunt Katie?"

"Almost. Is your watch timer set?"

"Yes, I just have to push it."

"Okay, Connor, one minute."

Caitlin came to watch the bubbling fruit expand into purple foam.

"Cool."

Step-by-step of the process the twins watched and assisted. After about two and a half hours they all stood together admiring 36 eight-ounce jars of wild blackberry jam.

"What are we going to do with all this jam?" Caitlin asked.

"This jam is yours. What would you like to do with it?" Katherine answered.

"All of this?" Connor asked. "Don't you want some, Aunt Katie?"

"I'll make another batch next week. This is for you."

"We could give some to Grandpa Daniel."

"I think your grandfather would enjoy it very much. Now, how about a lunch of blackberry jam on English muffins?"

As they all savored the fresh jam, jar after jar tinged to announce it was sealed.

"Isn't that a happy sound?" Katherine asked.

The twins, their mouths full, nodded their agreement.

"After this feast," Katherine announced, "when we have finished cleaning up the kitchen, I think this crew has earned a beach afternoon."

43

Katherine sat in the porch swing enjoying her morning coffee. There was a cool dampness in the dawn air that reminded her it was August. She reached for a beach towel which had been left outside and wrapped it around her bare legs for warmth. Leaning back in the swing she felt the pristine peace and solitude of the moment seep through her being. Indulgent personal reverie was a luxury she seldom afforded herself. She had hoped in retirement there would be time for contemplative projects and perhaps even writing. So far that hadn't happened. Last fall she cared for her mother, this summer there had been Connor and Caitlin, and family and more family. She wouldn't have traded a minute with any of them for an hour of quiet, but still it was a pattern in her life. There always was someone or something that was more important than personal time.

Katherine shifted her position. Her mind had already begun to wander to thoughts of what she should be doing. As much as she tried 'to be' she had always been a 'doer.' This morning in a surge of guilt, Aunt Elsa had surfaced in her thoughts. Katherine had been so focused all summer on the MacLeod branch of the family that she knew she had neglected an aunt on her mother's side. Aunt Elsa was in an Alzheimer's care facility and there didn't seem to be much she could do for her. That fact didn't alleviate the guilt Katherine felt as she reveled in doing nothing this morning. With a big sigh, and firm resolve, she got up, stretched, and went upstairs to dress. Today they would all go visit Aunt Elsa.

Katherine was busy packing a picnic lunch when the twins appeared in the kitchen.

"Good morning, Aunt Katie, what are you doing?"

"I am preparing for our day."

Connor came over to inspect the contents of the cooler. "Did you put in chocolate chip cookies?"

"Not yet, but if you would like we will have those for our dessert."

"Where are we going?"

"I will explain everything in the car. You two need to have breakfast while I go change."

"Do we have to change too?" Caitlin asked. Katherine turned to give them a thoughtful inspection; clean shorts and tees, hair combed, but barefoot. It was important they be comfortable on the long ride ahead.

"No, you are fine, except for your feet. When you go up to brush your teeth, put on some shoes, and as always grab a jacket. Okay?"

"Got it," the twins answered.

Katherine smiled as she left the kitchen. The twins had fixed their own cereal as usual, but today the bowls were mounded high with blackberries. She was pleased the berry outing had been so successful. She could only hope today would be okay. Visiting an old unknown relative in a care facility was never exciting for a child.

Thirty minutes later the car was loaded with picnic cooler and twins. Katherine locked the door and started down the steps. Out of the corner of her eye she noticed the soccer ball on the lawn. She picked it up and threw it in the trunk. Connor looked at her perplexed.

"Our soccer ball, Aunt Katie?"

"You never know," she answered, as she shifted the car into gear. They were on their way.

In the back seat Connor and Caitlin's faces expressed anticipation. She realized that without intending to, she had created a mystery trip for the twins. The weight of responsibility and guilt she was feeling were her own adult emotions. Perhaps she could make this fun for them after all.

"Aunt Katie, where are we going?" Of course it was 'Miss Factual' that demanded information. Katherine was amused again by the little girl's desire – her need – to be informed and in control.

"Well," she answered. "Sometimes when we start a journey we never know where it will take us. Anything is possible."

Katherine glanced at her watch, it was just nine a.m. She had a choice to visit Aunt Elsa before or after lunch. Her experience was that meals were always served early in facilities. She opted for after lunch, this way their visit would not be rushed. Her thoughts shifted to what detours en route would interest the twins. She had been so intent to just get there, get it over with, and get home, that she hadn't thought about diversions. Connor and Caitlin sat quietly waiting for her to continue. Please, Katherine thought, I need an inspiration.

To Connor and Caitlin's surprise she began to sing.

"May you step lively and quick,

May the Lord be with you on the water…"

By the time she started the chorus the fourth time, the twins joined her in the catchy tune. When they finished Caitlin asked the first question.

"What does it mean, Aunt Katie, 'step lively and quick on the water?'"

Yes! Katherine thought, I've piqued their curiosity.

"You have spent all summer learning about your Scottish heritage, the Clan MacLeod, my father's family. Today we will explore another branch of our family tree, the O'Reilly's, my mother's family."

"Were they Scottish too," asked Connor.

212

"No, they were Irish."

"Aunt Katie," Caitlin asked. "You're not going to tell us they were leprechauns and could walk on water, are you?"

"Let's go find their pot of gold," Connor added.

They all laughed.

"No," Kate answered. "Your Irish ancestors were not leprechauns as far as I know. My great-grandfather was an ordinary, hard-working man, who left Ireland as a young boy with his three older brothers during the potato famine. They arrived in Michigan in the 1850s about the same time as Ancestor Aonghus, but on the eastern side of the state. Like him they first worked in the lumber industry, but not in a sawmill, they were shanty boys."

Katherine launched into a history lesson about life in the lumber camp. How shanty boys were not allowed to speak during meals because of the possibility of fights. She explained how they lived with lice, worked from daylight to dark, but also amused themselves with songs and tall tales. She shared all the stories she had heard as a child, plus her own research into life in a lumber camp.

After her narrative Connor asked, "So shanty boys were really lumberjacks? They were the ones that cut down the trees to rebuild Chicago?"

"That's right! It sounds like you have studied the Great Chicago Fire of 1871 in school."

The twins both nodded.

"But what does cutting down trees have to do with walking on water?" Caitlin asked.

"Your great-great-grandfather, Peter O'Reilly, was known as the best log rider on the river and that's a story that starts here."

Katherine turned off the main road into a county park. She glanced at her watch; it was just after ten, a good time for a stretch. As she pulled into a parking place, Caitlin read the historical marker about "Roll-Away Park." Katherine waited for her to finish, and the questions that were sure to follow.

"So this is where they piled the logs during the winter, and in the spring they let the logs roll down the hill to the river? May we get out and look?" Caitlin asked.

"Absolutely! We can take the steps all the way down to the river's edge."

Both children bounded out of the car and ran to the first railing. Katherine heard them exclaim "whoa," and "awesome," as she locked the car.

"Aunt Katie, it's so steep! It's almost straight down," Connor said as she joined them.

"Aunt Katie, wouldn't the logs have caught on all the trees between here and the bottom?" Caitlin asked.

"No, these trees weren't here then. This bank was cut bare so the logs could roll freely."

"Oh." The twins started down the stairs ahead of her.

"Easy," she called after them.

Katherine followed at a slower pace. She could see the twins on the walkway below her and knew they would be okay. She smiled knowing that on the climb back up they would not be as quick. This has been a good break in the drive, she thought, a little history, a lot of exercise!

"Aunt Katie, this is so cool," Connor said as Katherine stepped down onto the bottom platform.

"Are you going to tell us now about riding the logs?" Caitlin asked.

"Of course," Katherine said. She explained about the spring river drives, the special spiked shoes the men wore, about birling and spinning the log in the water. She told them about the wanigan or floating cook shacks that followed the logs on the river drives. Katherine looked at the attentive faces on the bench across from her. The dappled leaves created a patchwork of shadows on their cheeks and the platform where they rested. The lives and future of these two children were so different from the lives she was describing of their ancestors.

"Aunt Katie, does walking on water really mean walking on the logs in the water?" Caitlin asked.

"Yes, it does."

"And," Connor asked, "do the words in the song 'Step Lively and Quick' mean that they had to be careful?"

"Yes, they do. Riding the logs was dangerous work and one of the highest paying jobs in the lumber camp. If a man misstepped, slipped or fell between the logs, he seldom survived. That is why great-grandfather O'Reilly was proud of being known as the best log rider on the river."

For a few moments the three sat and enjoyed the breeze and the sound of the river against the shore. Katherine hated to interrupt the quiet moment, but they had steps to climb and places to go.

The twins nodded and stretched.

"Where are we going next?" Connor asked.

"I bet it's a lumber camp," Caitlin answered.

Katherine smiled, "No, but if you would like, perhaps we could go another time. There are several wonderful parks and monuments to the lumbering era in Michigan."

"Where then?" asked Caitlin.

"We are going to visit Aunt Elsa."

"Another relative?" Connor asked.

Katherine winced inside. She heard a tone of dismay in the boy's voice. She had hoped the diversions in route would soften the reality of visiting an old aunt in a care facility. Yet the second half of his question was inquisitive.

"Who is Aunt Elsa?"

"I'll tell you about her in the car, now up the stairs."

The twins raced up the steps. Katherine climbed one step at a time, and at the fourth landing found the twins panting and waiting for her. Together they climbed the remaining stairs. At the top, the twins collapsed in mock exhaustion.

"Aunt Katie, we should have counted how many steps there were."

"Next time."

"Okay, let's go," Connor headed for the stairs.

"No!" Katherine managed to say before he disappeared, "another time. Who would like a cold drink?"

They enjoyed a glass of lemonade as fresh air blew through the open car doors.

"Okay, port-a-jons that way, and then it's all aboard for Aunt Elsa."

Once settled and underway, Katherine thought the twins might doze off. They did. She had some quiet time to formulate her thoughts and questions for the facility's care group. It was almost an hour later when Caitlin opened her eyes.

"So, Aunt Katie, who is Aunt Elsa?" she asked. Her question roused Connor.

"Yeah, who is Aunt Elsa?"

"She is my aunt, your great-aunt. She married my mother's brother, so she is an aunt by marriage, not a blood relative."

"Does that mean she's not a real aunt?" asked Caitlin.

"No, I consider her my real aunt. In fact she is my favorite aunt, just like Uncle Gus was my favorite uncle. I was clarifying for you where she fits on the family tree."

"Oh! How come you never talk about her? Caitlin and I talk about you all the time."

Katherine smiled at the implication. "I think we have been so absorbed with the MacLeod Reunion that I haven't taken time to speak of her and ..." Katherine stopped.

"And what?" Caitlin asked.

"Well, Aunt Elsa is still living, in a care facility, but in many ways she left two or three years ago."

"What do you mean?" It was Connor's turn to ask.

"Aunt Elsa suffers from Alzheimer's."

"Oh, that's when someone doesn't remember any more."

"No, Connor, they remember just not everything, right, Aunt Katie?"

"Basically, the disease is different for every person and sometimes different on different days. Aunt Elsa remembers very little of recent years, yet her memory of earlier years is still clear – for now. Sometimes when I visit she thinks I am my mother, and will call me Margaret, because I look a little like my mother, and she will ask about me. What grade I am in school, if I went to summer camp for example. She doesn't remember that I'm all grown up." Caitlin giggled. "Yes, it is silly sometimes, but Alzheimer's is never funny. I want you to remember that this afternoon, okay? Two heads nodded. "How about lunch? There is a park by a lake just ahead, sound good?" Two heads nodded again.

So far so good, Katherine thought, as she set out the picnic lunch. The twins were nearby climbing on an elaborate jungle gym. She glanced at her watch. They were right on schedule to arrive at one p.m.

Forty-five minutes later she parked the car outside the Parkside Manor.

"Okay, everyone, let's go visit Aunt Elsa."

The twins followed as Katherine walked down a long corridor. They peered into the rooms as they walked past open doorways. Most residents were enjoying a nap, a couple called out a greeting, and one came out to follow them. Connor and Caitlin crowded close behind

Katherine as she entered a room. 'Elsa O'Reilly' was printed in block letters on the door. The room was neat, and a bright quilt covered an easy chair by the window.

"It appears Aunt Elsa isn't back from lunch yet. Have a seat for a moment while I check to see if she needs anything." Both twins squeezed into the easy chair and watched as Katherine looked at the clothes in the closet and dresser. She held up a few tops, checking for stains and worn places.

"Next time I will bring Aunt Elsa a new outfit or two," she said. "These are looking very tired. Let's take a walk and see if we can find her."

Again, the twins followed close behind. As they passed the dining room, Katherine stopped and entered. At a far table one old lady sat primly in a chair.

"Hello, Aunt Elsa," Katherine said in a bright voice as she approached.

The old woman turned, her face broke into a smile. "Margaret, what a nice surprise. How did you ever get on board?"

"We came to visit you, Aunt Elsa."

"I am delighted, but how did you get on board? I thought we didn't come into port again until we reached Nassau."

Katherine heard giggles behind her. A quick glance at the twins quieted them. She pulled up a chair, sat down by Aunt Elsa, and motioned Connor and Caitlin to do the same.

"Are you going on a vacation, Aunt Elsa?" Katherine asked.

"Yes, to the Bahamas."

"That should be a nice trip."

"I thought so. I wanted to feel the ocean breeze one more time and maybe buy a new straw hat in the market."

"You always wear a hat well, Aunt Elsa."

"I do, don't I?"

Katherine looked at her dear aunt. Even here, and in the clutch of Alzheimer's, she was trying to live the life she always had. She wore earrings and a necklace, but they didn't match. Someone had given her a manicure and finished her nails with a coat of polish. Katherine shook her head, what an insidious thief was this disease.

"Margaret, what are you thinking, dear, and who are these children with you?"

"This is Connor and Caitlin, Aunt Elsa. How about if I ask if we can go outside?"

"That would be lovely, Margaret, I would very much like to go out on deck."

Katherine motioned to a passing attendant, exchanged a few words, and moments later a wheelchair appeared. Together they all went 'on deck for some fresh ocean breezes.' They spoke of what they would do when they docked in Nassau and, in general, enjoyed the fresh air.

Connor and Caitlin were very good and sat still until Katherine discreetly handed them the car keys and suggested they get their soccer ball. Caitlin returned the keys with a grateful smile as Connor started to pass her the ball from a side lawn. Katherine watched them as she took Aunt Elsa's hand in hers. She wondered, in thirty years, if she would be the crazy old aunt they would bring their children to visit.

44

The excitement of the children increased every hour as the time for their parents' arrival drew near. They were ready to put up their welcome signs right after breakfast on Friday morning.

Katherine didn't tell them "no," but cautioned them that their balloons might not hold up well for that many hours. They had agreed reluctantly. This could be a long day, she thought. What can we do? Her old bag of teacher tricks was beginning to run low. The twins had gone upstairs after breakfast, and before Katherine had solved her dilemma, they appeared with a solution of their own.

"Aunt Katie, may we pick some more blackberries this morning? We'd like to have some for breakfast tomorrow."

"Yeah," Connor added. "Mom really likes blackberries."

What children, Katherine thought. Here they are all dressed for berry picking. "That's a wonderful idea. I guess I was so intent on making jam I didn't save any for the weekend, did I?"

"That's okay, Aunt Katie."

"Let me change my clothes and we'll go."

That afternoon the wind was strong, so Katherine suggested a walk to the lighthouse to check for kite boarders. The twins were willing participants and eager to watch them again. Every time one caught some air they exclaimed.

"Aunt Katie, why don't you have a kite board?" Connor asked.

"Oh, I think a kayak is more my speed," she answered.

"Some day I want to kite board," Caitlin said. "Don't you, Connor?"

"I want to kite board today."

"No, not today, Connor, even if we could, look at your watch. We need to go back to Cloud Cottage and put up our signs."

Katherine agreed and offered to help them. In short order balloons and signs were in place. Katherine thought her driveway looked like an old 'Burma Shave' sign sequence, but she kept her thoughts to herself. She noticed Connor was still holding one sign.

"Did we miss one?" she asked.

"No, this one is for their bedroom," he responded. "Where are they going to sleep?"

"In the master bedroom across from your rooms."

Curious, she then asked, "May I see?"

Connor turned the sign around for her to read, "Sweet Cloud Dreams."

The arrival was a riotous moment of hugs, kisses, and conversations. The call of "Mommy" dominated the endless chatter. Dano stood back, watched, and listened. He waved to Katherine as she remained seated on the porch swing. She returned the gesture. She continued to watch the happy reunion unfold as it progressed up the path to Cloud Cottage, and was pleased to see Caroline's delight equaled the children's.

"Aunt Katie," Caroline greeted Katherine, "I am so happy to be here."

Katherine returned her genuine embrace and hoped she meant it. Dano placed their luggage inside the front door then announced "Alright everyone, sunset walk on the beach."

"Yaaaay!" the twins exclaimed.

"May I use the bathroom first?" Caroline asked, laughing.

In a few moments the family was ready to depart. Katherine remained seated and waved goodbye.

"Aunt Katie," Dano said, motioning for her to join them. In her ear he whispered, "I know what you are doing and it isn't going to work."

There were five MacLeods that walked into the sunset that evening, Connor, Caroline, Dano, Caitlin, and Katherine. The first four walked hand-in-hand, then Katherine felt Caitlin's hand slip into hers. All five were linked physically, but oh, by so much more as well. As the sun touched the horizon, they stopped to absorb the moment. Caitlin offered the first color of the night, *Dazzling Banana Orange*. Caroline looked perplexed. Connor explained.

"Mommy, with Aunt Katie we each name a color of the sunset."

"How lovely," Caroline responded. "May I name one?"

"Everyone names one, Mommy," Caitlin encouraged.

They all were quiet for a moment, then it was Dano who spoke.

"I name, *Rose Rapture*."

Katherine followed with *Shadow Pink*, as the last pink curve disappeared from sight. Connor then offered *Paradise Purple*. Everyone stood still, subconsciously breathing in sync with the pulsations of the breeze.

Caroline sighed, "*Lavender Twin Twilight*."

45

Upon their return to Cloud Cottage, Katherine excused herself and went up to her oasis. Settled in her easy chair, her computer on her lap, she realized she felt like she was off duty. She relaxed, reveling in the thought that tomorrow morning she didn't have any responsibilities. It was the first time in over two months. Amazed, she thought, I have loved every minute of this summer, yet this feeling is wonderful!

She opened her computer and thought for a few moments, reconstructing in her mind her current challenge. This had been such a busy week; she hadn't revisited the pages for several days. Oh, she had to learn Gaelic, she remembered. She thought that would be a good project for this coming week. A quick Internet search for Gaelic sites, yielded several sites for Gaelic word translations. Maybe she didn't have to learn it. She could just translate it.

"This should be a cinch, thank you Internet," she said.

Katherine typed the first word on the page in the designated box, hit search, and waited in breathless expectation. It took a moment but it processed and replied, "no match found." Intense, Katherine typed in the next word, searched again, "no match found" was the reply. She typed the third, fourth, fifth, the whole sentence of words, her heart sank lower as each one replied, "no match found." This can't be happening she said to herself. She was so sure this was Gaelic. These words look like the words on the Gaelic sites. Not all sites are created equal, so she tried another. Again she typed in the first word, "no match." Katherine repeated the process and on three different Scottish Gaelic sites, not one word was recognized or translated. Discouraged, she leaned back in the chair. Now what, she wondered? A good night's sleep, she decided was the answer. Ancestor Aonghus' book had become her Gordian knot and there still was another thread for her to unravel.

It was later than usual when Katherine went down to the kitchen the next morning. The family had already had breakfast and Dano was cleaning up.

"Hi," he greeted her. "I'm glad you're up. Are you okay?"

"Of course, I'm just lazy this morning."

"Good. You have a right to be lazy. But while you rested we made plans."

"What's on your schedule?"

"Right now the twins are giving Caroline a tour of your garden, and I expect demonstrating their prowess at weeding."

Katherine laughed, "They really have been good sports about the garden. I hope they haven't complained too much."

"Not at all, they are just plain proud of their rows."

"Anyway, we thought we would try a geocache site or two this morning and of course, spend the afternoon on the beach."

"Sounds like a great plan."

"We'll leave as soon as they return from the garden."

"Okay, I'll have something ready for lunch when you get back."

"Aunt Katie, *WE'LL* leave, that includes you. I told you last night…"

"No, Dano," Katherine interrupted him, "thank you but no. This week is about you as a family. I'll join you sometimes, but not all the time. You were right last night about my accompanying you to the beach. I think I'm right about not going on your geocache adventure."

"I'm not going to change your mind, am I?"

"No, Dano, you're not. Go and have a really good time together!"

"Okay, Aunt Katie, you win."

"Oh, Dano, there is one more thing."

"Am I going to like this?"

"I don't know, but it's what has to happen. You know Jennifer and John asked me to keep Blue for them and I agreed."

"Yeah, I remember. The more I think about it I don't really think it's fair to you," Dano stopped. "But what can I say about my sister dumping her dog on you when I dumped my kids on you, except that, Aunt Katie, you like Connor and Caitlin and you don't like dogs, do you, and for two years?"

"Dano, it isn't about what is fair or not fair. It's about being there for the people we love, to the extent that we are able. Now, I'm not crazy about dogs in general, but I did like Blue. I'll do everything I can to make it work. If I can't, then there will be a Plan B. Now, what I was about to tell you is that one day this week I'm going to drive downstate to meet Jennifer or John and collect Blue. They really don't have time to bring him here. I don't want to confuse the dog with an intermediary. Blue is smart. When he leaves them he needs to know I am his new 'pack leader.'"

"Sounds like you've been studying canine psychiatry."

"No, but after Blue was here on the Fourth of July, I was curious about the breed. I did a little reading long before I was asked to give him a home."

"Aunt Katie, you're amazing."

"Let's just hope Blue thinks so."

"Now I have one more thing for you, Aunt Katie. The twins told me you visited Great Aunt Elsa. How is she, really?"

"Physically, she is fine, Dano. She seems happy and content, not angry, violent, or hostile, like I've read can happen with Alzheimer's. I have no complaints about the facility or the care she receives. The disease is progressing but how fast is difficult for me to assess. I am sure the twins told you she didn't know me, and called me 'Margaret.'"

"Oh yes! It made quite an impression, as did the ship to Nassau. They think it's cool that you all pretended to be on board."

"Why not? To tell her she was mistaken would only upset her. Besides, Dano, if you were Aunt Elsa wouldn't you rather think you were on a wonderful cruise to the Bahamas?"

"Yes, I expect I would."

"Aunt Katie, Aunt Katie, one of the pumpkins has started to turn orange." The twins and Caroline appeared in the kitchen. "On Monday it was still all green."

"Funny thing about pumpkins and twins," Katherine responded. "They grow and change every day."

"Aunt Katie, you are so right," Caroline spoke. "I'm astounded by the growth in Connor and Caitlin since June. They have changed in ever so many wonderful ways."

"Speaking of Connor and Caitlin," Dano took over the conversation, "your mom and I have an adventure planned. I will explain in the den." He turned to Katherine, "Reconsider?"

Katherine shook her head. "I'll look forward to hearing all about it over lunch."

After the family left, Katherine decided to weed for a while. She needed time to think about the Gaelic – alleged Gaelic – writing of Ancestor Aonghus. Weeding time was good thinking time, besides she loved the garden in the morning. There was always a special quality during those hours. It was quiet and peaceful, but Katherine also sensed a hushed anticipation in the rows. She loved the idea that each plant began each day understanding with certainty that in this day it would grow, yet how, in what direction, under what conditions, or for how long was unknown. Katherine grimaced. She supposed that 'hushed anticipation' was also shared by the weeds she was pulling. That was another reason she always liked to talk to them, at least mentally, as she pulled.

It was about half way down the row of brussel sprouts that the practical underlying issues of Gaelic writing superseded Katherine's philosophic reflections about the garden. She had just started the row of eggplant when the obvious error in her logic occurred to her. Ancestor Aonghus learned to read and write during those winters in the lumber camp at Stony Creek and that would have been in English. How did he ever learn to write in Gaelic? Katherine finished the eggplant and moved on to the row of squash. The foreman, his future father-in-law, had spoken Gaelic. Perhaps he, or even Moira, had taught him, but they were Irish. Irish Gaelic was different.

Katherine's hands weeded faster. She now had another thread to follow to solve the writing, yet she would not, could not leave a row half weeded, even for Ancestor Aonghus. When she finished she picked a few ripe tomatoes. BLT's would be a good easy lunch. Connor had decided that Cloud Cottage tomatoes were not only edible but also very good. Caitlin preferred her sandwich sans tomato, but she relished a 'BL.' Katherine knew BLT's were a favorite of Dano's. She hoped Caroline liked them too.

Katherine left the tomatoes on the kitchen counter and hurried to the attic for her laptop. She had no idea when the family would return, but she was sure she had at least an hour. She went to work in the living room where she could watch for them. Her first search was for English Irish Gaelic translations. She selected a site, entered the first word, and held her breath, processing, processing, processing. "No match!"

"Damn," Katherine muttered under her breath. She entered another word, "no match," another word, "no match." "This has to be it, I'm sure it is!"

Unwilling to give up, she tried another site, same result. Even a third site couldn't translate a single word Ancestor Aonghus had written. If it isn't Irish Gaelic or Scottish Gaelic what can it be, an old dialect that this 21st century site doesn't recognize? Katherine pleaded for an answer. Did they speak a different dialect on the Isle of Skye? They still speak Gaelic there; at least one word should have been translatable. Perhaps she hadn't tried enough words. But Katherine didn't believe it. She was nowhere. I guess I need to weed in the garden again for a different inspiration. Discouraged, she shut down the computer and went to the kitchen to slice tomatoes.

She had just finished frying the bacon when excited voices announced the family's return. She knew by the pitch, geocaching had been a hit.

"Aunt Katie, Aunt Katie, it was so cool. There were these clues and …" Connor and Caitlin finished each other's sentences in such rapid succession Katherine could hardly keep track of who was talking. Then in a final flourish they announced, "You've got to come next time."

Katherine looked up to see happy smiles on the faces of Dano and Caroline. Dano gave a big "thumbs up" as Caroline moved into the kitchen.

"You've already prepared lunch, Aunt Katie?" she asked. "BLT'S? How perfect!"

Katherine sensed her sincerity, so far so good she thought. That afternoon Katherine joined the family on the beach. It was a perfect day.

The next two days were carbon copies. The mornings were spent on a geocache adventure and the afternoons on the beach. Katherine, upon unanimous insistence of all four, joined them on one geocache, and she also shared their enthusiasm. At other moments she remained adamant in her philosophy that this was their time, and she preferred to slip into the background. Besides, she had puzzles to solve and ingots to find. Another reason she had stayed at Cloud Cottage on occasion was she kept missing Gillian's phone calls. They had emailed and played phone tag, but Katherine was anxious to speak with her younger sister.

46

Tuesday morning she awoke to the sound of rain on the roof. She snuggled in her bed, listening and absorbing the soothing pattern. She did love the rain, but she wondered how it would impact the family. So far their time together seemed to be going very well. Katherine had been keenly observant for any sign of tension and had not detected anything. She remained hopeful that on Labor Day the twins would return to an intact home. She could hear their soft voices speaking to each other downstairs. The family was up. She knew Dano had been up for awhile because she had detected the aroma of pancakes. Yesterday, on their way home from geocaching, they had stopped at a local farm and picked blueberries. Dano had promised to prepare blueberry pancakes for breakfast. What a great way to start a rainy day, Katherine reflected. Her thoughts were interrupted by the phone. She reached to answer it, and was relieved it was Gillian's voice that greeted her.

"I'm so glad to talk with you," Katherine said. "Tell me everything."

"No, you first. How are things at Cloud Cottage?"

"Just fine. It is raining this morning, but it's a nice rain. You know, the kind of rain that refreshes."

"Dano and Caroline are there, aren't they?"

"Yes."

"And?" Gillian continued expectantly.

"I know nothing, but what I see looks positive."

"I hope so, Kate."

"Me too, now I want to know about you."

"I don't really know anything yet either. Radiation wasn't so bad. Chemo is tougher, but the waiting is the worst. I'm okay and Steve has been a saint, it's just some days I want to hear some good news, any good news. That's why I asked first about Cloud Cottage."

"Gillian, is there any chance you can come between treatments?"

"The thought has crossed my mind, but I don't know yet."

"At any moment you decide you can, you get in a car and come. Don't ever worry about calling first. Just get here."

"Thanks, Kate. A dose of Cloud Cottage would be wonderful medicine."

"It always has been, Gillian. Please come."

"At the first opportunity. I think I'm going to take a nap now, so I'll call again soon."

"Sooner than soon, get your rest and fight, Gillian."

Katherine pushed the end button to terminate the call. She sat holding the phone in her hand. Is this how it works in the cosmic universe, she wondered? Sometimes we talk, sometimes we listen, sometimes we push the end button, and sometimes perhaps, the end button just gets pushed. Then what? Stop it, Katie Ann MacLeod. This is no time to question your faith. It was just that Gillian had sounded so weak and sad. It really hadn't been much of a conversation at all. Katherine wondered if, after Labor Day, she should go and stay with her. She dressed and went downstairs. She was deep in thought when she entered the kitchen.

"Good morning, Aunt Katie, we're waiting for you."

Katherine forced a smile. "Sorry, no one should ever have to wait for their blueberry pancakes."

"Here we go everyone," Dano announced, as he set a platter of luscious pancakes on the table. They were so full of blueberries they were purple.

"Yum!"

"Daddy, these are the best pancakes ever."

"I agree, Dan, you outdid yourself this time," Caroline said, as she helped herself to another pancake.

Dano took a dramatic bow, then piled pancakes on his plate.

Katherine let the conversation swirl around her as plans were made for the day. An outing to Pentwater was the decision. Katherine declined the persistent invitations to join them.

After the twins left the kitchen, Dano demanded, "Okay, spill it."

Katherine didn't need to ask what. She knew her preoccupation during breakfast would not go unnoticed, at least by Dano. When she looked up she saw concern on Caroline's face too.

"This morning's phone call was Gillian. She just didn't sound good."

"I'm sorry, Aunt Katie. Are any of her early results back?"

"She says not, but I wonder." The group was silent. Katherine continued, "She says the hardest thing for her is waiting. I think the hardest thing for me is feeling helpless. For the first time in my life I don't know what to do or say. This morning there was a quality in her voice that was heart-wrenching."

"Can you describe it, Aunt Katie?" Dano asked.

"There was sadness, a wistfulness, a resignation. I guess I felt that I was hearing that she was dying, or at least that she thinks she is."

"That's scary stuff, Aunt Katie," Dano's voice was soft and kind.

Katherine nodded, "And a reminder of our own mortality. After just saying goodbye to Mother this winter, I'm not ready to lose my sister."

"Then let's think like Grandma MacLeod. What was her expression? 'Don't borrow trouble?' Let's think positive thoughts and pray for Aunt Gillian. There is no point going down a road of negative possibilities at this time."

231

"Give me a couple of hours and I'll climb out of my morass," Katherine answered with a forced smile.

"Are you sure you won't reconsider and join us, Aunt Katie?" Caroline asked.

"No, but thank you. Now go. I hear the twins coming downstairs."

Dano gave Katherine a hug.

Katherine wondered how she was going to shake off this gloom. She opted for yoga. She had been putting off re-establishing yoga in her routine long enough. She chose a protected spot on the porch and began with long deep cleansing breaths. Each inhalation filled her lungs with the freshness of the morning rain. Each exhalation purged her system of toxins and negativity.

An hour later Katherine still sat comfortable on her mat. She felt calm, renewed, and ready to face the world. Dano and the family would have lunch in Pentwater, so an empty stretch of hours was before her. Ancestor Aonghus came into her thoughts. Perhaps with a clear mind and no time pressure she might see something she'd missed. A few minutes later she was seated at the kitchen table, laptop open, a cup of tea in her hand. She wanted a fresh look at each line. She began word-by-word, line-by-line, searching for any variation in pattern, any repetition in pattern.

After two pages she stopped to rest her eyes and refill her mug. Half way through and she had found nothing. Think positive, she thought, and if you haven't found it yet that means it is in the last two pages.

In earnest she began again. At the bottom of the third page she couldn't help sighing, nothing. As she approached the very last sentence on the fourth and last page her heart was heavy, still nothing. Then she stopped and returned to the sentence she just finished. There were extra marks. The writing pattern and word formation was so full of accent marks or apostrophes she had almost missed them. These marks were not between letters of a word, but before or after a group of words. They seemed to delineate this group of words. With renewed intensity she studied the last sentence on the page. There was nothing there. This was the only variation she found. It might be significant.

Katherine wasn't sure just how to proceed, but she opened the Scottish Gaelic translation site on impulse. Perhaps the words within the marks were real words. She entered the first one, it translated into several possible words, but at least it was a recognizable word. She entered the second, the same result, the third, again the same. She stopped to think. The meanings of the words varied, depending upon the relationship with each other. She typed in all the words of the designated group. She held her breath and hit the 'Search' button. What came up on the screen caused Katherine to gasp, then burst out laughing. She read 'every gray cloud has a silver lining.'

"Ancestor Aonghus," she said out loud, "all this work to uncover a phrase that Uncle Gus repeated to me my whole life and said you always used too. Is this how you viewed the shipwreck? Was it your gray cloud and the ingots your silver lining? Oh ..." Katherine stopped. "Oh … Cloud Cottage has a silver lining; the ingots are inside Cloud Cottage." Again she laughed. "They're here, inside, protected all these years. Oh, Ancestor Aonghus, you were a clever man!"

When the family came home a short time later Katherine was standing in the middle of the dining room studying every feature, every crevice.

"Aunt Katie, what are you looking for?" Caitlin asked from the doorway.

Katherine turned to greet them. "Oh nothing. I just was considering new curtains. The sun is out, should we all go to the beach?"

"That's why we came back," Caroline contributed.

As the family went upstairs to change, Dano held back.

"Aunt Katie," he asked, "new curtains?"

"Dano, I am fine now, no worries. I just had to be reminded that every gray cloud has a silver lining."

The next morning Katherine left early to rendezvous with John. It had been determined that since Blue considered John the lead dog in their household, he should be the one to effect the transfer. A disappointed Jennifer had agreed.

As the miles ticked by Katherine found herself reveling in the feel of the open highway. In the five months since her arrival at Cloud Cottage she hadn't driven more than forty miles from home. It felt good to be behind the wheel. She switched the music to something with a strong beat and enjoyed the drive.

John was waiting for her at a designated rest area. He had wanted Blue to have some exercise in the middle of the trip. Katherine suspected he wanted to have one more romp together before he said good-bye to his dog. As she drove in the long curving approach, she spotted the two playing Frisbee. Oh my, Katherine thought, this is going to be hard for John. She slowed her speed to a crawl, then parked a short distance away to watch. John looked at his watch and scanned the parking lot. Katherine got out and waved. He waved back and motioned for her to come over. She was half way across the grass when Blue spotted her and came bounding over.

"Hello, Blue – sit – good dog," Katherine greeted him as she reached down to scratch his ears.

"Hi, Aunt Katie. This is a good sign. He knows you in a different environment."

"Is it? I hadn't thought about that. I have a lot to learn about dogs, John."

"You will do just fine. I wouldn't trust Blue with just anyone."

"I'm happy to have him, John, and I will do my best, just don't be surprised if I call Hong Kong with questions sometimes."

"Anytime. I can't thank you enough for taking care of him for me. Okay, this is it. Blue," he addressed his dog, "come." Then to Katherine, "Aunt Katie, may I ask you to drive over and park next to my car? I have a lot of Blue paraphernalia. This was like packing for a child. Also I want Blue to watch me put his things in your car."

"I understand."

In a short time the transfer had been accomplished, instructions shared, tearful goodbyes said – except by Blue – and Katherine was back on the road.

Blue sat on the back seat smiling. He, like John and the family, was on a new adventure. Katherine was somewhat apprehensive, and kept looking back and talking to him. After a while Blue seemed bored and settled down to sleep. While he slept, Katherine thought about the ingots and where they could be.

One of the biggest problems she realized, she didn't know what she was looking for. Her research indicated ingots came in all sizes. If the Confederate sympathizers had wanted to disguise what they were transporting they might very well have made the ingots a different size. Katherine kept thinking as the miles passed. For a moment a terrifying thought entered her mind. What if 'silver lining' meant the ingots were in between the double walls of Cloud Cottage where Ancestor Aonghus had placed sand? She would never tear apart those walls to find them. But no, Ancestor Aonghus had said they were "hidden in plain view." Katherine exhaled, relieved. They must be someplace he could always keep his eye upon them, she decided. Her thoughts took a virtual tour of each room of Cloud Cottage as she drove. When she pictured the den in her mind, she again panicked. It had been remodeled! The kitchen and the fourth bedroom too! No one would have had any idea what they were, and all the remodeling was done after Ancestor Aonghus died. Katherine groaned. In the back seat, Blue raised his head as if to inquire everything was okay.

"Good dog, Blue, go to sleep."

Blue didn't go back to sleep. He must have sensed they had crossed the Oceana county line and was on alert.

"Do you want to smell some of our good air?" Katherine asked as she cracked the window in the back seat. She rolled her window down as well. The air was warmer than the air-conditioned car, but neither dog nor woman minded. It felt and smelled wonderful.

47

Dano, Caroline, and the twins were playing badminton in the yard when Katherine pulled in the driveway. She decided to stop and let Blue out in front of the house. She opened the door. He jumped down, looked at her, then at the approaching family.

"Sit – wait," she commanded. "Good dog." Then, "say hello."

"Aunt Katie, we missed you."

"Hi, Blue."

"How was your drive?"

"The kite boarders were out today."

"Have you had dinner yet?"

The questions and comments were coming so fast and furious she couldn't keep track of who was asking what.

"Time out," Dano said. "Welcome home, Aunt Katie. You all go up to the house and I'll put the car in the garage."

Katherine nodded, then surrounded by chatter she started for the house, Blue was right by her side.

The remaining days of the week passed in a whirlwind. Katherine worked with Blue to establish boundaries, leadership, loyalty, and love. The family geocached, went horseback riding, played on the beach, and the grand finale for the twins was tubing down Stony Creek. Katherine met them with the car, where the creek emptied into Lake Michigan. The twins wanted to float down the creek again. They prevailed upon their father until he agreed. Caroline declared, laughing, she would keep Aunt Katie company. Together the two women stood and watched the tubes disappear down the creek, then walked to the car.

"Aunt Katie," Caroline spoke. "I have a confession. I wanted to have a few minutes alone with you."

Katherine looked at the young woman next to her. She was smiling, and seemed as at ease in her ponytail and flip-flops as she did in her power suits in the city. Katherine returned her smile and commented, "It has been a busy week, hasn't it?"

"Everything with the twins is busy. I don't know how you do it, Aunt Katie."

Katherine laughed. "Usually this is when people add – at your age."

"That's not what I meant," Caroline was serious and intent. "You are an amazing woman, and youthful. Most people would not guess your age within ten years. What I meant was I think this spring, between the twins, work, Dan, and the house, I was beginning to feel trapped, overwhelmed, inadequate, and I didn't know what to do. Inside I was panicking. All I could think about was running away. I did not have the sense of calm I feel with you."

"And now?" Katherine asked.

"I feel more in control. I have learned some things about myself and am working on some life skills that help. But what I want you to know is I love Dan and my children. I want for them and for myself what you and Cloud Cottage are all about. I am willing to work for it, and I will work hard. I am not giving up. I am not leaving my home, Dan, or my children."

Katherine studied the young woman's face. The set of her chin, her eyes, every feature, all expressed earnest determination and genuine sincerity. Katherine embraced Caroline.

"Aunt Katie, I want, I need, somehow, to convey to you my gratitude for sharing your life and Cloud Cottage with Connor and Caitlin all summer. It has been a gift for me. It has allowed me the time and space I needed to regain control, to find myself again. But the gift it has been for my children," she paused, "I don't know or have the words to express how formative it has been for them to be here with you. 'Thank you' seems like a hollow, inadequate thing to say."

Katherine responded, "Caroline, 'thank you' is never hollow when the words are filled with love, but a wise person once said that although appreciation may be expressed in words, true gratitude must be expressed in action."

"Aunt Katie, I do so love you, and I will try and live my gratitude every day with Dan, Connor, and Caitlin."

"Mommy, look at us!" It was Caitlin's voice that interrupted their dialogue. Their attention was directed to the creek where tubes were bumping and splashing against each other. Dano was right there bouncing and agitating with the twins.

"Look at them, Aunt Katie," Caroline said.

"Look at all of you," Katherine responded.

The next morning Caroline came down stairs wearing a MacLeod Proud shirt. The twins were delighted and raced upstairs to change into theirs.

"After breakfast, perhaps we should all change," Katherine suggested.

Dano looked at his wife with a big smile, then at his aunt with an even bigger smile. Katherine winked. On their last walk of the beach, before Dano and Caroline had to leave for the city, five proud MacLeods and Blue strolled together.

48

Monday morning Connor and Caitlin announced that since they had been on vacation last week they had two weeks of weeding to do. Katherine appreciated their eagerness but suggested they stretch it out over two or three days. She knew better than to wear out their enthusiasm in one day. These would be her last days with the twins this summer. She wanted no unhappy last memories. Dano was returning Friday and would depart with the twins on Saturday. Caroline had wanted to take the twins home with her when she left the day before. She felt she needed to shop for school clothes, supplies, and generally get the children organized and settled before they started school. That suggestion had been met with protests, the twins had been promised to stay until Labor Day. Saturday of Labor Day weekend was the compromise.

Katherine stood at the end of her row and stretched. Oh how she was going to miss these children. Caroline had spoken about how Katherine having the children had been a gift to her. Now at the end of the summer, Katherine realized she had been the recipient of the greater gift. This summer would forever be in her memory as the wonderful summer of Connor and Caitlin. Their enthusiasm, their intelligent minds, their energy had challenged Katherine. Like Merlin, she felt "youthened."

Katherine felt Blue press against her leg. As was their routine now, she scratched his ears in response. She realized she would be glad for his company in the coming days.

Caitlin looked up. "It isn't time for our moratorium yet, is it, Aunt Katie?"

"Not quite. I was just stretching. I'll get back to work now."

Katherine thought, as she weeded, about what activity they might do this week that would be special. Over lunch she asked the twins. They exchanged that look between them that she had learned to watch for. They had already discussed this with each other. Katherine waited to see who would be the spokesperson. It was Connor.

"Aunt Katie, we just want to be here at Cloud Cottage and do what we do with you."

"Except," Caitlin prompted.

"We would rather not go grocery shopping, and if we could, we would like to go to the band concert in Pentwater. It's the only thing we haven't done."

"And," Caitlin continued for her brother, "have ice cream cones, big ice cream cones to eat during the concert."

Katherine couldn't help laughing. It was true they hadn't gone to the Thursday night concert in Pentwater. They had talked about it, but somehow it had always been superseded by weather or other activities.

"Pentwater and ice cream it is. Now, who wants to go to the beach?"

All three hurried upstairs to change into their swimsuits.

"I want to make a phone call before we go, so I will be a few minutes," Katherine said. "Wait for me."

She knew Gillian was scheduled for chemotherapy later in the afternoon and she wanted to speak with her before her treatment. She dialed the number she knew so well. As she waited for Gillian to answer, she reflected on how natural it was for her generation to remember in their heads frequently dialed numbers. Yet with cell phones and electronically stored data no one dialed by memory any more. It isn't necessary; one just taps the name on the phone. Katherine hoped some other need for mental exercise and memory retention would replace memorizing phone numbers. Who knows what long-term impact this one aspect of technology might have. No one ever needed to remember anything any more because information was always at one's fingertips, literally!

"Hello," Gillian answered.

"Oh good, you're home. How are you?"

"Okay, a little apprehensive about chemo, but okay."

"I understand. That's why I called. I thought you might like some good news. Something happy to think about this afternoon."

"Please, what do you know?"

"Dano and Caroline are going to be okay."

"Oh, Kate! That is the best news. Tell me everything."

Katherine shared all the happy moments of the previous week, geocaching, blueberry picking, afternoons on the beach, tubing down Stony Creek, and also Caroline's conversation expressing her commitment to family.

"Kate, this news has made my day. I'll keep the image of their happy faces in my thoughts."

"Good."

"Aunt Katie?"

"Gillian, the twins are calling, they are ready to go to the beach."

"Go! Build a sandcastle for me and be sure and tell Connor and Caitlin that Aunt Gillian said hello."

"Please come soon, Gillian."

"One day at a time, Kate. Love you, bye."

"Love you too."

Katherine hung up the phone as the twins called again from the bottom of the attic stairs.

"Coming."

Katherine joined the twins and gave each one a big hug.

"That," she said, "is from Aunt Gillian."

Later on the beach they did build a sandcastle. Katherine asked a beach walker to take a picture of the three of them with their creation. That evening the photo would become a get-well card for Gillian.

Friday arrived too soon. The children were quiet as they sat on the porch with her waiting for their father.

"Do we have time for an Ancestor Aonghus story?" Connor asked.

Katherine hesitated. She had already shared all the stories she had been told, and the one that was unfolding about the ingots she couldn't share. Someday that was going to make a wonderful novel, and one, she hoped, with a happy ending. She was still tormented by the thought of all the remodeling at Cloud Cottage and the possibility the ingots could have been destroyed or lost. Before she had a chance to answer Connor the rev of a car engine was heard as someone approached Cloud Cottage.

"It's Grandpa!" Connor and Caitlin exclaimed together. "You didn't tell us he was coming!"

"He wanted to surprise you." She doubted they heard her because they were already running down the path. Having the twins at Cloud Cottage all summer had been wonderful for their grandfather too. She suspected he had spent more time with Connor and Caitlin in the past months than he had during their entire ten-year lives. It had been quality time, memory-making moments, as it should be at Cloud Cottage.

"Hey, Kate," Daniel greeted her.

"Grandpa, will you tell us a story until Dad comes?"

Oh, that's wonderful, Katherine thought. They are asking him, but before he could begin, Dano arrived. The twins ran to meet him.

"Did I make it in time for sunset?" he asked as he approached Daniel and Katherine on the porch.

"Absolutely. Let's go."

It was a quiet group that watched the final shades of pink fade to purple that evening. With a sigh Connor announced the last color of his wonderful summer.

"*Forever Blue.*"

Over an early breakfast Dano and Kate had an opportunity to share a few moments alone. They were quiet, content to just be together.

Dano spoke first, "Aunt Katie, this has been a summer of gifts. When I asked you to have the twins here at Cloud Cottage for the summer I saw it as a solution. My perceived solution precipitated gifts I never imagined."

"Dano," Kate interrupted.

"No, please, let me finish. We may be interrupted. I know you spoke about gifts with Caroline, but I want you to hear this from me. Of course this time has been a gift for Caroline and me to work through our issues and for the twins a whole summer of adventures at Cloud Cottage – well, I have been jealous – what a way to spend two and a half months. But, Aunt Katie, the children have grown and matured in so many ways since May. There is thoughtfulness for others now, and a genuine willingness to help. Connor has learned to express his thoughts, his feelings. It is a simple thing, but naming colors at sunset has been wonderful for him. Caitlin is a walking encyclopedia of the family tree. She knows and loves the stories, the roots you have shared. It has been grounding for her. For me, well, Aunt Katie, I didn't think I would ever have an in-depth conversation with my dad. Lying in our bunks at night in the boys' room, after Connor and JJ were asleep, we talked…really talked. Now that Jennifer and John and the kids will be gone for two years the time this summer with them seems priceless. I feel I know my sister as an adult. And my children know her children. These are all gifts to us because you and Cloud Cottage welcomed us here. Then there is the gift that is Aunt Katie herself." Dano stopped and looked at Katherine, tears welling up in his eyes. "I love you, Aunt Katie. I love you so very much."

Katherine extended her hands across the table and encircled his.

"I love you too, Dano."

There were footsteps in the hallway. This moment was ending, but she had just time to say, "Some day I will share with you the gift this summer has been for me."

Two long faces appeared in the doorway. Katherine looked at them.

"Come here, you two," she said. She wrapped an arm around each one. "No sad faces, Cloud Cottage is a happy place. It was for me when I was a child, it is now, and it will be on your next visit. Some day, when you bring your families here, it will be a happy place then too. Now, what would you like for breakfast?"

"Blueberry pancakes," Connor answered. A smile brightened both faces.

"Dano, you got this?"

"You bet."

"I suggest you make a big batch." More smiles.

"Where's Grandpa?" Caitlin asked.

"He drove out to make some calls on his cell phone. He will be back in time for breakfast." Katherine explained.

Every morsel of pancakes was relished that morning. No one hurried; no one wanted to proceed to the next activity of the day, yet even at Cloud Cottage clocks tick away the moments. Katherine initiated the next step.

"While you finish packing and load the car, I'll go pick some vegetables from the garden for you to take home. What would you like?" In a moment Katherine had a long list. Laughing, she said, "I'd better get started."

"I'll clean up here in the kitchen, or at least start it," Grandpa Daniel contributed. "You three go and do what you need to do."

Surprised, Katherine and Dano both looked at each other. A discreet Dano mouthed, "another gift."

Katherine proceeded, accompanied by Blue, to the garden. As she harvested the beans, radishes, tomatoes, and other vegetables the children requested, she thought about her brother. Perhaps an opportunity to contribute and to participate was important. Maybe she should ask for his help, instead of assuming he wouldn't want to be bothered, that he would resent the request. She needed to remember to not always be so independent. There was a blessing to be shared when one accepts, when one allows another to give. She needed to remember this in the future.

She had just finished filling the basket for the family when the children walked to the garden. Dano was loading their suitcases into the car.

"All set?" she asked.

"Yeah," was the quiet answer. Katherine noticed they were doing the twin thing again.

"Yes," she asked, "what is it I could do for you today?"

It was Connor who spoke up. "Aunt Katie, can we pick our pumpkins?"

"Oh," Katherine sighed, "I would love for you to have your pumpkins, but it's too soon. Even though one has started to turn orange, they are a long way from mature. I'm sorry."

By this time Dano had joined them. He understood the dilemma.

"Connor, Caitlin," he said. "I'm not going to promise, but maybe, just maybe, if it's alright with Aunt Katie, we may come for a weekend in October. The pumpkins will be ready to pick then."

"Really, Dad?" Caitlin exclaimed.

"Can we come, Aunt Katie?" Connor asked.

"Of course you may, remember you're Clan MacLeod."

Connor and Caitlin each took hold of a handle on the basket of vegetables and carried it between them as they walked to the car. Dano and Katherine followed.

"Do you really think you can come back this fall, Dano?" she asked.

"Yes. Caroline and I thought it would be easier for the twins to leave if they knew when they might come back. They're going to miss you, Aunt Katie."

"I'm going to miss them, and you. I'm happy to have a weekend to look forward to also. Make it happen, Dano."

The twins were giving their grandfather goodbye hugs. He had been waiting by the car and loaded their basket for them.

"Okay, Connor, Caitlin," Dano announced, as he and Katherine approached. "It's time."

Katherine was encircled by four young arms. She returned their embraces then knelt down.

"We have had quite a summer, haven't we?" It was a statement, not a question.

She reached into her pockets and pulled out two bags of sand, handed one to Connor and one to Caitlin.

"Some people would think this is only a bag of sand, but it is Little Point Sable sand, Cloud Cottage sand. It is the sand Ancestor Aonghus first stepped on when he shipwrecked here. It is the sand your grandpa and I, when we were children, used to build sandcastles. It is the sand you have played on all summer. Whenever you miss Cloud Cottage and Little Point Sable, let it flow through your fingers. It will bring your heart and mind back until the next time you walk on the beach, and you can return the sand to once again be washed by the waves."

Another round of hugs, a slam of car doors and they were gone. Tears rolled down Katherine's cheeks. She was aware her brother was watching her, and she felt Blue press against her leg. She wasn't alone, but the tears still flowed.

"I am still a mush head," she managed to say. "Remember when you called me that, Daniel?"

"I probably called you lots of things I shouldn't have," he answered. "How about if I take you out to lunch in Pentwater?"

"That sounds like a good idea. Cloud Cottage is going to seem very empty today."

Katherine and her brother shared a pleasant afternoon. Even though it was a holiday weekend, he had to leave the next morning, so Katherine hadn't escaped to her oasis that evening. They had sat and talked on the porch swing until long after the sun had gone down.

49

The next day, when Daniel left, Katherine thought, here I am again waving good-bye to a car as I stand alone on the porch.

"Oh, sorry, Blue, I apologize. I'm not alone am I?" She knelt by the dog, and gave him an uncharacteristic hug saying, "We will play later."

Today she was going to keep busy, very busy. She planned to start with Ancestor Aonghus. It had been almost a week since she had translated the quote. Since then whatever room she was in, she was always studying and looking for the ingots. This morning, however, she wanted to start on the next group of pages.

Katherine made herself comfortable, out of habit, in the living room by the window that looked towards the beach path. No Connor and Caitlin would come running up that path today. She forced herself to refocus her thoughts on the pages in front of her. There were only two this time. She wasn't sure if she was glad or not. It was less to work through, but it was also less content to find Ancestor Aonghus' clue/ message.

She scanned the pages. They were in English. That was a good start. It didn't take Katherine but a couple minutes to read the pages. Why is this never simple, she wondered? Once again she had no idea what she was supposed to find. The sentences were legible and formed cohesive thoughts. They rambled as they had on previous pages, but this time Ancestor Aonghus was talking about the MacLeod Crest. There was no mention of anything else. It was all about the red flags and the bull and the motto "Hold Fast." There were references like the bull is a worthy opponent, seek him, be challenged by him, then conquer him and hold fast. There were sentences that entreated one to hold fast to what one had achieved, one's possessions, one's accomplishments, and others to secure and hold fast to those things that we value.

In other words, Katherine thought, for two pages, he's saying if it's worth fighting for, it's worth hanging on to. Now what do I do with that? Is there some understanding of clan that I don't possess? Uncle Gus taught me to value family, clan, and tradition. He also said "Katie Ann MacLeod, hold fast to them."

Katherine tried a different tack. If she let go, if she didn't hold fast, what would happen? If it was the bull she let go, she could be injured. Does it follow that it may be harmful to let go of family and clan – perhaps? Could the bull have a different meaning? Katherine questioned it. The whole content of the pages was about the crest and the clan. The clan legend was that an ancient chief had wrestled a bull to the ground and the crowd had shouted out to him, "hold fast."

Katherine took a tea break on the porch swing. Blue was at her feet. This was the first quiet weekend in over three months. She remembered last spring, feeling nostalgic about giving up her solitude. Now here she was, reluctant to be alone.

"Blue, there I go again forgetting I'm not alone. Shall we play Frisbee?" She was rewarded by a vigorous thumping of his tail. "Let me finish my tea first. Blue, wait," she commanded.

The dog cocked his head as if to say "really?" then settled back down. Katherine's thoughts returned to the pages. What could Ancestor Aonghus want her to know? She sat in the swing, enjoying her tea and the quiet as she contemplated the pages.

"I give up. Blue, go find your Frisbee."

'Go find' was one of Blue's favorite things to do. Katherine opened the door to the mudroom and waited. It only took a moment before Blue brought his Frisbee to her.

"Good dog, Blue," she praised as they went outside to play.

It took Katherine a while to get past the dog slobber on the Frisbee every time Blue brought it back to her, but she did enjoy herself. She couldn't help but appreciate the gymnastics and acrobatic jumps that Blue employed to catch his toy. For a short time the fun of witnessing his pure joy supplanted thoughts of ingots and the clan crest. A half-hour later Katherine and a very happy Blue resettled themselves in the house. Blue went to sleep. Katherine sat back down at her computer with new resolve.

Starting at the top had worked before, so once again Katherine scrutinized every word, every sentence line-by-line. She looked for absolute meaning, for hidden meaning, implied meaning. There were no markings, no underlines, no patterns of repeated words, no strange system of capitalization or odd spellings. Katherine couldn't identify a single thing the whole afternoon that seemed unusual.

"That's it," she said. " I'm done for today. I quit." She fixed herself something to eat, put in a movie, and tried to forget that she felt frustrated and alone – even with Blue by her feet.

The next afternoon, Labor Day, Katherine took a long leisurely walk on the beach. There were people around, but fewer than a week or two before. She expected the highways already were full of cars, heading back to school and 'work-a-day' lives.

"Not me," she said to the wind and the waves.

She had anticipated she might be nostalgic or melancholy today, her first Labor Day to not be anticipating the new school year. So far she had only felt liberated. As she walked along the beach a familiar couple approached her. She had exchanged greetings with them often during the summer, and they had become acquainted.

"Hello," they called to her.

"Hi," Katherine responded.

"You're missing your walking mates."

"They left on Saturday," Katherine explained.

"Will we see you tomorrow night?"

"I'm planning on it."

"Good, see you then." They walked on.

Katherine had been invited to join a group of people for a 'day-after-Labor-Day' party. She had been informed it was a tradition among the cottage associations along the lakeshore for the year-round residents to gather and celebrate the departure of the summer people. These gatherings had various names, 'trunk-slamming' parties, 'tail-light' parties, but the sentiment was the same. Katherine as a new 'year-rounder' understood. She had loved every moment of every visit during the summer, but the peacefulness, the serenity of her first spring was fresh in her memory. After only a couple days alone she recognized she was looking forward to fall.

50

The gathering was to be a 'happy hour,' so Katherine chose to walk down the beach to the party. Even though it was September the sun wouldn't set until eight o'clock. A bottle of wine in a chilled tote swinging in her hand, Katherine started out. It always felt good to stretch her legs in long strides. She chose to walk on the harder semi-dry sand for speed, but she kept an eye on the waves. Normally she wouldn't care if an errant wave brushed higher on the beach and wrapped around her feet. She just didn't want to track wet sand into the home of her hostess.

Katherine was a little uncomfortable. She did not know Chris well. They had met walking the beach, first in May, then frequently over the summer. As their encounters became regular their exchanges became more than a casual hello. When Chris heard Katherine planned to stay all winter she insisted her new friend join the party at her home. Katherine realized she needed to develop friendships in the community, so here she was, strolling down the beach, wine in one hand, directions in another to spend an hour or two with people she didn't know.

The cottage Katherine had been invited to was a beautiful new home right on the beach. It looked like a featured design for a Home and Garden show, multiple angles and walls of windows. A wrap-around deck was already crowded with people. Katherine climbed the steps from the beach, hoping she'd see Chris before she reached the deck. She was relieved when she heard her friend call out a greeting. Katherine waved back and in another moment stepped up on the deck.

"Katherine, welcome. I can't believe you walked."

"It's a beautiful walk, and it didn't take that long," Katherine responded as she handed Chris the bottle of wine.

"Thank you. Let's go inside, get you a glass, and I'll introduce you to everyone."

The first half hour passed in a quick blur of names and a sharing of good food, wine and light-hearted exchanges. This was a group that knew each other well, yet they welcomed her with genuine warmth. Katherine was enjoying herself. She hadn't known that so many talented, articulate people had chosen to retire so close by. Each one had a comment or suggestion for her first fall and winter.

"Buy a pair of ice cleats to stretch over your winter boots."

"Get season tickets to the local artists' series."

"Plan your trip to town by the weather, not by impulse."

"Always keep at least two week's supply of everything you need on hand."

They even gave her the names of people she could contact to plow her driveway. Some things Katherine already knew, others were new contributions to her winter arsenal and she was grateful for the input. She was pleased this seemed to be a network that looked out for each other, and she had been welcomed in. What a delightful gathering this was.

Katherine was on the deck participating in a discussion of eagle sightings when Chris approached.

"Katherine, there is someone else I would like you to meet."

She turned and found herself face-to-face with him. Their eyes met, but Katherine was no longer a sixteen-year-old girl, and this time she would take control.

"Hello," she said, as she extended her hand. "I'm Katherine."

She wasn't quite sure where the presence of mind had come from to greet him this way. She hadn't thought about encountering him again. When she had seen him during the volleyball game she had just assumed he had been on a weekend visit. Yet here he was, still handsome, but in a different way. There was softness to the smile he returned with a handshake.

"Hi, Katherine, I'm David."

"Katherine has just retired and is planning on living here year-round too." Chris interjected. "You two should get to know each other."

This is interesting, Katherine thought. There had been a time in her life when she would have given anything for a moment like this to tell him what she thought of him. Yet perhaps this was better, maybe even perfect. She would carry on as if she didn't know him, didn't remember him. Let him think, feel insignificant, not worthy of being remembered. Katherine was pretty sure by the way he was looking at her that he did know who she was.

"Well, welcome to the winter warriors, Katherine," David continued. "Have you been here in the winter before, at least for a weekend?"

"Yes, many times, and sometimes for Christmas too. I have experienced winter at the Point, yet I understand it will be different to be here every day."

"True, but don't let people scare you. Not every winter is challenging. Some have been quite mild. The key is to be flexible, to get out whenever you can, and be active."

"That sounds like a good mantra for life, wherever one lives," Katherine responded.

"Yes, I guess it is."

"So how many winters have you spent here?" Katherine asked. She was determined to ask the questions, not to be questioned.

"This will be my fifth, and I love it."

"And what do you do to be flexible, keep active, and get out?"

David laughed. "Well, it varies. I do cross-country ski, but not as much as the first couple years. I walk whenever I can, and I volunteer in town with a couple programs. Once or twice a week I go to Ludington to swim at the college pool. There really is no shortage of things to do. The issue from out here is always can we get in to do them?"

"I understand, the flexible aspect."

"You got it. Sometimes, almost always, it's worse when the snow melts. One can usually maneuver on snow if it isn't too deep, but when these hills and these gravel roads freeze every night after a day of melting – well – it can be a dicey ride down and impossible to drive up."

"Yet you choose, after five winters, to spend a sixth? That at least is heartening."

At that moment they were joined by others and the conversation changed to politics so Katherine excused herself to find Chris and say good-bye. She did want to be headed home before the sun set. She found her hostess inside, and after a lengthy thank you and goodbye she was on her way. At one point the steps to the beach turned parallel to the deck. She did not look up, but Katherine could see David standing at the railing watching her. Good, she thought, let him wonder.

Katherine was a little surprised at herself. She had never been vindictive or revengeful and that her attitude towards David had manifested itself in this way, after all these years, was perplexing. She reran the introduction and ensuing conversation in her mind as she walked home. It had been casual, general, and brief, like every other conversation she had engaged in during the gathering. It had been a typical, appropriate exchange between new acquaintances. Only they weren't.

51

Katherine was still enjoying a quiet morning reading in bed when the phone rang.

"Good morning, Kate."

"Oh, Gillian, good morning, what a good way to start my day. How are you?"

"Today is a good day, Kate."

"You sound upbeat. Have you had some results come back with good news?"

"No, not yet, I am just not feeling sorry for myself today. The kids were all here on Sunday and we had such a delightful time I've been counting my blessings ever since."

"Great. Have you thought any more about coming to Cloud Cottage?"

"Every day, but Kate, I think I will wait until I am through with chemo."

"How do you feel about me coming to visit?"

There was silence on the line. "Maybe later, Kate, I'm doing okay now."

"Gillian?"

"Really, Kate."

"Alright, I'll accept that for now, but please think about it. I can be there in six hours."

"Okay, now tell me something happy about Cloud Cottage?"

Katherine realized Gillian wanted to hear about people, life, and everyday comings and goings. So she told her about the trunk-slamming party, about playing Frisbee with Blue, but not about David. Gillian had only been ten the summer of David. She may or may not remember anything about him. That was an excuse, really. Katherine knew Gillian would love to hear every detail. It was she who wasn't ready to share.

"Gillian, I'm sorry, but I've got to go. I was so enjoying talking with you I've lost track of time. I still haven't taken Blue out this morning. I suspect he is crossing his legs by now."

Gillian laughed. "Go take care of your dog."

"Promise you'll call back again this week, or anytime, every day?"

"Yes, I'll call back. With all your company gone I won't be so concerned about disturbing you. It has been good to laugh with you, Kate."

"Your calls are never a disturbance, however your silence is very disturbing. Promise we will talk?"

"I promise. Bye, Kate, pet Blue for me."

Katherine didn't even take time to dress; she went right downstairs in her nightgown, apologized to Blue and went outside with him. She sincerely hoped no meter reader would come around the corner and see them. An extra biscuit for a treat assured Blue's forgiveness.

"Good dog, Blue," she told him. "Very good dog."

Together they settled down in the kitchen. Blue on his favorite rug, Katherine with a cup of tea and an English muffin. "If I could read tea leaves, what do you think I would see Blue?" she asked. "Do you think there would be anything about a tall handsome man?"

Katherine's thoughts about the previous evening's party were mixed. She was surprised how much she had enjoyed herself, and was very happy about connecting with other year-round residents. She wasn't sure how she felt about the David encounter. She concluded Ancestor Aonghus would be a good diversion for the morning.

Soon she had made herself comfortable in the living room and opened her laptop. Somehow she felt that she should zone out in order to tune in. She closed her eyes, relaxed, and allowed any and all thoughts to flow freely. After a few moments what came to her was to consider other meanings of 'hold' and 'fast.' She consulted a dictionary; both words had a myriad of meanings. 'Hold' as a verb could mean anything from to keep in one's hands or arms, to contain, to be firm or loyal in one's beliefs. As a noun it could mean a strong grip, a pause in music, a storage space below deck on ships…

The meanings of 'fast' were almost as numerous. When used as an adjective it could mean secure, but it also could mean ahead of time, loyal, quick movement, loose living …

'Fast' as an adverb could mean nearby, or soundly, and then as a verb, to refrain from eating. Hmmm Katherine thought, our English language!

She always assumed 'Hold Fast' in the MacLeod crest meant to secure tightly, 'hold' as a verb, 'fast' as an adverb. Could it mean something else? Did Ancestor Aonghus want her to go beyond the obvious meanings? Both words had a meaning that meant loyal, firm, and resolute. That is interesting, Katherine observed. But then the ingots had come out of the hold of a ship. They had come out fast because of the shipwreck. Could he be referring to the basement of Cloud Cottage as a 'hold?' Or would Ancestor Aonghus be telling her that they were in the kitchen, that she should 'hold fast,' not 'break fast?' It seemed like a stretch. Ancestor Aonghus has been cleverly deceptive, but straightforward in his clues. He never had been oblique.

"I'm not sure this is getting me anywhere," she said to Blue. "I think we should take a walk on the beach. Maybe the waves will tell me what I need to hear."

52

September was an extension of August, except the days were shorter and some nights were cooler. Katherine could still swim in the lake, her garden was producing copious amounts of vegetables, and her apple trees were ripening their first crop. She knew she should be starting to prepare for winter, but she wasn't ready to let go of summer. She canned tomatoes, tomato sauce, tomato juice, and salsa. She froze beans and peppers. She made zucchini bread, zucchini lasagna, eggplant Parmesan, and froze it too. She made and froze three kinds of squash soups and two different kinds of vegetable soups. Katherine filled her freezer with enough food to feed a family for a whole year. She washed winter squash, and placed them in the basement root cellar along with a few bushels of potatoes. When or how she would eat them all she didn't know. But at least she would have seed for next year.

"Enough!" she said one day, and called a food pantry to donate her excess production. Katherine hadn't needed to be concerned how she would feel during this first school-free September of her life, she was too busy doing things she enjoyed to miss it.

There had been almost daily phone calls with Gillian. Her sister appeared to have surmounted the initial shock of having cancer and seemed to be doing quite well. Katherine was thankful for each conversation.

She was also thankful for a growing friendship with Chris. They met often on the beach for a walk, and Katherine looked forward to her company. They enjoyed many of the same things. Chris was a few years older, but like Katherine, was fit and energetic. She was astute, insightful, respected the past, but lived in the present. Her career had been in social work at a university hospital. Katherine felt at ease with Chris and appreciated that at no time did she ask personal questions motivated by simple curiosity. Of course they had exchanged a few life details. Katherine learned that Chris first came to Little Point Sable when she had married ten years before. Her husband's family always spent summers at the Point, and she had fallen in love with the place as well as with him. They met in a grief-counseling group following the death of their spouses.

Katherine shared that she had been engaged once but never married. That she had been an ambitious amateur musician in her youth and had played the cello in various quartets for years. She no longer played. She had allowed music to be crowded out of her life by care responsibilities for her parents and administrative overload in the school district. Chris and Katherine both concluded that life happens, and it goes on.

As busy as September life had become, Ancestor Aonghus and the ingots were never far from Katherine's thoughts. One day, when she had been making soup, an image flashed into her mind of she and her Grandmother cooking together in the kitchen years ago. She gasped, because in that image, there was a picture hanging on the wall in the background. She had forgotten about it. It was a framed print of the MacLeod crest, and it had always hung on the wall between the windows. Could Ancestor Aonghus have been trying to say in his rambling about the crest, that a visual representation of the crest marked the spot?

Katherine turned down the stove and walked across the room. She ran her hand over the stone wall. It was one of the few places in Cloud Cottage where the stonework was exposed on the inside. She pulled a chair over, sat down opposite the wall to study it closely. Once again she wasn't seeing anything that looked to her like an ingot. She realized she could be looking at them and not recognizing them. She still didn't know what size they were. After a few minutes she heaved a sigh, she had a strong feeling the ingots had been lost in one of the remodeling projects. Ancestor Aonghus could not have anticipated the possibility of changing the inside of Cloud Cottage or the 21st century need for bathrooms and daily showers.

It was about the end of September when she received a phone call from Chris.

"Hi, how about joining us for dinner tomorrow night? It's going to be an Equinox Potluck."

"Thanks, I'd love to, but Chris, wasn't the Equinox last week?"

"Yes, but a lot of us weren't here on the actual date, so we agreed on an equinox event this week."

"Sounds like a good excuse to party."

"Why not, it's a long winter."

"Got it. What may I bring?"

"How about a pot of one of those soups you've been making?"

"Can do."

"Okay, see you about five for happy hour."

Hmmm, thought Katherine, I wonder who else is on the guest list, but I don't care, I need a diversion. I'm becoming obsessed.

That evening Katherine decided to look at the Ancestor Aonghus pages one more time. She was tempted to move on to the next group without solving this one, even though she had resolved at the beginning to never do that. One more time, she thought. She read through the lines from beginning to end. It was a casual read, instead of her usual dissecting read. There were very few words that were illegible. The overall content and meaning of every sentence was clear. Katherine was confident she understood what Ancestor Aonghus had written. It simply was a long-winded, rambling narrative about the MacLeod crest with repeated emphasis on 'hold fast.' Throughout his life, according to Uncle Gus, Ancestor Aonghus had stressed that concept to his family. These pages were consistent.

"Alright, Katie Ann MacLeod," she said. " 'Hold fast' has to be the key. Think!"

She sat for a few more moments, then reread the lines again. This time she noticed one variation. It was subtle. Every statement about 'hold fast' was directed to the reader, except one. The sentence structure was 'you,' the reader, either implied or explicit, as subject with 'hold fast' as verb/adverb. The sentence that had caught Katherine's eyes had Cloud Cottage as the subject. She reread through one more time to verify that no other sentence had a different subject. This was the only one. It was a mandate in the middle of the two pages, to hold fast to Cloud Cottage so that Cloud Cottage would 'hold fast.'

That could mean, Katherine surmised, that the ingots are an actual part of the interior structure. It confirmed what she had already suspected. If this was the clue it wasn't a great revelation. It would just mean the ingots aren't buried in a treasure chest in the dirt floor of the root cellar. Perhaps it was now time for a metal detector. No, Katherine decided, there was still one more group of pages. She was confident enough of this clue to go forward. During her next visit with Ancestor Aonghus she would read the last pages. Maybe, just maybe, they would tell her where the ingots were. Somehow, for Katherine, using a metal detector seemed like cheating. She wanted, she needed, to follow, and solve the clues Ancestor Aonghus had left.

53

At five o'clock the next day Katherine arrived at her friend's house. Chris greeted her at the door and made a show of looking around her.

"Well, did you walk or drive?" she asked.

"I drove, with a pot of soup, I drove," she laughed, as she handed Chris the kettle.

"Good choice. You made a splash at our last gathering with your beach entrance and exit."

"Why, isn't it natural to walk by the beach when possible?"

"It should be, but I guess we just get lazy and drive. Or maybe it was your girlish figure that caught peoples' attention."

"Get real, Chris."

"Oh, I'm serious, Katherine. You really made a positive impression. Even David couldn't stop asking questions about you."

"Oh," escaped from Katherine's lips before she could stop herself.

"What?" Chris asked.

"Well," Katherine scrambled. "I guess I'm not sure I like being the topic of conversation,"

"Katherine, it's okay," Chris said. "Everyone liked you and wanted to know more about you. They would like to get to know you, that's all. Besides, I don't know much to tell them, that's up to you."

Katherine nodded, but there was a lump in her throat. Maybe this wasn't such a good idea.

"Hey," Chris continued. "Come help me in the kitchen and stay with me, I've got your back."

It was a pleasant evening, once again Katherine enjoyed herself. There were questions interspersed in conversation, but no one was prying or inappropriate. She had overreacted. She did share stories about herself and Cloud Cottage, offered her opinions when appropriate and engaged in light-hearted exchanges with other guests. David was there, of course. She could tell he was listening whenever she spoke, even if they were engaged in separate conversations. It hadn't mattered, because as far as he knew he was just another new acquaintance.

Later she helped Chris clean up the kitchen.

"Did you have a good time?" her friend asked.

"I really did. Thank you for including me. You have such a wonderful group of friends. It was a delightful evening, and I'm sorry I overreacted earlier. I guess it's just a shy side of me that still emerges sometimes."

"I'm glad, and you didn't act shy."

"Perhaps because everyone is so welcoming."

"Here, I'll walk out with you."

"Thanks again, Chris, see you soon."

That night Katherine got an idea. The next morning she was on the phone with Chris.

"Good morning, Katherine, this is a surprise, what's up?"

"Well, I would like to invite you and the whole group to a party at Cloud Cottage."

"Great!" exclaimed Chris.

"I was thinking about a harvest party, in late October, before the weather changes." Katherine continued. "My driveway could be really dicey if I wait too long. What do you think?"

"I think a harvest party during the third week of October would be great."

"Terrific, but I'll need some help for contacts, and who knows what else."

"You got it, any time."

"Thanks, Chris. I'll check back in with you in a couple of days."

Done, Katherine thought. Now I have something to look forward to. I also have a deadline to finish projects and something else to think about besides ingots.

Katherine threw her energies into all the projects she had put on hold for Cloud Cottage. There were things she wanted to have done before hosting a party, and things she needed to have done before winter. Storm windows had to go on and screens had to come off. Cloud Cottage had the old-fashioned kind! There was a handle on the toilet that needed to be fixed. The kitchen rugs needed to be washed, the garden needed to be mulched after the last frost, and leaves needed to be removed from the lawn. It seemed like an endless list, yet Katherine attacked it. All the frustrations she felt about the ingots were expelled with a burst of energy to complete projects. Finally, one night, exhausted, she thought ENOUGH! I am missing the beauty of fall. Tomorrow I'm going to sleep in and take the day off to enjoy the foliage.

She started the day with a walk in her own woods, Blue by her side. The maples were showing branches of red, and the birches were yellow, but for the most part the trees were still green. Her walk had been invigorating, but she wanted more. She packed a lunch, her camera, told Blue to "come," then got in the car and started to drive. Wherever she saw a blaze of color, that was the road she turned onto. She found herself at little out-of-the-way county parks she didn't know existed. She and Blue hiked in a national forest and came across a pond with exquisite reflections. Blue was patient and waited while her camera shutter fired again and again. She even took pictures of Blue chasing falling leaves.

She chased colors and the perfect moment of autumn. At dusk when the colors of sunset blended with the colors of the trees, she stood still and savored the moment. The day had been what she needed, a complete immersion in nature.

Upon her arrival home there was a phone message from Dano, could they come this weekend? Katherine couldn't wait to return his call. It had been such a wonderful day she was delighted at the prospect that the family could come and share the fall beauty too.

"Hi, Dano," she greeted him. "I hope I'm not calling too late."

"Of course not. How are you, Aunt Katie?"

"I'm great. How are you?"

"Everything is good here. You got my message?"

"Yes, this weekend would be just fine. Blue and I have just come back from a day of color touring and the world is beautiful, Dano. Right here at the lake we still have a lot of green, but when one drives inland a few miles colors are at their peak."

"Sounds wonderful. Caroline and the twins and I will see you late Friday evening."

"Dano, Caroline will come too?"

"Yes, Aunt Katie, she is just as adamant as Connor and Caitlin that we come."

"I am so glad, now you really have made my day."

"We all need and want our fix of Cloud Cottage and Aunt Katie."

Katherine laughed. "I can't wait for you to get here."

"That's the way we feel too, but Aunt Katie, it will be a short weekend. We'll leave before noon on Sunday. Caroline feels the children should be home early on a school night."

"I understand, we will celebrate autumn on Saturday."

"You got it."

Katherine couldn't help giggling after she said goodnight to Dano. What a wonderful day this had been.

54

The next morning was as rainy and dreary as the day before had been bright and beautiful. Katherine didn't care; nothing was going to dampen her mood. Yesterday had been wonderful; the weekend would be even better because the family was coming. Oh, how she had missed them. Blue thumped his tail on the floor in agreement with her happy mood.

"That's right, Blue," she told him. "We can be happy on rainy days. You can be my blue sky today. That's it," she said as she scratched dog's ears. "You now have a middle name, but you are a MacLeod, so I am going to spell it like the Isle of Skye – Blue Skye MacLeod."

She hoped John wouldn't mind that she had just renamed his dog. Katherine was so tickled she decided it was an omen and that today would be a good day to solve the mystery of the ingots. She would build a little fire in the kitchen and work at the kitchen table.

Katherine stared at the pages. There were three of them this time. The rambling and disjointed qualities of the writing had increased. She studied the words on the pages as she had in the other groups, examining each one to detect any irregularities or variations. This time the only thing different was that the pages were numbered at the bottom. On the third page above the number three, a straight line had been drawn. Somehow these page numbers must be significant, Katherine pondered, and why is there a line drawn over the 3 on the last page?

She sat contemplating, convinced that these page numbers and the line were significant. She happened to reread the last sentence Ancestor

Aonghus had written, "If only I had known I would have been on Cloud 9." What caught Katherine's attention was that the placement of 'Cloud 9' was exactly over the straight line and the number '3.' Hmmm, she thought, coincidence, or significant? Her experience with Ancestor Aonghus' clues was that they were very carefully crafted. If that pattern holds true then 'Cloud 9 over 3' is my clue. 'Cloud 9' is a state of euphoria. The rest of the words on these pages are the words of a tormented man guilt-ridden by the failings connected to the ingots. They were words of a frightened man. Terrified he would be damned to Purgatory for some 'sin' of the ingots. Katherine's heart ached to read the pain the words he wrote implied. It was sad to think this good man suffered because of this secret. If Katherine understood everything he had tried to tell her in these pages, if she was right in her assumptions based on those understandings, Ancestor Aonghus had nothing to fear.

She had done a layman's search of the rights and ownership of found treasure. It appeared to Katherine, the law of finds, not the law of salvage, would apply to the ingots. There was no evidence that anyone knew they had gone down in a schooner off Little Point Sable, that anyone had ever looked for them, or that they had even existed – except Ancestor Aonghus. It was probable that everyone else with knowledge of the ingots died that night in the storm. The most definitive argument for ownership of the ingots was that the one man who died on the beach and who had whispered, "For the Cause," had given the ingots to Ancestor Aonghus. The ingots were as rightfully his by possession as anyone else who had them, including me. No government, no owner could come forth and claim them. She was in too good a mood to be frustrated today, so she decided to think about 'Cloud 9 over 3' while she did other projects. The day of the party was coming and Dano would be here for the weekend. She had work to do.

All day Friday Katherine felt like a little girl waiting for Christmas morning. She couldn't wait for the family to arrive. She made Connor's favorite cookies, lasagna for Caitlin, apple pie for Dano, and for Caroline she filled the house with bouquets of colored leaves and mums. She cleaned the last weeds away around the coveted pumpkins that the children had taken care of all summer. Then finally she took Blue Skye for a long walk.

Her eyes were absorbing the beauty of the woods as they wandered the deer paths, but her thoughts were with Ancestor Aonghus. 'Cloud Nine over 3,' was it the clue? What did it mean? She was no closer to a solution. The challenge of the clues Ancestor Aonghus placed in his book intrigued and frustrated her. She didn't understand why all the subterfuge, why clues and why so many of them? She realized she would never know and could only assume he had been so obsessed with his own fears that he felt it necessary to protect the ingots. That thought started Katherine thinking what she would do with them if she found them. Would she sell them, and if she did, what would she do with the money? What would be appropriate? She didn't think she could just keep it. It wouldn't feel right, not for her nor Uncle Gus or Ancestor Aonghus, or for the men who died and had been buried here on the beach. She began to feel the weight of an impending dilemma.

Upon her return to Cloud Cottage Katherine opened her laptop to research buying and selling ingots. By chance she happened upon a numismatic site that had auctioned an ingot from the 1800's. Oh my, Katherine thought. She hadn't realized the value of the ingots, for historical collectors, could be so much more than the actual current value of their silver content. She sat for a moment allowing this concept to sink in. The flash of car lights caught her eye. Good timing she thought. This ingot dilemma has just gotten more complicated. Her computer powered off. She went to the door to meet her family.

Connor and Caitlin hadn't stopped talking since they gave her their first hug. Over pie and ice cream Katherine learned about school, soccer teams, a history project on Scottish clans, and their likes and dislikes of middle school. Dano, Caroline, and Katherine exchanged frequent smiles as they sat and listened. Finally their mother announced it was bedtime and went upstairs with the twins. Dano and Katherine remained in the kitchen for a few moments. They said nothing, content to just share the moment together. Then they both started to speak at once.

Laughing, Katherine said, "You first, Dano."

"I was going to tell you how much I've missed you. It has been a long six weeks since Labor Day, for the twins too."

"Cloud Cottage has been very quiet without you."

"How has it been for you this fall? Have you enjoyed your time here as much as last spring?"

Katherine answered by explaining about the trunk-slamming party and her subsequent visits and new friendships, but not David. She told him about the food pantry she had given produce to, and all her other activities. She was still talking when Caroline returned.

"There are two happy children going to sleep upstairs," she laughed. "They told me they have the best dreams at 'their Cloud Cottage.'"

"Sweet Cloud Dreams," Dano remembered.

"Sweet Cloud Dreams," Caroline smiled and nodded. "It is so good to be here, Aunt Katie, thank you."

"You know, Connor and Caitlin are right, it is their 'Cloud Cottage.' I am just the current custodian."

"Well, Madame Custodian, do you have a plan for tomorrow?" Dano asked.

"I have a suggestion," Katherine answered.

"I agree already with whatever it is," Caroline said.

Katherine explained about her fall adventure a few days earlier. She proposed they start out around eight o'clock to catch the golden morning sun on the leaves. That they pack a picnic lunch, drive inland and north, and when they were ready to return, drive home along the lake as the late afternoon sun highlighted the fall colors from the west.

"Perfect."

Dano nodded in agreement, then teased, "Is the picnic basket all packed, Aunt Katie?"

"No, but I have several options for sandwich makings. I thought each one could build a sandwich of their choosing in the morning."

"Again, perfect!" Caroline said.

The plans made, all said goodnight. This time Dano and Caroline would sleep in the den and Katherine was back in her own room. She went upstairs alone, but before she went to bed she couldn't help herself. She opened the door to the boys' room and whispered, "Good night Connor, sweet dreams."

She was surprised when a voice answered her, "Good night Aunt Katie, I love you."

She opened the girls' room door and whispered the same words to Caitlin. The only answer was the soft breathing of peaceful sleep. "Sweet Cloud Dreams," she added.

Saturday morning dawned clear and bright. It was a glorious fall day. From the back seat there was a constant chorus of "oohs" and "aahs" as every mile displayed spectacular fall colors. They enjoyed their lunch by a small lake where the still water perfectly mirrored the trees that lined its shore. They hiked in the Ludington State Park, absorbing every detail of the beauty around them. They arrived home just in time to enjoy sunset at Cloud Cottage. The colors that night were declared to be *Autumn Red*, *Glorious Yellow*, *October Orange*, and from Connor *Sunset Duet*, because he thought the trees along the shore reflected the show on the horizon.

An early departure had been planned for Sunday, however no trip to Cloud Cottage is complete without a long walk on the beach. After a sleep-in morning, brunch, pumpkin harvesting, then their walk, it was early afternoon before the family departed. Katherine stood on the porch a long time after she waved goodbye. When they left on Labor Day the promised weekend in the fall seemed like forever. Now their next visit during the Christmas holidays really seemed like forever.

Sunday afternoon the house was very empty and Katherine decided to spend her time with Ancestor Aonghus. Sometimes she had been successful when she tried to put herself in his place.

"Ancestor Aonghus," she asked. "What was your Cloud 9? What was your place of euphoria? I think you would say Cloud Cottage. This was your happy place, but what's with the 3? What a minute," she paused. "9 divided by 3 equals 3. The last clue seemed to indicate the ingots were inside Cloud Cottage. Is this one telling me they are on the third floor, the attic? Oh, my gosh!"

Katherine raced up the stairs. She walked in circles around the space she had come to know so well this summer. Nothing! Nothing could she see that would resemble an ingot. She shone a flashlight way back under the eaves, under every rafter.

"I'm so frustrated I feel like pulling everything out of every box and trunk up here, but it wouldn't solve anything if the ingots were hidden in plain view. Maybe I've gotten all the clues wrong. Maybe I don't know what I'm looking for. Maybe they don't exist anymore. I don't really know when Uncle Gus wrote his letter." She had assumed he wrote it during his last years, but maybe he didn't. Maybe he found the ingots and just never wrote another note. Maybe they were actually lost in the remodeling projects. Katherine's frustration was rising. "No," she stopped herself. "Calm down. This is a good day to solve this. Think, Katherine."

She started again, trying to think of other 'threes' of significance around Cloud Cottage, 3 windows, 3 stair steps, anything that might be a 3. She wandered through the house looking, studying. I have never seriously considered the cellar, she realized, so down to the cellar she went. She shone a flashlight in all the dark corners, behind the furnace, the hot water heater, and in the root cellar. She looked at every union, every corner, and every ledge from floor to ceiling. Nothing caught her eye that she recognized as an ingot with or without a correlation to a 3. She vowed she would not get frustrated, but she was feeling very discouraged. Blue had followed her all around the basement.

"I need to see that happy tail and be reminded of blue skies." Ready to oblige, the dog wagged his tail to express his support.

"Good dog, Blue Skye, good dog. Well, maybe we won't solve this today after all, how about a walk, my friend?" Again the tail wagged, "I thought you would agree."

55

The day of the party arrived and Katherine was ready. She was happy about the gathering and was anticipating a fun evening. She walked though the downstairs checking the rooms for details. Inviting fires burned in the living room and kitchen fireplaces, dishes of nibbles were placed on end tables, arrangements of dried leaves, gourds, pumpkins, and the last fall mums and asters decorated each room. A wreath of cornhusks hung on her door. Cloud Cottage was ready for guests.

Katherine heard the first car door and knew it would be Chris. She had promised to come ahead of the other guests and Katherine appreciated her offer to help. This group was very easy-going, but she wanted things to be perfect. She opened the door to welcome Chris and found her standing with her mouth open. It was her first visit to Cloud Cottage.

"Katherine," she whispered, "this place is spectacular."

"Thank you, come on in."

She gave Chris a quick orientation tour so she could help direct guests later.

"Oh, Katherine, what a treasure you have. I can't believe I never knew it was here."

Katherine smiled, pleased that Chris appreciated Cloud Cottage. She was also amused at Chris's choice of words, little did she know!

The sound of cars outside alerted them both to the arrival of others, and together they went to greet guests. People had car-pooled so four to six people piled out of each car. Chris was down on the driveway, directing them where to park.

"Wait until you see this place," she told them.

Katherine stood on the porch to welcome her new friends to Cloud Cottage, every bit the Clan Chief of Little Point Sable.

As always among good friends, it was a wonderful gathering. Once again the event was a potluck and there was an abundance of good food. Katherine had provided beverages and made dessert, but everything else had walked in the door. Her kitchen was filled with tantalizing aromas as dinner entrées warmed in the oven and simmered on the stove. However, no one was in a hurry to eat a main course, there were too many appetizers to enjoy and Cloud Cottage to explore.

The men had gone back outside to walk around the structure amazed at the stonework. The women, though impressed, were charmed with the décor throughout, a blend of 19th century with modern finishes like the kitchen. Several guests settled in front of the fires and announced they were moving in. Of course they each had their own beautiful homes but their praise and good-natured jests delighted Katherine. It was fun to share her home. She circulated through the rooms, kept the table and bar stocked, stoked the fires, and shared stories of her Cloud Cottage.

At sunset everyone went out on the porch to watch. They all appreciated the vantage point of the elevation. Katherine noted that sunset was a moment observed by many people, but a special tradition among lake dwellers. Perhaps because each sunset is unique and sharing the transition from day to night is a reflective, spiritual bonding with nature.

The evening continued with dinner and more conversation. During coffee and dessert Katherine, by popular demand, agreed to tell the story of Ancestor Aonghus. She sat in a chair by the living room fireplace and began. The room was full. Some guests made themselves comfortable on the floor; others brought chairs in from other rooms. Katherine watched the expressions on their faces as she related a condensed version of the stories she had shared with the twins. She felt like Scheherazade, but her story was true.

This night the group lingered longer than usual. No one was eager for the evening to end. Katherine wondered if it was because it was her friends' first visit to her home, or if they too, could feel the warmth and magic of Cloud Cottage. She didn't know if Cloud Cottage had ever before held a gathering like this, but she was sure it would not be the last.

A yawn by one guest signaled the beginning of departures. Possessions were gathered, thank-yous expressed, and good-byes said. Chris stayed behind and helped Katherine put dishes in the dishwasher. She started to straighten the living room but Katherine reminded her that she was a guest too. She had helped enough.

On the porch Katherine gave Chris an impulsive hug as they said goodbye.

"Thank you so much," Katherine said.

"Thank me? Thank you, you hosted the party."

"This time. But you welcomed me into your circle of friends."

"If it wasn't so late, I would suggest one last toast to new friends and great gatherings."

"Next time then," Katherine laughed. "Good night."

56

A few days later, after running errands, Katherine returned home to find a strange car in her yard. A meter reader was her first thought as she pulled around to park her car in the garage. She hadn't seen anyone, and the car was still there when she deposited her purchases in the kitchen. How odd, she thought. She went out the front door; there simply was no sign of anyone. A load of firewood had been delivered while she was out, so she went to work stacking it while she continued to watch the car. She must have been very intent on her task because she never heard him approach.

"Kat," it was a quiet voice that had spoken.

Katherine froze. It was David. In her whole life he was the only one that had ever called her Kat. She had been called Kate, Katie, Aunt Katie, Katherine, and who knows how many names by her students, but only David had called her Kat. Katherine played dumb.

"Excuse me? Oh, hello, David."

"Yes, I apologize for not calling first." His eyes were searching her face, then he said, "May I help you finish stacking the wood?"

"Sure, it won't take long."

Neither spoke as they finished the pile.

"May I offer you something to drink in exchange for your hard labor?" she forced a cordial laugh.

"I would like that," he stopped. "I would like to, well," he hesitated again, then continued, "Is it really possible, Kat, that you don't remember that summer?"

Katherine's back was to him, and she stood still not trusting herself to turn around, not knowing how long to continue her charade. After all, it had been over forty years ago. It had been a brief summer romance, she, a typical teenager, head-over-heels in love with a senior headed to college. Why did she think it ever would have ended differently? Why, after all these years was she still angry?

David continued, "Did I hurt you so badly, Kat?" Still she didn't move. "I guess I should not have come, but at least...I would like to say I'm very, very sorry, Kat."

Katherine was struggling within herself. This was the moment. If she didn't acknowledge she remembered, every future meeting would be based on dishonesty. Her silence had lasted too long, David turned to go. Katherine also turned and said quietly, "I accept your apology."

David looked at Katherine, "You do remember!"

"Yes. Perhaps we should talk."

"Please," David asked, "I would like that very much."

Over cups of coffee, dinner, and finally glasses of wine, Kate and David talked. He admitted being a cad, that he should have told her he had to leave, but he also explained he had been drafted that August. It had been at the end of the Vietnam conflict and it had been difficult.

Katherine admitted she recognized him during the volleyball game, suspected he recognized her, but perpetuated the charade in part to protect herself, and yes, she admitted, to see him squirm. They shared details of the intervening decades, they laughed at each other's exploits, marveled at accomplishments, and recognized grief in each other's eyes when a loss was shared. It was late when David said, "I should go," but then asked, "may I come back?"

Katherine looked at the man whose eyes sought hers while he waited for an answer.

"I think the question is, David, will you come back or will you disappear again?" She felt she knew the answer but she could not help herself from verbalizing just once, the source of her anger with him.

"Touché, yes, this time I will come back."

"I will look forward to it and I'll have the wine ready so we may toast to old friendships and new beginnings."

David smiled that wonderful broad smile of his and said, "Deal, but I'll bring the wine."

"Deal," Katherine answered, as they walked out onto the porch.

"There is one more thing."

"What?" asked Katherine.

"May I still have the privilege of calling you Kat?"

Katherine nodded. David gave her a hug and a quick kiss on the cheek.

Katherine watched David's car drive out and exchanged a wave. This has been quite a night. Last year at this time she never could have envisioned that she would spend an evening drinking wine and talking for hours with David Grant. Back in the living room she picked up the wine glasses and said, "Hmmm, new beginnings."

Katherine yawned and stretched. She was being lazy this morning. There was a novel in her hand that she wasn't reading; thoughts of the previous evening with David preempted words on pages. It had indeed been an interesting few months at Cloud Cottage. She reviewed the high points: her experience of solitude and beauty during the spring, Dano's bombshell on Memorial Day, the arrival and summer with the twins. The next and major high point was the discovery of the book by Ancestor Aonghus. At this point she sighed. The whole story was like something out of a novel, only novels had an ending, and she, like

Uncle Gus, had failed to complete the last chapter. Perhaps this winter she would take another look at it and maybe something she had missed this summer would pop off the pages. After all there had been plenty of distractions: the family reunion, and the week Caroline had spent with the whole family at Cloud Cottage. This thought brought a soft smile to her face. Ancestor Aonghus' ingots could never be as great a treasure as family or the preservation of family. The summer concluded with her acquaintance with Chris, the gatherings, and now David.

Katherine was looking forward to the next months. No storm of winter could freeze the warmth of the sense of community she felt. She anticipated becoming involved and hoped she had something to contribute. Life at Cloud Cottage was at one with the seasons, she thought. Spring had burst upon her with discovery, invigorating energy and growth. Summer had been temperate days of maturation for everyone who came to Cloud Cottage. Fall had been the perfect harvest that follows growth, development, and healing. Winter? Well, time will tell. Katherine hoped it would be a time of quiet observation, peaceful rejuvenation and new beginnings.

"Now, Katherine Ann MacLeod," once again she addressed herself out loud, "you'd better get up, you have winter prep work to do."

Over her morning cup of tea, Katherine decided to spend her day closing up the attic oasis. She had only slept up there a few nights since Labor Day. She headed up the stairs, stopping at the linen closet to collect an armload of sheets as she went. She moved wistfully around the space she had grown to love this summer. She checked the drawers of the bureau and removed some remaining sweaters. Ancestor Aonghus's book, now secure in a protective envelope, was in a drawer too. Not hidden, but secure from casual exploration. She stripped the bed, covered it and the easy chairs with the sheets. "There," she said, as she looked around. "I think that's it. All that's left now are my plants."

During the summer Katherine had placed potted geraniums and other plants on the wide sill of the east-facing window. They had thrived, and she had enjoyed seeing them there when she opened her eyes in the morning. The head of her bed was opposite the window, and the flowers with the morning sun streaming upon them had been pretty. She debated leaving them for the winter, they seemed so happy, but she was concerned about temperature. She really didn't know how cold it would become in the attic. She resolved to leave them and watch temperatures.

Katherine picked up her watering can and turned to go downstairs to fill it. She froze. Could it be? She raced to the other end of the attic, to look at the other window. No wide sill! Back across the attic she ran. Is it possible? She ran her hand across the 'tiles' that comprised the windowsill and extended all the way up and around the top of the window. She collapsed into the sheet-covered chair that she had sat on so many times during the summer. She had even examined the pages of the book in this chair and looked out the window in contemplation. She burst into laughter and couldn't stop. "Hidden in plain view," "every cloud has a silver lining," "hold fast," and "Cloud 9 over 3," the clues were all there. How could she have been so dense, so unobservant, then of course, the name of the window, Silver View! She laughed until the tears rolled down her cheeks and she was almost gasping for breath. She considered going downstairs for a screwdriver to pry up one of the tiles/ingots. She knew she didn't need to see any marks or stamps stating the silver content that would be on the underside. She had found Ancestor Aonghus' ingots.

Katherine sat in the chair looking at the window and its extraordinary edging. Now she had other decisions to make. She sat still for a few moments. Then she got up, retrieved from the bureau the book that Ancestor Aonghus had written all those years ago. She went downstairs to the den with purpose in her stride. In the desk she found some blank note cards and sat down to write. She wrote slowly and deliberately, stopping occasionally as if to choose her words. When she laid down her pen she read what she had written.

I, Katherine Ann MacLeod, discovered this book written by my Great-Grandfather Aonghus MacLeod. It contained a note written by my Uncle Angus MacLeod. The content of both book and note concern the unusual circumstances that brought a young Aonghus MacLeod to Little Point Sable on a stormy night in November 1863. The pages written by his grandson, Angus MacLeod, clearly tell this incredible story. It also raised many questions. The answers to which are in the pages written by Aonghus MacLeod. They are cryptic, but decipherable. I have been successful in doing so. I found that which Aonghus MacLeod secured. If you who read this choose to undertake the same challenge, do so with integrity, honor the lives of your ancestors, respect the clan, and enjoy the journey.

Hold Fast,

Katherine Ann MacLeod

Katherine placed the notepaper in an envelope and on the outside in large letters she wrote "Clan MacLeod." She placed the envelope inside Ancestor Aonghus' book next to the envelope with the note written by Uncle Gus. Katherine, with special care, almost reverently, carried the book into the living room. She stood looking at the bookshelves. A chair became a stepstool as she placed the book on the very outside end of the top shelf. It was almost obscured by the large book next to it.

Katherine stepped down, stood back a few feet, and then spoke.

"Ancestor Aonghus, I have found your ingots. They are as safe and secure as the day you built Cloud Cottage. Uncle Gus, you did not fail. You preserved Cloud Cottage and in so doing preserved the ingots. I commit to you that I will "hold fast." I too will preserve Cloud Cottage and the clan, and the ingots may, in time, help me do so. Until then, like you, I will enjoy a Silver View."